A
RISKY
UNDERTAKING
FOR LORETTA
SINGLETARY

A Killing at Cotton Hill

The Last Death of Jack Harbin

Dead Broke in Jarrett Creek

A Deadly Affair at Bobtail Ridge

The Necessary Murder of Nonie Blake

An Unsettling Crime for Samuel Craddock

A Reckoning in the Back Country

A SAMUEL CRADDOCK MYSTERY

A RISKY UNDERTAKING FOR LORETTA SINGLETARY

TERRY SHAMES

SEVENTH STREET BOOKS®

Published 2019 by Seventh Street Books®

Cover image © Alamy Stock Photo
Cover design by Nicole Sommer-Lecht
Cover design © Start Science Fiction

Inquiries should be addressed to
Start Science Fiction
101 Hudson Street, 37th Floor, Suite 3705
Jersey City, New Jersey 07302
PHONE: 212-431-5455
WWW.SEVENTHSTREETBOOKS.COM

10 9 8 7 6 5 4 3 2 1

Library of Congress Cataloging-in-Publication Data

Names: Shames, Terry, author. Title: A risky undertaking for Loretta Singletary : a
    Samuel Craddock mystery / Terry Shames.
Description: Amherst, NY : Seventh Street Books, an imprint of Prometheus Books,
    2019.
Identifiers: LCCN 2018034389 (print) | LCCN 2018035085 (ebook)| ISBN
    9781633884915 (ebook) | ISBN 9781633884908 (paperback)
Subjects: | BISAC: FICTION / Mystery & Detective / Police Procedural. |
    FICTION / Mystery & Detective / General. | GSAFD: Mystery fiction.
Classification: LCC PS3619.H35425 (ebook) | LCC PS3619.H35425
    R57 2019 (print) | DDC 813/.6--dc23
LC record available at https://lccn.loc.gov/2018034389

Printed in Canada

To Karen Wright,
for all the good times and those to come.

CHAPTER 1

It has been a quiet week; so quiet that Wendy Gleason and I were able to sneak off to drive the bluebonnet trail yesterday. It's the peak of bluebonnet season, and the views across the fields were spectacular. Wendy kept wanting to stop to take pictures. I asked what she was going to do with so many photos. "You must have taken a hundred."

"When I'm a dotty old lady in a rocking chair, I'll take them out and remember how much fun we've had today."

We're at that stage in getting to know each other where everything looks a little brighter when the other one is around. We took a picnic and had lunch in somebody's field. We laughed a lot. I hadn't been that relaxed in weeks.

I should have known the lull wouldn't last. Today the weather blew up blustery and chilly, a weak winter storm making one last effort before spring sets in for good. I got caught in a rainstorm an hour ago, and before I had time to go home to change clothes, I got a call from Robert Caisson's wife. She said the Caisson brothers were in the backyard in a standoff with guns, and she was afraid they were going to kill each other.

When I arrived the two were still outside, sopping wet from the rain, both holding outsize pistols and shouting at each other. In their forties, they're big men, at least 6'2" and 230 pounds. I demanded to know what they were upset about, but they ignored me. Robert's wife, Darla, said it was too stupid for her to bother telling me.

It's starting to get dark and cold, which I hope will put an end to their nonsense. I'm standing on the back porch in wet clothes and wet shoes, getting madder by the minute. I'm scared if I get out there and try to talk to them, one of them will shoot me. Meanwhile, I have to listen to them holler at each other like third graders. The conversation so far has gone like this:

"Daddy always favored you and you think you should have anything you want."

"Bull. You're Mamma's little pet. No wonder you're so full of yourself."

"I'm going to shoot you and be glad to spend time in jail just so I don't have to listen to any more of that."

"You couldn't hit the side of a barn. You're mad because I was always a better shot than you."

"Fellas," I holler, "you sound like a bad TV western. You're acting like children. Come on inside and let's sit down and talk."

Neither of them so much as glances my way. If it weren't for me being the chief of police and charged with keeping the peace, I'd go home and let them keep this up all night. But I'm afraid eventually one of them is going to make good on his threat.

I go back inside. "Darla, where is T.J.'s wife?"

"She has the kids over in Bobtail. She took all of them to a movie."

"How many kids are there?"

"Each of us has a pair of them. The older ones are just a few months apart, and the younger ones are a year apart. They're good kids." She isn't looking at me while she talks. She's watching the door to the backyard, hoping as am I that the two men will come inside. "I swear to God, I hope they kill each other," she says.

I would protest that she doesn't mean that, but she might. Darla is a scary-looking chunk of a woman who wears cowboy outfits and motorcycle boots, and has dishwater blond hair down to her waist. She and her husband belong to a motorcycle club, and they tear around the countryside on weekends. Oddly enough, although all the motorcycle people look savage, I've never heard of them giving the law any trouble.

I asked about T.J.'s wife because, of the four of them, she's the most mild-mannered. I was hoping to call on her to help smooth things out.

With that option gone, I step back outside. "If you boys don't cut this out," I holler, "I'm going to take you both in and you can spend the weekend in a jail cell." I might as well have been yelling to an empty yard. "Lay the guns down!" I put all the authority I can muster into my order.

T.J. finally looks my way and says, "Chief, get out of here. We have to settle this between us. He'll come to his senses eventually."

"Like hell I will!" And just like that Robert's gun goes off.

T.J. yells and spins and drops to his knees.

Robert flings his gun down and leaps backward. "I didn't mean to shoot. The gun went off by itself."

Darla comes screaming out of the house and stomps to Robert's side and says, "You damn fool. You don't have the sense of a goose."

"Are you sorry he didn't shoot me?"

"I swear, you two . . ." She storms back into the house with Robert right behind her.

Neither of them has paid the slightest attention to T.J., who is moaning on the ground. I go over and see that he's bleeding pretty heavily. "One of you call 911," I yell. "He needs an ambulance."

"He can call the ambulance himself," Robert calls back.

"I'll call them," Darla says.

I put pressure on the wound, which is high on the right side of his chest and not life-threatening, until the paramedics arrive. I gladly hand over responsibility for the injured man to them. Then I go inside and tell Robert to get his jacket, I'm taking him to jail.

"What do you mean taking me to jail? I told you I didn't mean to shoot."

"Mean to or not, you did. Now are you coming quietly or do I have to call for backup?"

"Robert, you better go with the Chief because if I have to look at you for one more minute, I'm going to kill you."

11

CHAPTER 2

Loretta Singletary usually drops in unannounced, but this morning she called and asked if she could come over before I leave for headquarters. Seemed a little formal to me, but I told her to come at eight o'clock. I intend to take my time going in today to give Robert Caisson plenty of opportunity to consider his situation.

I don't linger seeing to my cows in the dewy morning. It was chilly last night from the passing storm, but at seven o'clock, it's already warming up, and a few scattered clouds tell me it's going to be hot and humid today.

Loretta knocks on the screen door promptly at eight, which is no surprise. She prides herself on being punctual. She looks different, although it's hard for me to pinpoint exactly what she's done to herself, except that she looks more dressed up.

"New blouse?" I venture, as she steps inside. I'm living dangerously. If the blouse she's wearing isn't new, she'll be disgusted with me for not remembering it. This time I'm in luck.

"Do you like it? I bought it last week."

"It's nice. Whoa, Dusty!"

My six-month-old pup, Dusty, has come skidding in from the kitchen to greet her. He never loses hope that she'll be happy to see him. As usual, she shies away, glaring at him.

"Go on, Dusty. Go lie down." He backs up a step or two, his tail wagging. "I'm going to have a cup of coffee. What can I get you?" I ask Loretta.

Her smile fades. "Nothing. I'm here on a particular errand."

"Where do you want to sit for this formal pow wow? Living room? Kitchen? We could sit on the front porch. The weather's pleasant."

"I think the living room would be fine." Uh-oh. This really is a formal pow wow.

I get my cup of coffee and fetch Dusty's bed from the kitchen. I toss it down near the fireplace and tell him to lie down on it. I'm trying to teach him manners, when I happen to remember to. Loretta's aversion to him always reminds me.

We sit in armchairs in front of the fireplace, even though there's no fire. I scoot my chair to see Loretta better. "What's all this about?"

She takes a deep breath. "I've been asked to have a talk with you about the rodeo."

Of all the things she could have brought up, this is the last one I would have guessed. It's only April, and the annual goat rodeo is two months off, the middle of June, right after school is out. "What's the problem?"

"Don't rush me." She fiddles with the sleeves of her blouse while I wait. "You know we got a new preacher at the beginning of the year. Arlen Becker."

"I do know that, although I haven't met him." It seems like the Baptist Church turns over its ministers every year or two when one faction or another gets riled up and votes to oust him. The one Reverend Becker replaced only lasted nine months. I don't know whether Becker will be any more successful. He has already made a few people uncomfortable because he's a stickler for Baptist doctrine.

"He's . . . he's learning his way, that's what I think. Anyway, he has brought up a situation that we in the Ladies' Circle decided we need to address."

With me? Surely he didn't sic them on me to insist I start going to church. Not that I would let him bully me, but he wouldn't be the first to try to get me to be "a good example." And what does this have to do with the rodeo? I wait for her to enlighten me.

"You know everyone likes Father Sanchez, even if he is a Catholic. And we support the goat rodeo. We know it's popular with the kids and the parents, and uh . . ." She grinds to a halt.

I'm completely baffled. "Loretta, just tell me what the problem is."

"All right I will. Reverend Becker thinks we shouldn't let the Catholic Church run the rodeo without participation from the Baptist Church."

I would laugh if Loretta didn't look so anxious. "Why in the world would Becker care?"

"Reverend Becker doesn't like having the Catholic priest in charge of an event that members of his congregation participate in. He says he doesn't think the Catholics should get all the glory."

Now I have to swallow hard to keep from laughing. There is little glory involved in being in charge of the annual Jarrett Creek Goat Rodeo. It's a lot of hard work. Raymond Sanchez is the latest in a line of priests who seem to be dedicated to doing it though. I say, let him.

"Loretta, I cannot comprehend why anyone wouldn't be thrilled to let somebody else do the hard work of organizing and running the rodeo. Is Reverend Becker afraid that Father Sanchez is going to lure members of his church away?"

"Maybe."

"That makes no sense. That little Catholic Church has fifty members at most, and as far as I can tell, it has rarely varied from that number. Father Sanchez is not a proselytizer. Even if he was, he's not likely to lure any members away from the Protestant churches."

"Maybe," she says again. I don't remember when I've seen her look so uneasy.

"What does this have to do with me?"

"We all know that you give them money to run the rodeo. We want you to use your influence as a backer to get him to let the Baptist Church have equal billing."

We stare at each other, and I blink first. "I have to get another cup of coffee. You sure you don't want one?"

"I guess I will." She sounds discouraged, which makes me feel bad. I wish they hadn't put her up to this chore. They're using her because everybody knows we're good friends.

Dusty follows me into the kitchen, where there's always the possibility of a treat. I pour myself a cup and then pour Loretta a half-cup and add another half-cup of hot water and a good slug of cream. Loretta likes her coffee pale. Meanwhile, I'm trying to figure out how to wriggle out of this proposal without making Loretta lose face with her church circle.

When I'm settled again, I say, "Loretta, you know I more or less live by the adage to let sleeping dogs lie." I shouldn't have said "dog." Dusty leaps up, startling Loretta. She grabs the arms of the chair as if she thinks he might knock it over.

"You mean you won't help me?"

"I didn't say that. I'll have to think about it. But consider this: If the Baptist Church gets equal billing, all the other churches are going to want it too. Imagine what a mess that will be with every church wanting a little piece of the action. One organizing the concessions, another the three-legged race, another the goat-roping. You know how it is when there are too many people involved."

She nods, light dawning in her eyes. "I hadn't thought of that. I'll bet when I put it that way to the preacher, he'll change his mind."

I wouldn't count on it, but for now the crisis is averted.

She jumps up. "I'd better get going."

"Doing something special?"

"What makes you ask that?" Her tone is sharp.

I meant it as an innocent question, and I wonder what I've stumbled into. "Nothing in particular. Just passing the time of day."

Her cheeks are pink. "I'm meeting a friend, that's all."

"Have a good one," I say. I'm relieved when she's out the door.

Dusty has come to my side to watch her go down the steps. I close the door and say, "Dusty, sometimes it's best not to ask questions."

I call the hospital in Bobtail, and the nurse tells me that T.J. Caisson will be released later today. I tell her not to let him go until I've questioned him. Robert Caisson refused to say what the argument was that led to the shooting. I need to go to the hospital to find out if I can get anything out of T.J.

On the way to the hospital, I go by headquarters to leave Dusty there, knowing that Maria Trevino, my chief deputy, will be in at nine o'clock and will watch him. I also want to tell Robert that his brother is going to give a statement, even though I don't know if he actually will.

"He's okay?" Robert asks. His hound-dog eyes are red-rimmed, but whether that's from being hungover or because he lost sleep after shooting his brother is anybody's guess.

"The nurse I talked to said he'll live."

"I'm not surprised. That son of a bitch is too stubborn to kill."

"You want any coffee?" I ask. I've heard enough from Robert.

"I don't suppose I could get something to eat too."

"I'll give you coffee, but you'll have to wait until Maria gets here at nine o'clock to get breakfast. If she's in a good mood and you be-have yourself, she might be persuaded to go over to the café and get you a bite."

"Well, goddammit," he says. I'm not sure what that refers to, but I don't have enough patience to ask. I bring him the coffee and tell him I'll be back after I talk to his brother. "You have anything you want to say to him?" I was thinking there might be an apology lurking.

"Tell him he can go to hell for all I care."

T.J. and Robert look so much alike you'd think they were twins, but T.J. is the older one. In their forties, they grew up on a big ranch to the northwest of town. They never got along, and since their parents died, their animosity has only gotten worse. T.J. inherited the home place, and Robert inherited money equal to the value of the house and lives in town. Each seems to think the other one got the better deal in the will.

"T.J., I'm glad to see you're going to recover," I say. "The nurse tells me they're going to release you this afternoon."

He scratches at the edges of the big bandage on his shoulder. "I told 'em they had to. I can't be off work long."

Tomorrow is Sunday, so I doubt he'd be going in anyway. "What kind of work do you do?"

"Robert and I run our daddy's garage. We've always got a string of vehicles waiting to be taken care of. Can't keep folks waiting or they'll go somewhere else."

"You can't do a lot of car repair with that shoulder."

"I don't know a thing about fixing cars. That's Robert's part of it. I do the office part. I can do it with one hand." He grimaces. "I hope you haven't told my brother I'm still alive. He might come over here and try to finish me off."

"He knows you're going to be okay. But I put him in jail, and he's not going anywhere until I sort this out."

"In jail? What for?" He glares at me.

"For assault with a deadly weapon."

"I'm not going to press charges against my little brother." He's growing more outraged by the second. Like a lot of kinfolks, they can squabble like crazy among themselves, but let someone from outside threaten them, and they're suddenly united.

"You don't have to. He broke the law by shooting you, and that's my business."

"Well, goddammit." They really could be twins.

T.J. claims he doesn't remember any more than Robert does why they were arguing. I suspect he does remember, but he isn't talking. The argument didn't create the crime anyway; alcohol and handy guns did.

"Listen, I'm mad at the son of a bitch, and his wife can go butt a stump as far as I'm concerned, but there's no need to hold him in jail. We'll get over it."

On the drive back to Jarrett Creek, I argue with myself about whether to charge Robert. We can't have people shooting each other, but I can't see him as a threat to anybody but his own brother.

When I walk into headquarters, Maria is playing tug of war with Dusty. He breaks it off to dance around me and welcome me back. He's getting to be a rangy dog, not big, but all legs. I called him Dusty because he was dust-colored when he was a pup, but he's starting to get spots and look like a border collie, which is what the vet said he mostly is.

"Did you give the prisoner anything to eat?" I ask.

"I did not. He was rude, and I told him he could go hungry."

"Won't hurt him," I say.

I tell Maria what I decided to do with Robert, and I'm relieved when she concurs. Maria has only been a police officer for a little more than a year, and her rookie spirit of strict adherence to the law hasn't worn off yet. She often has opinions contrary to decisions I make, and she's happy to share those opinions with me.

The prisoner is lying on his back, hands behind his head, staring at the ceiling. He sits up when he hears my boots on the floor.

"Robert, I'm letting you go with a fine, but I'm keeping your weapon," I say.

"You know, she wouldn't get me any breakfast," he says, nodding toward the front in case I don't know who "she" is. "I've got low blood sugar, and I could faint and hit my head and you'd have a lawsuit."

"Did you hear what I said?"

"Well, let me out then."

"I don't think you fully comprehend what I mean when I say you owe a fine. It means you have to pay it before I'll let you out."

"Call my wife. She'll get the money."

"You want to know how much it is?"

He comes close to the bars and clutches them, eyes narrowed. "How much?"

"Five hundred."

"Five hundred!" He slams his hand on the bars. "That's robbery."

"Would you prefer that I charge you with attempted murder?"

He blusters around for a while, but finally tells me to call his wife. Darla comes down with the cash so fast that I figure they must keep money on hand. She slaps the money down and says, "I'm taking this money out of his hide. Both of them ought to have to pay for disturbing the peace."

"That would be a start. One of them is going to end up dead if they can't figure out a way to settle their differences besides gunning for each other."

"Whatever. You going to let him out?"

After they leave, Maria asks what the fight was about. I tell her that neither of them would say.

She rolls her eyes. "We haven't seen the end of this."

"You're probably right." I loll back in my chair sipping coffee and consider an early lunch.

CHAPTER 3

"I told you that you were going to get into trouble if you broke up with Ellen and started dating Wendy." Jenny Sandstone, my next-door neighbor and friend, is using her stern voice. Jenny is a prosecuting attorney with the District Attorney's office in Bobtail, and I can imagine the dread that her voice strikes into the heart of anyone she thinks worthy of prosecution. In this case, it's me.

"You think that's what's going on? Seems crazy to me that anyone would care who I date." Until last fall, I was going out with Ellen Forester, who moved to town a few years ago and opened an art gallery and workshop. She has made a lot of friends in town, and apparently some women saw it as a betrayal when Ellen and I broke off and I took up with Wendy Gleason, who lives in College Station. They seem to be of the opinion that I am a cheater and a womanizer.

"People like Ellen," Jenny says. "They had the two of you all set up. What has Loretta said about it?"

"Not much. She and Ellen are good friends, and I expect Ellen told her it wasn't a big blowup or anything. Ellen and I get along fine."

"Humph." She raises an eyebrow.

Jenny and I don't have our Wednesday wine evenings as often as we used to, since she's been dating Will Devereaux, but we try to get together once a month. We haven't known each other that long, but we've been through experiences that bonded us. In particular, she saved my art collection from being destroyed when someone set fire to my house. For my part, I pulled her out of a destructive situation of a different kind after her mother died. We are comfortable friends who can read each other whatever riot act needs to be read.

This warm spring evening, we are sitting out on her back deck sharing a bottle of pinot noir and munching on snacks that Will made last night, knowing we were planning to get together. I bite into a spicy cheese puff. I appreciate his efforts because Jenny's idea of cooking is slicing cheddar cheese and slapping it onto crackers.

"I'm surprised you disapprove of me dating Wendy, seeing that I met her at your house," I say. Last Thanksgiving, Ellen went out of town unexpectedly, and I was feeling sorry for myself when Jenny invited me over. I met Wendy that day. Nobody was more surprised than I was when we fell for each other.

The conversation tonight started innocently enough. I haven't seen Loretta Singletary in a few days. She usually brings baked goods around most days, and this morning was the fourth day she hadn't shown up. I wondered if I had offended her, which is why I asked Jenny if she had seen her. That's when I got the earful about dating Wendy.

Jenny laughs. "I'm giving you trouble, that's all," she says, smirking at my discomfort. "I don't think that's why Loretta hasn't brought you any goodies. Why don't you call and ask her?"

"I would have phoned her this morning, but I had to go help Melvin Pritchart haul his car out of a ditch. He and his son went out celebrating his son's twenty-first birthday last night."

"Men," Jenny sighs. "Everybody survive?"

"They're fine. Embarrassed."

"Back to Loretta, you could ask your neighbors if she has stopped baking for them."

"It's not that big a deal." That's not true. I actually wondered whether she's mad that I declined to get involved with the goat rodeo situation. She didn't seem mad when she left my house, but maybe the Baptist ladies persuaded her that I had not done the right thing. "Has she brought anything to you?"

"No, Samuel, she hasn't. She never does because I asked her not to. I leave for work early, and once she left a plate on the porch and Bess's dog next door got into it and ate all four cinnamon rolls. Bess described to me the results of that dog's greedy feast in detail." She shudders.

I laugh, although it isn't funny. I've had to deal with a greedy dog a time or two now that Dusty is old enough to get into things.

"I guess if she doesn't show up in the morning, I'd better go over and ask her what's going on."

"That seems like a reasonable idea. She's probably been busy with something else. And speaking of busy." Jenny sighs and sits forward, running her hands through her flame-red hair. "I've got an early court hearing in the morning, so I can't sit here all night."

As soon as I get up, Dusty leaps to his feet and cocks his head. He's always ready to go somewhere. "Let's get on home, boy."

Before we go into the house, we take a nice walk. Spring is in the air, and at 9:30, it's still warm. We stroll by Loretta's house, and I see that it's dark. Seems early for her to have gone to bed. Maybe she went away and didn't tell me, although that's odd. She usually keeps me informed of her plans.

CHAPTER 4

It's eleven o'clock Thursday morning, and things are quiet. "I want to ask you something," I say to Maria. "Have you talked to Loretta? Do you know if she's out of town?"

Maria chuckles. "She could be, but I don't know for sure."

"What do you mean?"

"Not that you'd notice, but Loretta has been a little cocky in the last few weeks. I think she's got a boyfriend."

I lunge forward in my chair. "She what?"

"Don't get excited. Why are you surprised? I've known that Loretta is on the lookout for a man ever since I met her. I'm glad for her if she has found somebody."

"Well, I'll be damned."

"You've been around Robert Caisson too much. You sound just like him." Maria doesn't approve of salty language.

I tell Maria I'm going over to Town Café. "Loretta hasn't brought any baked goods around the last few days, and I didn't get any breakfast." She's laughing when I leave.

The few people in Town Café are there for late breakfast, and I don't know any of them. Later, at lunchtime, it will be full of regulars. It's a typical small-town café with chrome and Formica tables and vinyl-padded chairs. The walls are decorated with pictures of past football teams and members of the high school booster club. The place has changed hands a number of times, but it hasn't changed the way it looks. It also hasn't updated the menu, although the food quality has improved under the current owner.

I order a plate of enchiladas and use the solitude to ponder Maria's observation that Loretta has been acting a little cocky. We get to know people so well that we don't always look at them, and I remember now how shocked I was several months ago when Loretta showed up with a new hairstyle. She had changed her hair from gray to a kind of blondish color and stopped wearing it in tight curls. But how was it different? Straighter? I try to picture her hair but can't. I just know she looked younger, softer.

Another change, even more startling, is that she wears slacks occasionally. She has always maintained that women ought to stick to wearing dresses. I thought she made the change because she was taking painting classes from Ellen and wanted to be able to get dirty without worrying about her clothes, but now I wonder whether it's a sign of a basic change in attitude. There's no reason she shouldn't be looking for somebody to date. She's in my age range, and some people might say we're too old to find romance. It's not true. I'm a good example of it not being too late to have a good time with a partner. But for some reason, it bothers me that Loretta is dating. I guess because it means I don't get my bakery goods. That's plain selfish.

Lurleen brings me my enchiladas. She has worked here for years, and she knows me. Usually she's so busy she sets the plate down and speeds off, but it isn't busy right now.

"Everything okay?" she says. "You look like you've got things on your mind."

"The usual. But mostly right now I'm hungry."

"Eat up."

She's walking away when Ellen Forester steps into the café. I'm surprised to see her here. She's usually busy with art classes all day. She looks around the room, and when she spies me she hurries over.

"Don't get up," she says. She waves at my food. "And don't let your food get cold. Go ahead and eat. You mind if I sit down? I need to ask you a question."

"Of course I don't mind."

For a short time through the winter, relations were strained between Ellen and me. She and I had been seeing each other for a year or more, but then I met Wendy Gleason, and things took a different turn. Like Jenny said, women around here haven't forgiven me for what they perceive as me throwing Ellen over for Wendy, but they don't know the truth of it. In fact, Ellen had been keeping important matters from me that had a bearing on our relationship. We might have gotten over it if I hadn't met Wendy, but I did. Ellen told me she was glad I had met someone else. I believe her.

Lurleen comes over, and Ellen orders iced tea and a cheese enchilada. She's a vegetarian, and I like meat three times a day. That was another little glitch that I think we are both glad not to have to navigate anymore.

"I'm surprised to see you," I say. "No classes?"

"I have to be back in 30 minutes. I stopped over at headquarters to talk to you, and Maria said I could find you here."

"What's up?"

She clasps her hands on top of the table and grimaces. "I don't want to be nosy and silly, but I'm worried."

I've got a mouthful of enchilada, so I nod to her to keep going.

"Have you talked to Loretta recently?"

I swallow and wipe my mouth. "Maria and I were discussing that a few minutes ago. Loretta hasn't been around with baked goods the last few days. You know how she is, trying to fatten everybody up with those rolls and coffee cake."

She nods. "Samuel, have you ever known Loretta not to show up when she's supposed to?"

"The opposite. She's never late, and she always keeps her word."

"Exactly. Well, we had planned to go shopping over in Bobtail yesterday afternoon, and she was supposed to pick me up. She never showed up. I tried calling her, and she didn't answer. So I did something I probably shouldn't have done. I drove over there and went into her house to check on her."

"How did you get in? Was the house unlocked?"

"I know where she keeps a key. Anyway, she wasn't there, and it looked like she had left in a hurry. She left dishes on the table and a pan unwashed in the sink."

"That's odd, but there's probably a good explanation." Is there? I hadn't worried when Loretta made herself scarce the last few days, but Ellen's concern puts a different spin on it. I've known Loretta a long time, and I've never known her to be late—or to not show up at all.

"Probably, but it's not like her."

"Did you check upstairs to make sure she wasn't sick in bed?"

"Yes, and I called the hospital in Bobtail in case she had an emergency, but they didn't have a record of her coming in."

"Did you call her cell phone number?"

"Yes, but it went to voicemail. You know she hardly ever uses it. Most of the time she doesn't even take it with her."

I've lost my appetite and shove my plate away. "Did you call any of her friends?" Although it isn't like her, it's possible that a problem came up at the church, and she ran off to take care of it, forgetting that she had an appointment with Ellen.

"No. It wasn't that important. I figured she forgot, and that I'd talk to her today. I left a note asking her to call when she got home. But I haven't heard from her this morning. Maybe I'm being silly, but I'm uneasy."

I lay money on the table for the bill and get up. "I'm going to go talk to her neighbors."

"Good. I wish you would," Ellen says. "It's not like her to be so careless."

I start to walk away, but then I pause. "Maria said she thought Loretta might be interested in finding a . . . a . . ." The words stick in my throat.

Ellen smirks. "You mean finding a man to date? You know, it isn't out of the question. Loretta has a lot to offer. A man could do a lot worse."

"Has she met somebody?"

"If she has, she didn't tell me."

I go back to headquarters and tell Maria where I'm going, and she insists on coming along. She and Loretta are the most unlikely pals ever, an elderly white woman and a young Hispanic cop, but they hit it off as soon as Maria started working for Jarrett Creek Police Department. Loretta admires that Maria has the spunk to be a cop, and Maria admires that Loretta doesn't mince words.

We take a squad car over to Loretta's neighborhood, with Dusty tucked in the back. When I knock on Loretta's door, there's no answer.

"Look at that," Maria says, pointing to the front yard.

"What?"

"Look how droopy those plants are. She waters almost every day, and it looks like it's been a few days since she tended to it."

"Maybe she went out of town."

"If she was going away, she'd ask somebody to water."

We go around into the backyard and see nothing amiss. I peer into the garage, and that's our first break. "Car's gone," I say, turning to Maria.

"Maybe something happened to somebody in her family, and she left in a hurry to be with them." She frowns. "Still seems funny that she wouldn't tell anybody."

"Let's see if her neighbors know anything."

We leave Dusty tied up in the shade on Loretta's porch while we go next door.

We don't bother her neighbor to the west, Irwin McIntire. He's deaf as a post and wouldn't likely hear when Loretta comes and goes. Her neighbor on the other side, Sharon Page, answers the door, drying her hands on a kitchen towel. She's in her sixties, tall and big-boned, with bright eyes and a warm smile. "Well hello, what brings you all here? Has Ken gone and killed James? He has threatened to do it so often that I expect it any day now." We laugh. Her husband, Ken, sold his real estate business a while back, but couldn't stand retirement. He went back to work for James Crowley, the man who bought it. I've heard they don't see eye to eye on the way the business should be run.

She invites us in and gives us a cup of coffee in the living room, which has a cheery, lived-in feel to it with a sofa and chairs that seem to me to have just the right amount of wear and tear to make them easy to sit in. I ask Sharon when she last saw Loretta.

She taps a finger to her lips and looks out the big front window. "I see her pretty much every day one way or another. She works in the yard most days, but come to think of it, I haven't seen her out there in the last couple of days."

"Did she mention that she might be going out of town?"

A light dawns. "Yes, she did. I completely forgot. I guess it was, what's today, Thursday? Last weekend she told me she had something to do this week. She seemed excited."

"Did she say what it was? Was she going on a trip?"

"Let me think." She shakes her head. "No, I don't believe she said anything specific. Why are you asking?"

"I don't want to alarm you because there might be a perfectly good explanation, but nobody has heard from her in a few days."

"Like I said, she told me she had something to do, but whether it was going out of town or. . ." She bites her bottom lip. "Now I don't want to be foolish, but I remember when she told me, something struck me funny. Or different anyway. I'm trying to think what it was. Oh, I know. I told Ken that she seemed like a young girl. Her eyes were all sparkly. I told him I wondered if she had met a love interest."

"Ever seen any men come to visit her?"

She flushes. "Goodness, no. Loretta wouldn't like to have a man come to her house unless she knew him really well. You know what I mean."

I do know what she means, because Loretta is even skittish for me to come into her house alone, and we've known each other for years. She was very kind to my wife Jeanne when Jeanne was in her last days, and I feel like we got to know each other better than most.

I thank Sharon for the information and ask her to call if she sees Loretta.

When we get back to the car, we both pause and look back toward Loretta's house. "What do you think?" I ask. I have a feeling Maria feels the same way I do—that Sharon's information was helpful, but we're still worried.

"It's not like her."

"Ellen Forester told me where Loretta keeps a spare key," I say. "I think we should go inside and look around. We have probable cause."

Maria nods. "You do that, and I'll water her yard. Wherever she's gone, she's going to be unhappy if she comes back and her flowers are dead."

I retrieve the key from under a flowerpot on the screened porch. When I go inside Loretta's house, I feel like the place disapproves of me being there without her. It's deadly quiet and smells a little musty, the way houses get when they are shut up for a few days. I go into the kitchen and take a long look at the unwashed dishes in the sink. There's not much—a couple of small plates, a coffee cup, and a spatula. On the stove, there's a skillet that looks like it hasn't been washed either. It is absolutely not like her to leave the dishes undone. Why would she leave in such a hurry?

In the back of my mind is a possibility no one likes to contemplate, but when we get to a certain age, it is one of the health issues we have to consider. Is it possible that Loretta's mind is slipping and she simply forgot a few things? I can't believe that she would forget so much all at once. Forgetting the date with Ellen to go shopping in Bobtail, forgetting to tell anyone where she was going, and leaving the dishes undone. I could see one of those things happening, but not all of them at the same time. I've seen absolutely no sign that Loretta is slipping mentally. Something made her hustle out of here, leaving her work unfinished.

On the countertop, there's a loose-leaf, page-a-day calendar, not the tear-off kind. The day showing is Monday, three days ago. Either she forgot to turn it to Tuesday or she went away Monday. Monday has a note that says, 10:30—Ladies Circle Meeting. I flip back a day and see that Sunday 4:30 is circled, but with no note about what was going on then. On Tuesday, 2:30 p.m. is circled, again with no indication of what she was doing. I flip back a few more pages and see lots of notes with times circled, all saying what is happening. Those two are the only ones that have no hint as to what she was going to do at that time.

Loretta keeps her phone numbers on a hanging pad next to her wall phone. The numbers for both of her sons are at the top of the list. Her younger son lives out in North Carolina, and Loretta wouldn't have driven all the way out to see him—or at least I don't think she would have. But the older son, Scott, and his family live out in the hill country, and she could make that drive easily. I hesitate before I dial Scott's number. If she isn't there, it's going to alarm his family for me to ask whether they know where she is. Maybe I should wait a little longer. But for what? I dial the number, and the voice-mail kicks in with the voice of Loretta's daughter-in-law. I've met the daughter-in-law, Marcie, a friendly, well-kept woman. Loretta likes her "fine," although I think Loretta mostly likes that she gave her grandchildren.

I leave a noncommittal message asking her to call me about "a quick question." Ellen said she went through the house to make sure Loretta hadn't left any signs of where she might have gone, but I go through it again. Her bedroom is tidied, the bed made and all the clothes put away, but the closet door is ajar. I approach it and ease it open, hoping I won't find anything unexpected. Everything looks in place, but I notice that there are a few empty hangers. One hanger is on the floor, as if she took the clothes off in a hurry and didn't notice that it had fallen. Then I look up at the top shelf. She keeps small suitcases on the shelf, and there is a gap between two of them. Wherever she is, she packed a bag.

In the bathroom, I find more evidence that she left on her own. There are gaps in the neat row of items on the counter. Plus, there's no toothbrush in the holder, and no toothpaste sitting out or in the medicine cabinet.

I don't know why she didn't tell anybody she was going away, but it's obvious that she left under her own steam. I feel a weight lift off my shoulders, and I laugh to myself thinking how outraged Loretta will be if she happens to come home now and find me snooping in her house.

CHAPTER 5

I may be satisfied, but Maria isn't. When we get back to head-quarters, she says she's going to make a few calls to see whether any of Loretta's church friends know where she is.

After the second call, she hangs up and says, "Why do some women have to be so coy?" With her dark eyes and jet-black hair, Maria is a pretty girl, except when she scowls, which she's doing now. With her heavy brows together in one line and her mouth turned down in a pout, she looks like a statue of a Mayan warrior.

"What do you mean?"

"I called Jolene Ramsey—you know Loretta thinks she hung the moon because she's the Baptist Ladies' Circle treasurer—and she hinted around that she *might* know what Loretta has been up to."

"If she thinks Loretta has been 'up to something,' that's a good thing."

"What do you mean?"

"I mean if Jolene knows Loretta is keeping a secret, then her going off without telling anyone is more understandable."

She shakes her head. "Leaving the dishes undone is not understandable. That is not Loretta, and you know it."

"Maybe. Her neighbor said she was excited about whatever she was going to do, so maybe she really did forget. But unless she told somebody where she was going, I don't know what we can do to find her."

"At least you can go talk to Jolene. She's more likely to tell you than she is me."

She's right. Some older women don't like the idea of a female police officer or a female doing any job that is traditionally male, and Jolene Ramsey is one of them. One reason that Maria is friendly with

Loretta is that when she first came to town, having been assigned to us by the state on their minority outreach program, a few citizens resisted her joining the department. They claimed that they didn't like the state of Texas, or any other government entity, telling the town what to do, but I knew it was the gender issue. That was even more of an issue than her being Hispanic.

Loretta would have none of it. Generally, she tends to stick to tradition, but she firmly believes that women should be able to do any job they want to. She defended Maria fiercely, and gradually the hubbub died down.

"Okay, I'll go talk to Jolene. Was she at home?"

"Yes, but she said she was leaving her house soon on her way to the church."

"You want to go with me? It will make the point that you are a police officer and that she ought to be forthcoming with you as much as with me."

Maria declines. She's more interested in getting the facts behind Loretta's disappearance than in making a point with Jolene. I leave Dusty with her while I go to the church, ignoring the mournful look he gets when he knows I'm going in the car without him.

Loretta told me that Jolene practically lives at the Baptist church. I'm not a churchgoer, but if I were, I wouldn't join the Baptist Church. They say it's the same basic church as the Methodists, the Lutherans, and the Presbyterians—just with different trappings. But the Baptists have a habit of making a fuss over every little thing and demanding that people do things their way. A case in point is the stir over the goat rodeo.

If Baptists had their way, the school wouldn't let kids dance at their prom, wouldn't let anybody have a glass of wine at a town function, and would ban beer from the events out at the lake. I've discussed these strictures with Loretta, but she says it has nothing to do with being Baptist; it's the fault of a few do-gooders who don't want anyone to have any fun.

I've only met Jolene a few times, and she strikes me as being one of the do-gooders. She's got that narrow-eyed look, like she's keeping score of what's going on around her so she can tattle to God. She's in the church office, sitting at the desk with the computer open, surrounded by receipts and spreadsheet printouts. She's a scrawny woman with iron gray hair worn like a helmet. She's dressed in a prim dark skirt and white blouse.

"Hello, Chief Craddock. This is a pleasant surprise."

"Jolene, hope you're well."

"I know why you're here. That girl called me earlier asking questions about Loretta's business. I guess she wasn't satisfied with my answers." At the end of this speech, she presses her lips into a thin line and pins me down with her stare.

"You look like you've got your hands full," I say, gesturing toward the papers on the desk. I'm trying to soften her up so she'll be cooperative.

"Nobody knows how much work it is to be a church treasurer. People assume that all you have to do is take in the collection money and it pays the bills."

These are matters that are foreign to me. "I'm sure you're up to the task," I say.

"I certainly intend to be." She has to have the last word.

"Do you have time to talk to me for a few minutes?"

"You *are* the Chief of Police. I suppose if I said I wouldn't talk to you, you could run me in."

Coming from anybody else, I would have thought this was a joke, but Jolene looks dead serious.

"It probably wouldn't come to that," I say. "I can come back later if you're too busy."

"Go ahead and sit down," she says.

I look at my choices of seating. Severity seems to be the message imparted by pretty much everything in the office, from the sharp-edged metal desk to the metal file cabinets. I take the armchair next to the desk, which is more comfortable than it looks. I note the framed Biblical quotations on the walls. Loretta told me that strict Baptists don't believe in having pictures of saints or Jesus because nobody actually knows what they looked like. Makes sense to me, but it doesn't keep a lot of people from hanging pictures of a blond, blue-eyed imaginary messiah.

"I don't know whether Officer Trevino told you, but we're a little concerned because Loretta Singletary hasn't been in touch with any of her friends in the last few days. Have you talked to her by any chance?"

"I told the girl that I hadn't talked to Loretta since last week, but I don't find that cause for alarm. We don't see one another every day." She glances at her computer, and I wonder whether she's thinking about her numbers rather than my question.

"Officer Trevino said you indicated you might have an idea where Loretta is."

She lifts an eyebrow. "Well, the girl got it wrong. I don't know where she is."

"Did Loretta indicate to you that she might be going out of town?"

"Not really." I wonder what Jolene said to Maria to make her think she did.

"I see."

She levels a pert look at me, and I realize that she's enjoying being obtuse. She doesn't want to be an easy mark. "Do you have a list of the members of the Ladies' Circle?"

She glances at a stack of papers on her desk. "It may not be completely up-to-date."

"I'd like to take a look at it. Please."

She sighs and gives an eye roll before she plucks the top sheet off the stack and hands it to me. Nothing like a little obstruction to make someone's day.

I glance over it and see two names that Loretta has mentioned. I get out a pen and my little notebook and jot them down.

"Who are you going to talk to?" Jolene asks.

"Michele Orlander and Sunny Jones." Loretta has mentioned their names.

"They won't be able to tell you anymore than I can."

"What is it you can tell me?"

She drums her fingers. She has beaten herself at her own game and she knows it. "Loretta told us at the last sewing meeting that she was going to have coffee with a man she had met online."

"Online? You mean on the computer?"

"That's what online means." Her tone would wither a healthy plant.

"How do you meet somebody online?"

"A dating website." She looks at me like I've just swung down out of a tree.

I have heard of dating websites; I'm not entirely out of touch. But I don't know much about them. I'm not even sure what the right question is. How do you find out the names of such websites and where they are? And how to get in touch with them? But I've had enough of begging Jolene for information. "Good to know," I say, mustering as much dignity and goodwill as I can.

It's late afternoon, and when I leave the church, I call Maria to tell her I'm coming by to get Dusty, and then I'm leaving for the rest of the day. "Anything going on?"

"Connor and I are having a little discussion." The surly note in her voice and her emphasis on the word "discussion" tells me that the two of them are at it again. Connor Loving is the newest cop on our force, hired after Zeke retired for good last summer. Maria and Connor argue over everything. If she says it's hot, then he argues that it's not as hot as it could be. If he says the coffee is weak, then she says it's too strong. There is nothing too insignificant for them to rag each other over.

"I don't want to hear it," I say. "If it comes to blows, whoever survives has to take the other one to the hospital."

When I get back to headquarters, Dusty leaps up and barks with excitement. I assume when he gets a little older he won't act like I've been gone for a week when I leave him for a half hour.

An hour later, when I pull into Wendy's driveway, Dusty whines and can't wait to get out of the car. I don't know which one of us likes Wendy better, but at least I try to show more dignity.

Wendy always surprises me when she comes to the door. I've never seen anybody who loves clothes the way she does. Tonight, she's dressed in plain old blue jeans, but she's wearing a ruffled blouse the color of the ocean. "Oh, I'm happy to see you!" she says. She stoops down to pat Dusty, who flings himself onto his back so she can scratch his belly. Finally, she grabs my hand, and we go inside.

"Something smells good."

"I decided to branch out. I tried a new recipe I found for osso buco."

"Whatever that is, I'm ready for it." I hand her the bottle of red wine I've brought.

"This is perfect," she says. There's nothing like having a woman who thinks you're the best at everything, especially because I feel the same way about her. When I'm with her, I feel like whatever I say will be okay. And if she disagrees with me in a discussion, she doesn't hold back, but she also doesn't make it into a war. More important, she doesn't brood or pout.

When we sit down to eat, I ask her whether she knows anything about online dating sites.

"Are you planning to dump me and put yourself out there on Match.com?"

"Could happen unless you play your cards right."

I tell her that Loretta is missing, and that someone said she was going out with a man she met through a dating site.

Wendy frowns. "I don't like the sound of that. I don't know Loretta well, but she seems smarter than that. You know those dating sites can be tricky."

"What do you mean?"

She shrugs. "Every now and then you hear a story of a woman meeting up with a date through one of those sites and she gets attacked." And then she laughs. "But I expect Loretta has enough sense not to get sucked into a situation like that. I wonder what site she's on?"

"There's more than one?"

"Oh, honey, there's more than twenty. There might be fifty."

I groan. "How do you figure out which one somebody is on?"

"After we eat, we'll sit down at the computer and maybe we can narrow it down."

We never get around to it because we end up, as we often do, in the bedroom. I don't usually sleep over because I have to be up early to see to my cows. Wendy has never complained about it. Maybe it's because we were both married for a long time, but we don't feel the need to spend every second together.

CHAPTER 6

Maria isn't coming in until later. She has gone to Bobtail to track down information at City Hall on a cold case she's working on. I'm at headquarters on the early shift with Connor. I ask him what he knows about online dating sites and am surprised when he blushes as red as a tomato. Connor is an awkward young man, chunky, with a tendency to blush easily. He is quick with a sharp reply at what he perceives as little slights. Sort of like Maria, actually. But Maria has a better sense of humor.

"Why would I know about that?" he asks. His beaky nose twitches and his eyes narrow.

"Because you're young."

"Oh." He relaxes.

"Most people your age are a lot savvier on the Internet than us older citizens. I'd like you to help me research Internet dating sites." At least I can dazzle him with my knowledge that there's more than one site.

He favors me with a speculative look, and I know he wants to ask me why I'm interested in dating sites. Before I can formulate a reason that doesn't sound lame or implicate Loretta, he opens his computer and starts pecking away. I'm envious. I never got the hang of typing and still have to hunt and peck. "Here," he says, and turns his computer to face me.

I look at the screen. It's a list of dating sites. Like Wendy said, there are a lot of them, with names like "Match," "Elite," and "Eharmony."

"Is this all of them?" I'm reading down the list. There must be twenty-five, all with cute names.

"Heck, no, there's a lot more. This is just the most popular ones."

"Would they all appeal to everybody? How about older women?"

He screws up his face, thinking. "These are more for younger people." He takes his computer back and types some more. "Here are five that Google says are popular with older women."

Google says. Why didn't I think of that? I look things up on Google, but sometimes I still don't think to do it. "What kinds of people use them, and how do they get their names in there?"

He shrugs. "Anybody can use them." I appreciate that he takes the question for what it's worth rather than acting smug because I don't know what I'm looking at. Another siege of typing. "Here's one of the websites. It tells you how to sign up. It isn't hard. They all make it easy."

"Why?"

"Because they want to sell you a subscription. They're not in it to make people happy, no matter what they say. They're in it to make money."

The one I'm looking at is a site called "Fifty and Beyond." It asks for your email address and zip code, and then it asks for gender and whether you are looking for a man or woman. It seems to me if you put your gender in, that's all you need. They would know you are looking for someone of the other sex. But then I realize I'm being narrow-minded.

"You mean if a man is looking for another man, they'll know that?"

He shrugs. "Sure."

I don't want to stare at him, but for a few seconds, I think I've stepped into alien territory. I'm no prude, and I believe it's best to live and let live, but his attitude surprises me. It isn't even the idea that same genders are looking for each other online that brings me up short; it's that Connor is so casual about it. He grew up in Bobtail, not in a big city. How is it that he takes such things for granted? It occurs to me that I don't know a thing about his love interests. I shut the door on my speculation. It's none of my business.

"People don't have a problem putting in their email address? Aren't they afraid these websites will start hounding them?"

"That goes with the territory if you sign up for anything at all on the Internet. But they have to know basic information, like what area you live in. It doesn't make sense for them to show you the profile of somebody who lives in Arkansas when you're here in Jarrett Creek."

"People could lie."

"Sure, they could, but why would they? You go on a dating site to find somebody to date. You're not going to find anybody if you aren't willing to share a little bit about yourself."

"What if I just want to check whether someone is on their database?"

"Who?"

I hesitate, not wanting to drag Loretta into the conversation. But Connor is a cop, even if he's young. There's no need to keep things from him. I tell him that no one has seen Loretta in a few days, and there is a suggestion that she was looking at dating sites. "I want to look through and see if she signed up for this one."

Connor wags his finger. "Unh, unh, unh. No can do. It's pay to play. You have to sign up to browse through the members."

"I need to know which site Loretta is on. Do I have to sign up for every one of them? Can I send whoever runs the site an email asking if she's there? Or do I have to get a court order to be able to look?"

"All you have to do is sign up as if you are a man looking for a woman like Loretta. But you'll have to sign up for as many sites as it takes to find her."

I sit back, considering the number of sites I might have to sign on to. "How much does it cost?"

"It varies, but most aren't expensive. At least not at first. I've heard that the sites will offer all kinds of gimmicks for finding a mate, and it can get costly." He taps vigorously into his computer again. He looks like he enjoys searching. "Here's an article that says they charge anywhere from $25 to $50 a month or less if you sign up for several months."

My phone rings. It's Loretta's son, Scott. Thank goodness. Saved by the bell.

"Hi, Chief. My wife said you called with a question?" His voice is hurried, like he has taken a minute out from something important.

"Scott, did your mamma tell you she might be going away?"

"No, I haven't talked to her since last weekend. Why are you asking?"

"I don't want to alarm you, but nobody has seen her for a few days, and she didn't tell anybody she was leaving town. I was hoping you might have an idea where she is."

"Hold on a minute." He hollers, "Marcie? Where are you? Can you come here for a minute?" Kids are squabbling in the background.

"This better be important," she says loud enough for me to hear. "I'm trying to get the kids ready for school."

Scott asks Marcie whether his mom mentioned to her that she was going somewhere. I hear the anxious tone in his voice. Marcie says she hasn't talked to her since Scott did. "Why? What's going on?"

He comes back on the line. "You sure Mamma didn't just go over to Bobtail to go shopping?"

"It doesn't seem that way. She was supposed to meet a friend and didn't show up. I took the liberty of going to her house, and she wasn't there and the car's gone."

"Have you called the hospital? Maybe she had a wreck."

"We did call the hospital in Bobtail but not farther away. Do you know if she keeps emergency information in her purse? Who to call, that sort of thing?"

He hesitates. "I guess I never thought about it, but Mamma's careful. It's hard for me to imagine her not having information like that with her." He has gotten increasingly agitated. "Listen here, I don't like the sound of this. Let me call into work and cancel a couple of appointments, and I'll get back to you. I think I'd like to come down there."

Twenty minutes later, he calls back. "Marcie wondered if you've talked to her friends. You know, they might have gotten it into their heads to go down to Fredericksburg to look at the bluebonnets or go shopping in Houston."

I always wonder why people think they know more about police work than police do. What kind of fool would neglect to call a missing person's family, friends, and the local hospital? "I contacted a few of her friends, and the ones I talked to didn't know of any plans."

"Well, where the hell is she?" I realize this is a rhetorical question. "I think I'd better come over there."

"Look, Scott, let me put a little more time into it. I called you in case someone in your family had an emergency and she took off to go be with you and didn't have time to tell anyone. Let me get a little further along before we start to worry. I don't want to get you all fussed up over nothing."

"I don't know . . ."

I would have the same concerns in his place. But he's a man with a family and a job, and I don't want him to waste his time, when his mother might just be gallivanting around somewhere.

"You go on to work, and I'll pursue this. I want to talk to a couple more people."

"Call me the minute you know anything. And if you haven't located her by, say, two o'clock, I'm driving down there."

I get his work number and hope that I'll be able to call him soon and tell him the mystery is cleared up—that Loretta is back home and mad because we were too nosy for our own good.

Loretta seems to know everybody, but when it comes down to it, she doesn't have what I think of as a "best friend." She and Ida Ruth Dillard get along well though. Maybe she confided in her. She knows Ida Ruth can keep a secret. Ida Ruth was close to a friend of mine who died a few years back, and it turned out Ida Ruth had kept a secret about her for many years that no one else knew. Loretta was impressed and said if she had a secret, she'd surely tell Ida Ruth before she'd tell anyone else.

I've barely hung up from Scott when Ellen Forester calls. "Samuel, I still haven't heard from Loretta. Have you?"

"No. I spoke with her son Scott, and if she was planning to leave town, she didn't tell him."

"I'm so mad at her I could spit. Why would she go off like that and not tell anyone?" She sounds close to tears. I need to give her a task to keep her busy.

"Would you do something for me? She's taking that watercolor class from you, right? Would you ask the people in the class whether she might have mentioned to any of them that she planned to go away?"

"That's a good idea. I'll be glad to. She and Kathy Weinman are both in the intermediate watercolor class, and they chat a lot with each other. Maybe Loretta confided in her."

I have my doubts. It seems like she would be more likely to confide in Ellen. "Don't get too worked up," I say. "We'll find her. She'll probably be aggravated because we poked our nose in." I tell her I'm going over to talk to Ida Ruth right now.

"I suppose you have to," she says. I don't know why Ellen doesn't like Ida Ruth, but the few times she has come up in conversation, Ellen has had a sour face. It's unusual. She usually likes most people. I've never asked what the trouble is.

I'm lucky to find Ida Ruth at home. She has been a pillar of the First Baptist Church in Jarrett Creek for many years, and she's gone a lot, traveling all over the state attending meetings. I don't know what they do that involves so many meetings.

Ida Ruth and Earl have lived here all their lives. They have a nice little place right in the middle of town. Unlike Loretta, who is an avid gardener, Ida Ruth and her husband are clearly in my gardening camp—simple is best. A lawn with a few trees and a couple of potted plants on the porch do the trick. I wonder whether it's Ida Ruth or Earl who decided on the dazzling yellow color of the house. I suspect it was a mistake and neither of them had the nerve to admit it to each other.

Ida Ruth gives me a cup of coffee, which I always appreciate. She says Earl is in Bobtail looking at property. She laughs. "I don't know what he thinks he's going to do with land if he finds acreage he likes. We're too old to build a new house, and farming never appealed to him. No telling what he has in mind. He always was one for big ideas."

We sit in her living room, which is as full of knick knacks as you can cram in. She favors Hummel figurines and must have two dozen of them. "Now I'm going to warn you," she says. "I may have to answer the phone. We've got a little argument brewing down at the church, and I'm trying to settle it down."

I can tell by the way she raises her eyebrows that she wants me to ask what the argument is about, but I suspect it has to do with the rodeo. I'm not going to let myself get into that subject with her. "I'll get right to the point then," I say, "so I won't have to keep you long. I'm concerned because nobody seems to know where Loretta is. I was hoping she might have told you if she had plans."

"Loretta is missing?" She reaches up in an unconscious gesture to stroke the side of her face where the skin is wrinkled from a burn she got as a child.

"I can't exactly say that. But I haven't seen her in a few days, and she didn't show up for a date she had to go shopping with a friend. Her car is gone, so it appears that she left under her own steam, but it seems funny that she didn't tell anybody where she was going."

Ida Ruth nods her head. She's worrying her bottom lip with her big buck teeth. "I expect she'll be back before too long. You know how Loretta is. She's an independent person, and I don't think she believes she has to answer to anybody."

That's an oddly defensive comment, and it makes me wonder whether Ida Ruth does have some idea where Loretta is. "I would really appreciate it if you could set my mind at ease." I meet her eyes, and she glances away.

I persist. "Somebody suggested that she might have met a man through an online dating site. Do you know anything about that?"

She straightens her spine. "Samuel, sometimes women want to keep their business to themselves. It isn't against the law to go out on a blind date."

"Is that what she did?"

"I don't know for sure. But yes, I do know she registered for one of those dating sites. For seniors. But I don't think she has to broadcast the news all over town if she signs up and goes on a date." She gives me a pointed look.

"All I want is to make sure she hasn't met a man who's up to no good," I say.

"Tsk. She's a grown woman, and she can take care of herself."

The phone rings, and she rolls her eyes at me. "I'll be right back."

Her conversation with whoever called is one-sided, with Ida Ruth interjecting an occasional, "We'll work it out" or "I wish you wouldn't get so riled up."

She comes back in but doesn't sit down. "I have to go down to the church. You need anything else?"

"Yes. Do you know the name of the website she was using?"

"Oh, let me think." She raises her eyes to the ceiling. "Something to do with small towns. Oh, right, Smalltownpair. She said they specialize in small towns in Texas, and they have a separate section for senior citizens."

"You think it's on the up and up?"

"I have no idea. It all seems shady to me. Not that I judge Loretta. She has been single for a long time. I think whatever people have to do to try to make themselves happy, they ought to do it. You know, the Lord put two by two in the ark, so I think He likes for people to be together." She pauses, pursing her lips. "I'll tell you this though. I personally would not get involved with anything like that. The idea of going out with a stranger bothers me."

I get up. "Thank you for your time. If you hear from her, would you tell her she's got a lot of people worried and to at least call me to let me know she's all right?"

"I sure will."

I have my hand on the doorknob when she says, "Can I get your opinion about something?"

Here it comes. I turn back to her. "What would that be?"

"It concerns the rodeo. I'm not sure everything is going well with that."

"What do you mean?

"I hate to say it, but I believe Father Sanchez thinks he owns it. That's not right. It's time for him to share some of the glory with others. Loretta was supposed to bring it up with you. Did she?"

The glory. I suspect those are Reverend Becker's words. "Yes, she talked to me last week. She told me the Baptist preacher wanted to participate in putting on the rodeo. I told her that I worried that if the Baptist Church got to be a sponsor, then all the other churches would want in on it."

"The other churches didn't think of it first, though, did they? They're willing to go along with the Catholics getting the glory. Since the Baptists are taking the initiative, they ought to get to be part of it if they want to."

More about the glory. "I haven't had much time to ponder on it," I say.

"It shouldn't take that much pondering. It's a matter of principal." She's on the warpath now.

"Does Reverend Becker think Father Sanchez is doing a bad job?"

"I don't think that's the point."

I find myself turning my hat around and around. "I guess I can't help thinking if something isn't broken, why fix it?"

She sniffs. "Well, you aren't a church going man. I can see how you might not appreciate the nuances."

"Yes, ma'am, that's probably right."

I open the door, and Dusty springs up.

"My goodness, look at that cute dog. Oh, no, no, you stay outside. Good dog." She flutters her hands at Dusty, and he backs up with his ears back.

Why is it that when I leave one of the church ladies, I always feel like I've barely escaped?

CHAPTER 7

I'm walking into the station when my cell phone rings. It has only been an hour since I talked to Loretta's son, but he's calling again. "Have you heard anything from Mamma?"

"I got a little information, but I haven't found her yet. It's only been a short time, Scott."

"I know it, but I can't get anything done for worrying. I'm going to come to Jarrett Creek."

He won't be dissuaded. It will take him a couple of hours to get here, by which time I hope his trip is unnecessary.

I turn on the computer to look up the dating site that Ida Ruth told me Loretta was involved with.

I find the site easily and go into the senior citizens section, which is for those fifty and older. The header has photos of toothy, healthy-looking men and women who look 50 years and one month old. They are holding tennis rackets and wearing crisp-looking white shorts, or they are dressed in swimsuits with bodies that 20-year-olds would envy. No truth in advertising here. I bite the bullet and sign up for a month.

Next, they ask me to fill in a description of myself. It's not mandatory, but if I'm going to do this, I might as well go all in. And it will help me to get an idea of what Loretta had to do to find a date.

I can't say I'm a chief of police, so I put "retired." Description: Gray hair. I wear glasses to read. I'm slightly over six feet tall and weigh 190 pounds, which is what I've weighed since I was forty, but I don't put that down. Marital status? That one is easy. Widower. Likes and dislikes: I like my cows and my cat and my dog. I like the woman I'm dating, too, although I doubt that would help me in my search. I write down that I don't like sharp-tongued women, although I don't mind a woman who speaks her mind. Should I have put that in? I doubt it. I sigh. I don't know why people subject themselves to this.

The next section is likes and dislikes. Why would anybody care what kind of food I like? I put down meat. What kind of clothes do I wear? I skip that one. What do I like to do? One thing I know I don't like to do is fill out questionnaires like this. Is it really going to help me find Loretta? Finally, I copy the words from the sample. I like sunsets and drives in the country and walks on the beach. What beach?

Now it gets harder. It asks for my preferences as to what kind of woman I am looking for. If I hope to find Loretta's profile, I have to figure out how somebody would describe her. I'm annoyed with myself because the truth is, I'm not sure what she looks like. I mean I know she changed her hair so that it's a blondish color and she no longer wears it in tight little curls, but how would you describe it—straight? Short? She has brown eyes. I think. No, they're blue. I'm pretty sure they're blue.

What would she write down as her hobbies? I know she likes to bake, garden, and paint, but is that something she thinks a man would be looking for in a woman? Would she think it was a good idea to describe herself that way? I would hope that she would think it's best to be honest. I read a few of the samples, and they are long on romantic notions (love moonlight dinners and interesting conversation) and short on concrete facts. What I end up with is that I want to find a good cook, a good conversationalist, and a woman with a sense of humor. I think Loretta has a sense of humor. She makes me laugh.

I finally grind to a halt and ask the site to find me a match. It warns me that it will take several minutes. I picture a bunch of people on the other end writing down all my information and then searching a bunch of cards that match. Of course, I know that's not the way it works, but it's soothing to picture something other than a bunch of electronic signals doing mumbo jumbo. It's only three minutes before a list of women gets presented to me. And none of them is Loretta.

A RISKY UNDERTAKING FOR LORETTA SINGLETARY

I'm gnashing my teeth over this when Maria walks in carrying a couple of fat folders. She has been researching the cold case. She said she was glad to have a case to take her mind off worrying about where Loretta is. She throws the folders on her desk, pours herself a cup of coffee, and flops down.

"What's up?" she asked. "You look like you could bite somebody."

I tell her everything that has transpired this morning. "Loretta's son is on his way here, and I'm trying to find her on the dating site that Ida Ruth told me she joined."

"Let me see what you've got," she says, in that bossy way she has that usually tickles me but occasionally annoys me. In my current state of mind, it's the latter.

I push my computer around to give her a look at it. She asks me the password I set up and then reads the entries I took such pains to enter. Pretty soon she starts laughing. "How in the world do you think you're going to find Loretta with all that?"

"What do you mean?"

"First of all, it makes you sound like an old fart looking for a cook and a maid."

"It does not." But I can't help laughing.

"And second, you didn't really need to put all this stuff in. You can simply scroll the site and look at profiles. Like Connor, she starts typing a mile a minute and then pauses while she waits for results. "Here you go."

She turns the computer around, and there is Loretta staring out at me. But this is a Loretta I haven't seen before. She has on make up, her hair is fixed up, and she looks twenty years younger.

"She looks cute, doesn't she?" Maria asks.

"She looks different," I say. I sound like a curmudgeon. She doesn't look like the Loretta I know, and the idea that she thought it was a good idea to publicly announce that she's looking for a date just seems wrong.

"Makes sense. She wanted to look her best."

"She looked fine the way she was," I grumble.

Maria glares at me. "If you think she looked so great, why didn't you go out with her?"

"It would be like going out with my sister," I say. "I wonder if anybody did respond and she went out with them?"

"I imagine they did. We could go back to her house and see what kind of email replies she got."

"We'll wait until her son gets here." I look at my watch. "I'm going to get lunch. You want to come?"

"No, I got myself a hamburger to eat at my desk. I need to go through these files."

Maria would happily eat hamburgers three times a day. "How did your search go?"

"There wasn't a whole lot, but I did get these files. I have to have them back by tomorrow."

"You mean they let you take them out?"

She grins. "Took some sweet talking. Anyway, I'll know before too long whether Howard Mosley had a financial incentive to kill that hired hand."

The case she's working on transpired twenty years ago, when a hired hand disappeared from Howard Mosley's ranch. Last year the ranch was sold to a Houston attorney who decided to have a pool built in the backyard. During the excavation, they dug up a body that, not surprisingly, turned out to be the missing hired hand, an eighteen-year-old drifter by the name of Doug Lantana. He had been shot at close range. Howard Mosley, who moved to Bobtail several years ago, seems like the likely suspect for the killing, but twenty years is a long time for evidence to show up. Still, Maria had a yen to tackle the case and see if she could make anything of it. She reminds me of myself at her age.

A RISKY UNDERTAKING FOR LORETTA SINGLETARY

I join my usual bunch at Town Café for lunch. Gabe LoPresto is there, along with Alton Coldwater and a couple of others. When I sit down, I see that they have been hot onto some subject. They're all red in the face and tight-lipped. If this is about the goat rodeo, I've a mind to get up and walk right back out.

"What's the subject?" I ask, after I give Lurleen my order.

Turns out they're arguing over which quarterback should start next fall. In other words, the usual. It doesn't matter that the first football game isn't until late August. I'm perfectly content to listen to them squabble about it. But then Alton says, "Not to change the subject, but is anybody else's wife making your life miserable over that goat rodeo problem?"

Gabe snorts. "Anne says we're going to start going to church in Bobtail if it doesn't simmer down. Last Sunday the preacher actually brought it up in his sermon."

They're Methodists, and why their preacher should get involved I don't know. "Why does he care?" I ask.

Gabe wads up his napkin and throws it on the table. "You have to ask him. Sometimes I think preachers jump in on things just to keep everybody riled up. Job security."

Pete Briskin, in his forties and owner of a heating and cooling repair company, sits tall and looks daggers at Gabe. "What do you mean by that?" I had forgotten his brother is a preacher in a small town down on the coast.

"I don't mean anything by it, Pete. I'm aggravated because half the town is stirred up over it."

"Well, you ought to watch what you say."

Gabe is pompous about a lot of things, and he'll argue with a rock on the subject of the football team, but in general he doesn't want trouble. He's the biggest building contractor in the county, and he likes to keep peace with potential customers. "You're right, and I apologize." He eases to his feet. "I'd better get on back. We're almost finished framing the place we're working on."

There's more rodeo talk, but it has turned to more practical matters, such as whether it is financially sound and whether it's time to retire it. That's not going to happen. It has been a popular event for the last quarter century.

In the rodeo, goats take the place of cattle, and it's a lot tamer than a regular rodeo. Kids of all ages chase the goats and try to catch them—or, in many cases, the kids get chased. There's a milking contest and a riding contest for little ones. Goats are pursued on foot, wrestled to the ground, roped, and then let go. For their part, they get in a good bit of butting, but the horns on the young Billy goats are wrapped so nobody will get gored. Old Billy goats don't get to take part in the "fun." There's even a variation on the three-legged race, where two contestants are tied together and have to carry a baby goat to the finish line. Needless to say, the goat isn't amused and tries to wriggle out of their arms. I usually get a kick out of it, but this year I'll be glad when it's over so I don't have to hear any more about who sponsors it.

"Samuel, do you think the Catholic priest should share sponsorship with other churches?" Alton asks.

I get to my feet. "Alton, I don't have an opinion on the subject. And my advice to you is that you steer clear of the controversy too." I normally wouldn't say that to anybody, but Alton has a knack for getting himself into hot water, including a disastrous stint as mayor a few years ago, when he managed to bankrupt the town.

Back at headquarters, while I wait for Scott Singletary to show up, I research information on online dating sites. What I find both surprises and troubles me. Apparently, even though the sites try to maintain security, predators slip through. In the younger population, people, mostly women, get preyed on by liars and cheats. A certain percentage of both men and women on the sites are married and claim to be single. Then you get people who claim to be more attractive or wealthier than they turn out to be. And now and then you get really bad actors who are looking for vulnerable people to hit up for money.

A RISKY UNDERTAKING FOR LORETTA SINGLETARY

Worst of all are the sexual predators who have been known to rape or even kill women respondents.

But when you get into the senior area, the incidence of financial predation goes way up. In particular, older women get fleeced out of their savings by younger men. The stories are disturbing. I'm getting worried. Where is Loretta?

CHAPTER 8

Scott Singletary, Loretta's older son, looks like Loretta except that he's at least a foot taller and outweighs her by 100 pounds, even though he isn't heavy. He has two teenaged boys who, according to Loretta, are the best-looking, smartest, most loving grandsons ever born.

He eyes Dusty when I walk onto the porch. "Would Mamma let that dog in the house?"

"No, and I hadn't planned to bring him in. He'll stay out here on the porch. He'll be fine."

Inside, Scott gives me permission to get onto the computer, which Loretta keeps at a kneehole desk in the kitchen. He leaves me alone so he can go through the house to see whether he can spot anything missing or disturbed.

Maria stays with me to take command of the computer. "I'll see if she exchanged emails with any men she met through the site," she says. "Also, we should see if she took notes on men she was interested in."

"I have a hunch she wouldn't keep notes on the computer," I say. She knows how to use a computer, but like the rest of us fogies, I think she prefers to write things down. "I'll bet if she kept a list at all, it would be handwritten."

The top of the desk is bare of any papers except a tidy stack of bills. I open the top side drawer of the little desk. The top drawer contains address books, church fliers, handbooks, and a stack of business cards held with a rubber band. And Loretta's cell phone. "Look at this," I say.

"It's probably dead," Maria says.

She's right. It's out of juice. The cord is connected to the computer, and I plug it in. Nothing happens.

"It's probably completely out of power," Maria says. "It'll take a couple of minutes to get enough juice to open it."

The second drawer turns out to be a file drawer. I start thumbing through the file folders. "Bingo." I pull out a folder marked "Pairs." It contains a small spiral notebook with a yellow cover, and the first page contains a list of men's names. Maria and I pore over it. One by one, Loretta has marked off the entries, with notes: "Too old." "Too young." "No." "Silly." Maria laughs at that one.

There are two that have question marks beside them: A man named John Markham and another named Frederick Hastings. Two possible dates. That shouldn't be too hard to trace.

When I turn the page, my hopes are dashed. On this second page, she has written down more names, but she abandoned her earlier, complete profiles in favor of names only and no descriptive notes. Just yes, no, or maybe. There are two more pages—more of the same. Who would have guessed there could be this many men in small towns willing to go on the Internet to look for a date?

"There must be thirty names of men here," I say. "Is that possible?"

"These sites are very popular," Maria says.

"Do you suppose she contacted any of them, or was she just making notes of men whose profiles she liked?"

"On her computer here, there are emails back and forth from ten men."

I peer over her shoulder and we go through the emails. They all seem innocuous enough, asking each other mundane things, like where they live, if they have been married before, if they have kids, and what they like to do.

Two haven't been married before, and Loretta rejected them, kindly, telling them she wants to date people who have been married before so they have shared experiences of losing a spouse.

"Ha," Maria says. "I suspect that's a nice way of saying that if a man has never been married by his age, he's probably got something seriously wrong with him."

Another two tell her they are not religious, and she writes them back and says that probably wouldn't work.

Two men she emailed never wrote back. Another one wrote such a weird email, full of his likes and dislikes, heavy on the dislikes, that apparently she decided not to even reply. Or hadn't had time to. One said he had changed his mind about meeting. And she set up a meeting with one man two weeks ago, at a church gathering in Bobtail. It turns out they were both Baptists. I print out that email. "It's possible that when they met they decided to meet again, and he swept her off her feet and they ran away for a fling."

"I doubt it." Maria gives me a disgusted look. "But he sent her his phone number. Let's give him a call."

She dials the number and puts the call on speaker. We identify ourselves. Maria does the talking. "I'm calling because you were in contact with Loretta Singletary through the dating website Smalltown-pair."

"Yes, I guess I was. What's this about?" He's got a reedy voice, and his profile picture shows an older man with a thin face and little hair.

"Did you meet with her?"

He's quiet for a few seconds. "I'm sorry, but I don't have any proof that you are who you say you are. Why are you asking?"

"Mrs. Singletary is missing, and we're trying to ascertain her whereabouts."

"Missing? I don't have any idea where she is. I only met her that one time. We chatted with one another at a church social."

"Did you plan to meet again?"

"No. She was nice, but it was awkward. Neither of us had ever tried a blind date before, and we couldn't figure out what we were supposed to do. I was there with my sister, and I don't think my sister took to her all that much." He gives a huff of laughter. "I think we were both glad to get out of there."

"Did you leave with Loretta?"

"No, we had driven there separately, and I left with my sister, Lena.

And to tell you the truth, I don't think I'm going to try meeting a date that way anymore. It was, well, like I said, awkward."

"Do you mind giving me your address in case we need to ask you more questions in person?"

"I tell you what. I'll call the Jarrett Creek Police Department and leave my information there. That way if you are who you say you are, you'll have the information. And if you're not . . ."

"That will be fine."

She hangs up and shrugs.

"I don't think he ran off with Loretta," I say. Especially since his sister didn't approve of her. "But I don't think we can depend on making judgments from just calling people. I'm not looking forward to having to visit each man Loretta might have met, but we may have to."

"Wait. Here's something." Maria has found a printed-out photo stashed in the notebook. "I guess she liked this man's photo."

The man in the photograph is distinguished and looks friendly. "How are we going to find out who this is?"

"We can look through all the profiles on the site. I didn't see anything on her list to indicate that she thought any of these men were particularly appealing."

"Is it possible that this is someone she didn't contact through the dating site?" I say.

Scott appears in the kitchen looking flustered. "Everything looks normal. It's like she just was . . ." he throws up his hands, "teleported out of here."

"Except she packed a suitcase," I say.

I take him back upstairs and show him the gap in the collection of bags in the closet and point out that her toothbrush and toiletries are gone.

"That makes me feel better," he says. He mops his forehead with his handkerchief. It isn't that warm. He's upset.

Downstairs, Maria is holding Loretta's cell phone. "I can't believe she doesn't have a security code," she says. "That's not smart. But at least that meant I could get right into it."

"And?"

"And nothing. She hasn't used it for two weeks." She sets it down. "What's the point of even having a cell phone if you aren't going to use it?"

"She must have used her landline," I say. "Let's get a printout of her phone records for the last month."

While Maria uses the computer to access Loretta's landline account, I show Scott the list of men's names that we found. He gets a glass of water and sits down at the kitchen table and looks at the notes she made. I also show him the photograph. "Do you recognize him?"

"No." He stares at it for several seconds. I expect he's having the same response I have—a strange kind of possessiveness. He groans. "Oh, Mamma, what have you done?"

Maria looks like she could cry. "Scott, it's possible that she's off on a lark. Sometimes people meet someone and get swept off their feet. It happens even to older people." She cuts her eyes at me as a prime example. I met Wendy several months ago, and she wowed me from the first day I met her. "Swept off my feet" describes it just right.

"Not Mamma. She's too practical."

Maria smiles. Scott doesn't want to think of his mamma in that way. But even though Maria is right that people Loretta's age can meet someone that they take to right away, that's not the part that bothers me. I'm bothered by the statistics I saw regarding the number of over-sixty women who get bilked by men on these dating sites. It's appalling. But I'm not going to tell Scott that. "We'll figure this out," I say.

"How?" He practically begs.

"First of all, I'm going to call the Department of Public Safety. They need to know we've got a missing person. I'll get them to put out a bulletin to look for her car. And I'll get them to tag her credit cards. If she went any distance at all, she's bound to need gas at some point. Or she'll stop to buy snacks or a meal. We have to hope that she uses a credit card, and when she does, we'll have an idea what direction she went." I also want to find out what kind of action they take if it looks like someone has been duped by a person they met online, but again I don't feel the need to say that to Scott.

"Good. That sounds like a start." Scott is clutching at my words.

"Then, depending on what they say, I'll call the FBI."

"The FBI?" His eyes widen. "What do they have to do with it?"

"In specific cases, they handle Internet fraud. Mostly it's a state concern, but there are circumstances where they'll step in. I don't know if they'll think this qualifies, but it won't hurt to talk to them."

"Meanwhile," Maria says, "I'm going to go over her phone records and match them to the men on her list. I'll also try to contact the men on the list that she marked 'yes' or 'maybe' to find out if they heard from her."

Scott nods. "I guess you have a plan. What can I do?"

"Call your relatives and see if anybody has heard from her. Her sister, your cousins, your brother. Or any old friends she might have mentioned recently."

"Good. I'm glad it's Friday so I can be here all weekend."

My heart sinks. It's hard to have a feverish relative looking over our shoulders. "Try not to get your relatives too worried." They might descend on Jarrett Creek in droves, and we surely don't need a whole posse of worried relatives.

"I got you."

"I'm going back to headquarters to make my calls," I say. "It's getting on in the day, and I want to try to get some responses before they close up for the weekend."

Maria stays behind to dig deeper into Loretta's computer. "Maybe I'll find something more."

"Like what?" Scott asks.

"I'll look through her Internet history. She might have checked a map or looked up the name of someplace where she was thinking of traveling. I have your permission, right?"

"My permission? Absolutely."

Back at headquarters, I call the regional office of the Texas Department of Public Safety (DPS). I have a good friend in the local office over in Bryan-College Station, but I want to get to a higher level. It turns out the honcho I reach is not too interested in my story.

"We don't usually get involved in problems with those dating sites," he says. "Unless we find out for sure that somebody has been defrauded. Or attacked. We get a lot of calls from people who are worried that a loved one might get into trouble, and we simply don't have the manpower to look into all of them."

"Well I'd like you to put out a notice to be on the lookout for her car anyway."

"That I can do." He takes down the information.

"And I'd like to have you tag her credit cards." Scott looked through her bills and gave us the numbers of two cards she uses.

"You can do that yourself," he says.

"Yes, but they'd pay more attention if it comes from DPS."

"If you think so, I'll get that done too."

"Would the FBI give me any help?"

He hesitates. "It's not a bad idea to talk to them. They won't do anything straight off, but they do look at patterns. If something has happened to your friend, they'll want to record the information in case there is a rash of problems." He gives me an 800 number to call.

When I finally reach the proper FBI department and talk to a live person, he listens patiently. Then he chuckles. "I wish I had a dime for every time I hear that story. I get a call from Mary Smith telling me her mother is hooked up with a guy she doesn't trust or Joe Jones telling me his wife has run off with a boy taking their retirement funds with her. And so on."

I don't appreciate his being amused. "But this woman is missing."

"She's most likely hiding out because she's embarrassed that she got caught up in fraud. She'll come back with her tail between her legs, along with a lighter bank account."

"I don't mean to argue, but I know this woman pretty well. She's smart and she's careful."

"And she lives alone, right? Religious? Generous?"

"Yes, but . . ."

"Let me fill this out a little more for you. In the last few weeks or months, she has started dressing a little younger, maybe had her hair fixed different, started a new hobby. And people have noticed that she has a sparkle in her eye?"

I'm momentarily stunned into silence.

"Fit the profile?"

I sigh. "I guess it does."

"One thing is a little different though," he says. "She at least has people worried about her. Some of these poor women, and men, too, are just plain lonely. Nobody pays any attention to them until it's too late, and they've lost their money and are either too embarrassed to call us or they wait until the trail is cold."

"You're right. Loretta has a lot of friends, and we're all surprised that she went on one of those websites, and now we're getting worried."

"I'd suggest you sit tight. It won't take too long before this guy gets enough money and he'll suddenly disappear or send her packing. That's when she's going to need friends and family."

That night over spaghetti, I tell Wendy what the FBI said.

"That makes me feel bad," she says. "I never would have thought of Loretta as lonely, as social as she is, but it wouldn't hurt for us to pay more attention to her. We could ask her to have a meal with us or maybe drive to a music festival or something."

She's right, but we grin at each other, knowing it probably won't happen, at least not right away. We like to spend time alone together. We're still getting to know each other. We haven't even gone out with her daughter and son-in-law, and they live in Bobtail. Not that we spend every minute together. We both have busy lives; me with work and Wendy with family and travel plans she made months before we met. We like it that way. "We're not teenagers," she said one time, "and there's no need to rush anything."

"How worried are you?" she asks. "I mean, do you think Loretta's in danger? I don't mean financially; I mean bodily."

"I don't know what to think."

When Maria got back from Loretta's house late this afternoon, she said she hadn't found anything helpful in the computer history or by going through the rest of the desk. She said that Scott was going to spend the night in his mamma's house and hoped that she'd turn up.

"I tried to steer him in the direction of going home and letting us take care of it," she said.

When I told her what the FBI said, she was dismayed. "They can't do anything at all?"

"Not at this point."

She had brought the list of men and the phone list from Loretta's house, and she went to work trying to contact them. By the time I left for Wendy's place, she hadn't gotten very far.

CHAPTER 9

I'm glad Dusty is old enough to go down to the pasture with me when I feed the cows in the morning. He has learned not to bark at them, but he watches them as if he thinks they might make a false move. They ignore him. The weather is glorious this time of year: cool in the mornings, although already with a hint that the day will be warm. I spend a little extra time in the pasture, cleaning up and checking on the herd's hooves. We've had a wet spring, and soggy ground can lead to problems.

Next week I have to start considering which cows I'm going to take to auction. Truly Bennet will be back from west Texas, where he has been helping a newly rich retiree put together a herd. He usually helps me with the selection process.

Wendy is off to Houston this morning. Her younger daughter, the one with wanderlust, is back from India and is stopping in Houston for an unspecified number of days before she pushes on to the East Coast. That means I'm at loose ends this weekend.

When I get back to the house at ten o'clock, the land phone is ringing. I snatch it up.

"Samuel? This is Ida Ruth. I heard news I think you'll want to know."

"What is it?"

"A woman from Bobtail is missing. About Loretta's age. The circumstances made me think of Loretta."

An older woman missing. My heart thuds. It may not be anything at all to do with Loretta. "I'm glad you called. What circumstances do you mean?"

"According to my friend, the missing woman had a date to go out with a man she met on the Internet, and nobody has heard from her. I wasn't worried about Loretta before, but this makes me wonder."

"How did you find this out?"

"I've got a cousin who works in the accounting department at City Hall, and her husband is a police officer. She called me and told me."

When I get off the phone, I call the Bobtail Police Department and ask to speak to my old friend Wallace Lyndall. He's likely to be more forthcoming with me than an officer I don't know. I'm glad when the duty officer says he's in and puts me through.

"You're mighty quick on the draw," Lyndall says, when I tell him what I'm calling about. "We just heard this ourselves an hour ago. The chief hasn't even had time to send an officer over to talk to the woman who reported her missing. How did you hear it?"

"You know how the grapevine works. I have a particular interest because a woman I'm friends with seems to have gone missing under the same circumstances."

"Uh-oh." He tells me their missing person is a widow who lives alone. "She lives in a nice subdivision that went up twenty years ago."

"How did you find out she was missing?"

"Her next-door neighbor called us. Said the woman wasn't answering her phone or her doorbell. She was worried that something had happened to her, so she went into her house, and it looked like the woman hadn't been there for a couple of days. Cat hadn't been fed. She's alarmed."

"I'd like to tag along to talk to the neighbor. Would there be an objection to that?"

"Let me talk to Brent Hogarth. He's the one with the assignment." He comes back on quickly. "He says if you can be over here within thirty minutes, he'll wait for you."

Twenty minutes later, Lyndall introduces me to Hogarth, a lanky man of forty who looks easy in his skin. "Lyndall said you have a friend who's missing?"

"At first we weren't too concerned, but it has been a number of days, and when I heard about your missing woman, I thought I ought to look into it. I understand your woman was on one of those Internet dating sites. Looks like that's what Loretta was doing too."

Hogarth grimaces. "I had hoped to keep that quiet. How did you hear that?"

"Grapevine. You know how small towns are."

He nods. "I don't like the sound of this. Like you, I didn't make much of it when the neighbor told me our missing woman was supposed to go on a date with somebody she met online, but the fact that two women are missing under the same circumstances raises questions."

"I've been looking into it," I say, "and it turns out that meeting people through those sites can be dangerous for older women. The DPS and FBI said a lot of older women get taken in by con men on dating sites. They're mostly fleeced out of their money. A few were attacked, but that seems to be a bigger problem for younger women."

"Well, this one's older. How old is your friend who's missing?"

"Late sixties."

"Same as our woman." Hogarth jacks his hat back. "Lord, what did those two women get themselves into?" He shakes his head. "We're going over now to search her house and talk with the neighbors. Be glad for you to join me and my partner."

"I assume you called the hospital?"

"Yes. They don't have any record of her. I also called her kids to find out whether she had talked to them about any plans, but she hadn't. And as you might expect, they're all stirred up now. Not that I blame them."

Lyndall is working on another matter and can't join us. Outside, I tell Hogarth I'll take my pickup because I have Dusty with me.

"Good-looking dog," he says. "He doesn't get in your way?"

"He's only six months old, but he already knows the drill." Or at least part of the drill.

I follow Hogarth and his partner, a much younger officer, David

Marks, over to the woman's house. I brought my pickup rather than a squad car, so I can leave Dusty in the pickup bed. As we pull up in front of the house, I realize no one has told me the missing woman's name.

Her house is a one-story sandy-colored brick home bordered by a flowerbed. The yard is shaded by a big pecan tree. Inside, the place is neat as a pin, but with a heavy scent that turns my stomach.

"Whew. Potpourri," Officer Marks says. "My grandmother has that stuff stuck in bowls in every room in the house."

"Marks, open some windows," Hogarth says.

"What's the victim's name?" I ask.

Hogarth smiles. He knows it goes down better for a cop if you know the name of the person you're investigating on behalf of.

"Elaine Farquart. Her husband was a city councilman. Died ten years ago. He was young, sixty-two. Mrs. Farquart was sixty-eight on her last birthday."

On a table pushed against one wall, Elaine Farquart has set out a couple dozen framed photos. It's easy to pick out Elaine and her husband, with her kids and grandkids. She's attractive, slim with a youthful haircut and a glowing expression. She doesn't look like a woman who is ready to call it quits with life. The question is, why couldn't she have met someone the old-fashioned way? Why go for a stranger?

Suddenly I hear a "meow," and a tabby comes slinking into the living room and immediately sidles over to rub up against my leg. I reach down and pet it.

The Bobtail officers split up to search the place, and I stick with Hogarth, keeping my eyes open and myself out of his way. Elaine's place reminds me of Loretta's, although a little messier. Her desk is in a small room off the hallway. In the middle of the desk, her laptop is surrounded by piles of notices of events like the theater and a fundraiser, travel brochures, and bills. Hogarth sorts through the bills. "The usual," he grunts.

He sits down and opens the laptop and then pulls up her email program with ease. Twenty years is the line of demarcation between those of us who struggle with computer technology and those who have no trouble with it. I do wonder if he has permission to look into her computer files. As if he read my mind, he says, "Her daughter told me to go ahead and look through anything in the house."

Hogarth starts to type and says, "If you want, you can go through the drawers, see if there's anything that catches your eye."

I'd rather watch what he does with the computer, but I'm an interloper on his patch, so I do as he asks.

There's nothing of note in the drawers, but the more I see, the more I notice similarities between Elaine Farquart and Loretta. Their kitchens are both spotless, and they have little knick knacks on countertops and windowsills. An apron is hung on a hook near the stove, much like Loretta's. How do their similarities account for their decision to go on an Internet dating site? And if they have been abducted, how will they respond—if they get a chance to respond? Loretta is fierce—like a banty rooster. Was Elaine like that, or was she more vulnerable? The more I compare the two, the more uneasy I get.

"Here we go," Hogarth says, breaking into my thoughts.

He pushes the computer to his left so I can see. "It's the same website Loretta was on," I say. "How did you find it?"

"Looked in her history." Hogarth takes a deep breath and taps his finger on the bottom of the computer. "I don't know how to find out who she met or where." I give him the benefit of the little I know. Hogarth tells Marks to go through her emails to see who she might have corresponded with.

"Maybe the neighbor can tell us more," I say. It sounds like Elaine confided her plans more than Loretta did.

The neighbor, Amy Martin, is a long-legged forty-year-old with blond hair tied back in a pony tail. She's wearing baggy pants and a ragged T-shirt. "Sorry," she says, indicating her clothing. "I've got three teenaged boys who are like wild animals, and Saturday is my day to clean up the zoo." She leads us into a living room, where two boys are playing a video game in front of a big TV. They don't look up when we walk in.

"Gavin, you and Freddie make yourselves scarce."

One boy glances over at us. His eyes widen when he sees we're police officers. He sets down his game gear, but the other one says, "Aw, Mom, just let us finish this game."

"Gavin, now!"

Freddie punches Gavin, who reluctantly sets down his controller, too. Then he glances up, and like his brother, he hastily gets to his feet.

"Thank you, Freddie," Amy says. "You're now officially my favorite son."

"Suck-up," Gavin says, and punches his brother as he walks past him. The two boys scramble out of the room, tussling and growling at each other.

Amy watches them, rolling her eyes. "See what I have to put up with?"

"I got a couple of boys of my own," Hogarth says. "And a couple of girls too. I don't know which is worse."

"Sit wherever," Amy says. "As you can see, I haven't cleaned up in here yet. Coffee?"

We both say yes, and she comes back with coffee that is my style—it could wake the dead.

As soon as she sits down, Amy's expression turns sober. "I'm glad I have cleaning up to keep me busy. I can't stand to think that something bad might have happened to Elaine."

She tells us that they are good friends. They hit it off when Amy and her family moved in ten years ago, and they have remained close ever since. "When the boys were little she'd babysit on a second's notice. She has two grown kids and she said mine were no trouble—even though I know they could be a handful. And if either of us has something on her mind, we can share it. I love her."

She says the last without tears, but her voice is husky. "The boys call her Ms. Cool. They're too old to need her to babysit anymore, but she makes cookies for them . . ." She unconsciously reaches over and scoops up a bunch of papers spread out on the coffee table and stacks them neatly.

"Ms. Martin, we'd like you to tell us what you know about Elaine Farquart's activities on the dating site she was on. First of all, did she tell you the name of the site?" Even though we saw it on her computer, it's possible she went onto more than one site.

"It was called Smalltownpair. We both thought it was probably best to use one of the smaller sites. And they had a special senior section."

"How long had she been registered there?"

"She started around the first of the year. I'm actually the one who suggested it. She complained that it was hard to meet men. She said they're all either married or looking for a nurse to take care of them in old age."

"Do you know how many men she has gone out with?"

"Not many. Some of those guys are sketchy." She shrugs. "We've had a lot of laughs over some of the replies she got to her profile. I mean, what is it with men who think they are God's gift to the female species?" Her smile is rueful. "Present company excluded, of course."

"We assumed that," Hogarth says dryly, and we all chuckle. It's good to break the tension.

"She brought over pictures or printouts of a few of the replies, and we'd make fun of them. And then a few days ago, she was all flustered. She said she thought she might have a live one."

"You mean a man she was interested in going out with?" Hogarth says.

"Exactly. She said he seemed like a real gentleman. He was exactly the right combination of friendly and private." Amy splays her hands out. "You know, you don't want someone who seems too eager, but you also don't want them to be too reticent."

"Did they interact by email or phone calls?" I ask.

She shakes her head. "I don't really know. We didn't talk details. She just said he sounded nice. Maybe it was on the phone."

"Did she show you his profile on the website?"

She hesitates. "Yes, but that was the one thing that bothered both of us. He was really handsome."

I think of the photograph we found in Loretta's desk. It's possible women would think he was nice-looking, but it's a stretch to say really handsome.

Hogarth frowns. "Why would that bother you?"

Amy tilts her head to one side. "Look, Elaine knows she isn't a spring chicken, okay? I mean she looks great for her age, but she didn't think a man that looked like this guy, Andrew, would need to be on a dating site. We both figured there was probably something wrong with him that he wasn't being truthful about."

"Like what? Did she have any particular thoughts?"

"Like I said, we could get pretty silly. We wondered if maybe he was really five feet tall instead of the six feet he said he was, or maybe that was an old picture and he was really ninety, or he'd gained three hundred pounds, or he was living on the streets . . ." She shivers. "I wonder if we should have been worried about something worse."

"Even though the two of you were dubious, she decided to go out with him anyway?"

Amy hugs her arms to herself. "Not at first. She said she told him she wasn't sure. She said he wrote back a really nice letter, telling her he understood and that if she changed her mind, he'd like to meet her. He suggested they meet at a coffee shop, so in case she wasn't comfortable she could leave and there'd be no hard feelings."

"He wrote her a letter?" Hogarth asks.

She blinks. "She did say letter. Although she might have meant an email. People use them interchangeably these days."

I presume if it was an email, Hogarth's partner will find it.

"But she changed her mind about meeting him?" Hogarth asks.

"She came over a few days ago and said she had decided to go ahead and meet him. They were planning to meet at a coffee shop in Bobtail on Thursday. But this is where it went wrong."

"What happened?"

She sighs. "Thursday morning she phoned and said that Andrew called and told her he twisted his ankle and he couldn't really go out. He wondered if she would drop by his place. He said it would really help him if she could pick up a couple of things at the grocery store and he'd pay her back." She bows her head as if in defeat. When she lifts it again, she looks stricken. "She asked me if I thought there could be something shady going on. But she didn't want to leave him high and dry. I told her it sounded okay, but to get out of there if she felt uncomfortable."

"So she went," Hogarth says.

"Oh, why didn't I tell her not to go? Or I wish I had gone with her, but to tell you the truth, it never occurred to me. Besides, she would have thought I was being silly if I told her I wanted to go with her."

"You can't blame yourself."

She shrugs. "But I do. I meant to call her Thursday night and ask how it had gone, but Buster—that's my oldest son—got hit by a baseball, and I spent a couple of hours with him in the emergency room."

"I hope he's okay," Hogarth says.

"He's fine. I call him my hard-headed one, and I guess in this case it was a good thing. He didn't even have a concussion, which the doctor said was a miracle. And then last night I had a meeting. I'm on the prom planning committee for the PTA. We met for four hours. Four hours! Drives me crazy how long-winded some people can be. I didn't get home until after ten. This morning I realized I hadn't heard from Elaine, so I called to ask how things went. I've been kicking myself ever since I realized she wasn't home."

"How did you know she wasn't?"

"She usually calls me back right away, so after an hour, I thought I'd pop over and see whether she was home. The thing is, I noticed that she hadn't picked up the mail. She usually asks me to get it if she's going to be gone. I decided to take it inside, and to tell you the truth, I wanted to check and make sure she wasn't sick and couldn't get to the phone. At first, I thought everything was okay. Her cat seemed fine. He has one of those perpetual watering fountains, but then I realized he was really hungry. That's when I got alarmed and called the police. I feel responsible. I should have called her Thursday night."

"No ma'am," Hogarth says firmly. "You can't blame yourself. Even if you had sounded the alarm with the police, we most likely wouldn't have paid much attention to the idea that a grown woman hadn't come home for one night."

The same way I didn't take it seriously when Ellen first told me Loretta was missing. It's easy to assume that everything is fine. Usually it is.

"If I might ask a question?" I defer to Hogarth. He nods. "Did she mention a last name for Andrew?"

"If she did, I don't remember," Amy says.

"And besides this man Andrew, did she ever mention any other names to you?"

"A few, but only first names, and Andrew was the first one she was really interested in."

"Last question. Does she have a cell phone?"

"Yes, but she hardly ever used it. I tried calling it, but it went straight to voicemail."

We get up and thank her. She looks around at the living room with a bereft expression. "I guess I'd better get busy. My husband gets home tonight, and he won't like it if the house is a mess."

"Gets home from where?" Hogarth asks.

"Oh, he's a salesman. On the road a lot. I didn't mean to make it sound like he's strict with me. He thinks I'm too easy on the boys and I ought to get them to help me. He's probably right."

Back at Elaine Farquart's, we search for the photo Amy mentioned of the man Elaine was supposed to meet, but we don't find any photos at all.

"Maybe she took it with her," Hogarth says.

"Why would she do that?" Officer Marks says. He had been waiting for us on the steps and followed us back into the house.

"Where else would it be?" Hogarth asks. "She wouldn't have thrown it away. Tell you what. I'm going to ask DPS to send us a sketch artist from San Antonio, and I'll ask Amy Martin to come down to the station to see if she can remember enough about him to make a sketch."

Hogarth asks Marks whether Farquart exchanged any emails with potential dates.

"There were a few, but nothing that raised any alarms. But I used her printer to print a few that she exchanged emails with. I'll get on that back at the station."

We ask if there was an email from the man named Andrew, but there wasn't. And we don't find a regular letter in her desk.

"Her neighbor said she has a cell phone. Did you find it?" I ask.

"No, sir. I wondered about that. I knew she had one because I saw the bill for it, but I didn't find it."

"Let's see if her cell service can get a read on where it might be," Hogarth says. "Could lead us to her."

Marks shakes his head. "Not likely, unless she has a smartphone. And even then, if the phone battery is dead, it might not get us to her exact location."

Back at Bobtail Police Department, there has still been no report of Elaine's car, a late model, red Acura, being found.

It's time for me to get back home. I ask Hogarth to keep me up to date.

"You do the same. I hope there's no correlation between the two women." But I'm not counting on that.

CHAPTER 10

Maria is supposed to be on the afternoon shift, but she has come in early and is sitting at her computer. She says she was too restless to stay home. I dread having to tell her that a woman from Bobtail is missing.

"Any luck getting in touch with any of the men on the list?" I ask.

"Two of them wrote back and said they had not heard from her." Her dark eyes are full of gloom. "Then I realized there's no way to know whether they are telling the truth."

"I'm afraid you're right. By the way, you remember that photo we found in Loretta's notebook? Do you have it?"

"It's right here." She has it paper-clipped to the four sheets of Loretta's notes.

"Do you think this man is good-looking?"

She stares at the photo. "Not really. I mean, some women, older women, might find him attractive, but not super good-looking."

I'll show Amy the photo. I glance over at the third desk. "Where's Connor?"

"He went to Arlo Stevenson's. Arlo's wife called here an hour ago and said Arlo broke his leg. EMS was on their way from Bobtail, but she wanted somebody there with her."

"How did he break it?"

"His tractor hit a stob and tipped over."

I smile to myself. Maria is a city girl and a year ago probably didn't have any idea what a stob was. I don't even know if it's a real word, but every farmer knows it's a tree stump that was hewn level with the ground, but the roots weren't removed. Grinding out the roots can be a big job, and a lot of people choose to leave them. It's usually not a problem, but every now and then, somebody runs into one that is hidden and fouls their tractor plow or, like in the case of Arlo, tips the tractor.

"Lucky he wasn't killed."

"I'm sure Connor will be a big help," she says sarcastically.

"Now Maria . . ."

"Okay, okay. Where were you this morning? Have you talked to Loretta's son?"

My heart sinks. I've been so involved with the Elaine Farquart disappearance that I haven't given any thought to Scott Singletary this morning. I've been stalling Maria too. "I'll call him in a few minutes. I have something to tell you."

When I tell her that a woman from Bobtail is missing, she jumps up and starts pacing. "We've got to find Loretta! And we don't even know where to look! What do you suppose happened to those two women?"

I shake my head. None of the options seems good. "We have to hit the dating website angle harder. If we have to, we'll go question every single person she had any email exchanges with. I agree with you that calling them isn't going to be good enough."

For once I wish Loretta revealed more about herself. She likes to gossip about other people—not mean gossip, just news—but I have begun to realize that she keeps a lot of personal information to herself.

"Maria, I have a list of the names of the women in Loretta's church circle meetings. I'd like you to call them and ask if anybody knows anything. Maybe she confided in one of them."

"I'll get right on it." Her expression is grim. I don't envy these women. Maria can be relentless. If any of the women is reluctant to tell her what they know, they'll regret it.

Now that Maria has a task, I need to figure out my next step. Elaine was originally supposed to meet her date at a coffee shop. And if she had followed through, I could have gone there and shown her photo around to find out if anybody had seen her there with a man.

But Elaine didn't follow through. Instead, she bit on the man's ruse to get her over to his place. Or at least it looks like that's what happened.

Looking at it with a wider lens, it's possible that Elaine bought groceries, went to the man's house, visited with him, and then was attacked by someone completely unrelated after she left the man's house. But for now, the most likely explanation is the first one. I'd give anything for a copy of the photo Elaine had of her date. I'm sure Hogarth wishes the same thing. We can only hope that Amy can give a sketch artist enough of a description to get a good idea of what he looked like. It would be a win if it matched the photo that Loretta had, but that's probably too much to hope for.

I wonder if there's anything I can do to find out more on the dating website. Is there a way to send out an announcement to women, asking whether they were contacted by someone who claimed to have twisted his ankle? Would the attacker use that excuse more than once? It even occurs to me that this man might have had more than two victims, and the others haven't been found.

Although Maria said she was going to look through the history on Loretta's computer, I want to take a look myself. I don't know that I'll find anything useful, but with Elaine Farquart missing, I want to go back and make sure I've got a good handle on Loretta's online footprint. On my way out, I grab the list of men's names that Maria was going through in case I want to match them up.

I'm not looking forward to telling Scott Singletary that another woman has gone missing, but I have to. In fact, I wonder why he didn't call to nudge us this morning.

When I get to Loretta's, Scott is outside with his cell phone to his ear. Although he isn't shouting, his body language and flushed face tell me he'd like to punch whoever he's talking to. He waves me closer, and I hear him say, "You haven't heard the last of this. Do what you can to make it right." He listens for a few seconds. "I'll hold you to that. I have to go now. I'll talk to you later."

He hangs up and mops his brow. His face is sweating, and he didn't shave this morning. He looks like an angry, bristly hedgehog in a kids' storybook. "If this thing with Mamma isn't bad enough, five minutes after I left work, the shit hit the fan." He grimaces. "'Scuse the language."

When I tell him what I was up to this morning, it turns out he already knows at least part of it—the easy part.

"I answered Mamma's phone, and it was one of her friends telling her that a lady was missing in Bobtail." He grimaces. "I don't know why these ladies like to gossip about things like that. I remember when I was a kid, always being creeped out by perfectly nice ladies telling all the gory details of a trial or a news report they saw on TV." He frowns, searching my face. "Why are you telling me this? Why did you get involved with something that happened over in Bobtail?"

"I don't want to scare you, but the woman had arranged for a date with a man on the same match-up site that your mamma was involved in."

He takes a gasping breath. "Well, goddammit, we need to talk to the people who own the site and find out who this man is."

I tamp him down with my hands. "Let's go inside. Did you eat breakfast?"

It turns out Scott has been on the phone all morning and hasn't eaten. Feeling like an interloper, I take eggs out of the refrigerator. Loretta doesn't have any bacon, but there's some patty sausage, which I fry up along with scrambled eggs and toast. While we eat, I try to calm Scott by telling him that it's actually helpful that two women are missing. "We have a lot more people looking for them. We're going to figure out what happened."

"But will it be in time? I mean . . ."

I look him straight in the eye. "You know, your mamma and I are real close friends. I'm going to work nonstop until I find her."

"I know it," he mumbles. "I just worry that we won't find her in time."

"We're all worried and, believe me, we're on this. You know, it might be better if you go back home. There's not a thing you can do here."

He hunches over a cup of coffee, and I can see that he's at war with whether to leave. I know how he feels. I'm feeling helpless at the moment. But at least for me, I know there are things I can do.

"Why don't you consider it, and meanwhile, I'd like to take another look at your mamma's desk and go onto her computer again."

"Maybe I'll call my wife," he says. He heads outside again to make his call. I feel sorry for him. He seems like a man who's used to taking charge, and there's nothing he can do.

The desk hasn't magically grown any leads since I last looked through it, even though I go through the file folders more carefully. I log into Loretta's computer and pull up her history. Well, there it is. She went onto the dating site many times in the past couple of weeks. I hit the latest entry, but when I get to the site, it wants a user name and password.

I find the information on a Post-It in the middle desk drawer. And I'm in. This is where I should have been all along, and I would have been if I'd taken her disappearance more seriously from the beginning. Loretta may have felt the need to write down names on a yellow pad, but the dating site has kept them for her in her own file. I scroll through profile after profile. There are men of all shapes and sizes. Bald, wrinkled, smooth-faced, silver-haired, glasses, no glasses, smirks, shy grins, slick, angry, and even gloomy. You'd think if a man was trying to attract a woman's interest, he'd at least manage a smile. But then I suppose there are women who like serious men. It's all there, including a couple of men who I recognize, to my chagrin. I match the profiles with her list of names and see that she rejected both of them. If circumstances weren't so grim, I'd laugh.

Most of the profiles have pictures with them, but among them I see no one who looks like the photo we found in Loretta's desk. That means I have to contact each of the eight men with no profile picture to find out whether he's the one in the photo.

The profiles show only a first name—and there's no one named Andrew in the list. I hope that means that whoever Elaine Farquart was meeting was not the same person Loretta was meeting. But it seems farfetched that two different women would disappear around the same time with two different men. What I suspect is that whoever "Andrew" is, he used a different name on his profile and then when the women replied to him, he told them his real name was Andrew. I go back through the photos slowly. Is there anyone here who I think a woman would consider almost too good-looking? I should ask one of Loretta's friends.

What strikes me is that Loretta is a social person. It's hard for me to imagine her doing this computer dating completely on the sly and not confiding in anyone. If she did tell somebody, though, she might have sworn them to secrecy, and they might not be aware that it's high time to break that promise. As word gets out, they'll know.

Scott comes back in, looking better from having talked to his wife. "Marcie says I should come back home. She says I'm most likely underfoot here. Is that right?"

"I wouldn't say that," I say. "But I don't know what more you might do to help right now if you stay. You're not that far away, and if we need you, you can be back here pretty fast."

"That's what Marcie said."

"You haven't told me what your relatives said when you called them. I assume you got nothing from them."

"Nobody knows anything. I swear my younger brother thinks it's my fault she's missing. He told me I ought to keep better tabs on her. How am I supposed to do that?"

"He's worried."

"I know it. He's all the way back east." He grimaces. "I know him. He thinks everybody but him is an incompetent fool, and if he was here, he'd find her in nothing flat."

"If it comes to that, maybe I'll call him and get him out here."

CHAPTER 11

B ack at headquarters, I'm stewing over what steps to take next, when a phone call comes in from Ellen Forester. "You were right! Loretta did tell one of the members of the class that she was trying out a dating website. It's Kathy Weinman. Kathy said she doesn't know much, but Loretta did mention that she was going to go out with a couple of the men she met through the site."

"Is Kathy at the studio now?"

"She'll be here for a two o'clock class. I figured you'd want to talk to her, so I asked her if she could come in early."

I don't have time to sit down at the café for lunch, but I stop by and ask Lurleen to have the cook make me a roast beef sandwich before I head over to meet Kathy.

Kathy is a tall woman with red hair shot through with gray. Ellen lets us use her office to talk. It's a working office, with stacks of papers on the desk and paintings leaning against the wall, some framed and others not. I bring the chair out from behind Ellen's desk so it doesn't feel so much like an interrogation. Kathy is one of those tall women who seems to be uncomfortable with her height. She slouches in her chair, knees together primly and hands in her lap, like she's trying to make herself small.

"Did Ellen tell you what's going on?"

"She said Loretta is missing."

"We're going to find her. Ellen tells me that you might have information for me."

"I'm afraid it's not much. I take a Wednesday afternoon class with Loretta, and last time she was in class, I went over to her house for cake, and she told me she had been looking online for companionship." She shoots me a quick glance. "You know, like a man to go out with sometimes. She said she was going to meet one or two men she contacted through a dating website."

"Did she tell you anything about the men?"

"Well, back up. I told her I thought she ought to have coffee with a man before she went out with him on a real date." She flashes me a hesitant smile. "You know, in case he's not a good match. Or if he turned out to have lied to her."

"What did she say?"

"She was way ahead of me. She said she had already met one man, and they had gone for coffee. She said he was nice, but nothing special. She was planning to meet three more of them for coffee."

"Did she say when?"

"I don't remember the first one, but I think she was going to Bryan last Sunday afternoon and then to Bobtail on Tuesday."

I remember Loretta was dressed up last Saturday when she came to see me about the goat rodeo. That must have been what she was up to. "Isn't that kind of crowding it? Three men in five days?"

Kathy chuckles. "That's what I said. But you know Loretta. She's efficient. She said if she was going to make a serious effort, there was no reason to fool around, and she might as well get on with it."

"Sounds like her." I laugh, but my pulse speeds up. I may be looking at a lead at last. "Did you talk to her after she went to Bryan?"

"No, we don't usually see each other between classes. I mean we aren't close friends, we just enjoy meeting after the workshop to go over the techniques we learned and problems we're having with painting. To tell you the truth, I was surprised that she brought up the business about her dates. She said she didn't want people in town to know what she was up to, in case it didn't go well, but that she was dying to tell somebody."

"You didn't think anything about it when she was not in class last week?"

"I asked Ellen, and she said she didn't know why she hadn't come.

But she seemed funny about it. I guess I shouldn't have been surprised when she told me Loretta was missing."

"You have any idea what coffee shop Loretta was going to with either man?"

"She asked me if I knew the one in Bobtail, which I do. It's the one by the courthouse, The Hot Spot."

I nod. I know that one well because I've been there with Jenny from time to time.

"The one in Bryan, I didn't know, and I can't remember the name. It was a funny name for a coffee shop. Reminded me of a Greek name. Like Constantine or something like that, but that wasn't it."

"If you think of it, give me a call." I hand her my card. "You've been a great help. I appreciate it."

"I hope everything is okay with her. She's a good person." She squares her shoulders. "I have an idea. I know this sounds silly, but have you thought about putting out a flyer asking if anybody has seen her?"

"I did think about it, and I think it's a good idea. I haven't had time yet." And until this morning, I didn't feel the urgency.

"I could help. I'll get some friends to tack them up around Bobtail."

Back at headquarters, I've barely sat down at my desk when a man comes striding in. He looks familiar, although I don't know where I've seen him. He's my height, in his fifties, with a full head of silvery-gray hair, a hatchet nose, and a sparkle in his ice-blue eyes. He strides over to my desk. "Don't bother to get up. You're Chief Craddock, I bet."

"That's right."

"I'm Reverend Arlen Becker. It's a true pleasure to meet you. I've heard so much about you."

"I've heard about you too."

He throws his head back with a hearty laugh. "I'll bet you have. Seems like I've stirred things up in town."

"What can I do for you?" I'm impatient to get on with the search for Loretta, and I hope he's not here to prod me about the rodeo. I'm in no mood. But I'll bet that's it.

"Dropped in to say hello. Won't take but a minute of your time."

"I was just going to pour myself a cup of coffee. You want a cup?"

"I never drink the stuff myself, but you go ahead." When I come back with my coffee, he looks like he's settled in for longer than a few minutes, leaned back in his chair with his fingers laced behind his head and one leg crossed at the knee. All in all, he looks like he owns the place.

"Reverend Becker, I've got a situation I'm working on, and I don't have a lot of time. Did you need something specific?"

"Oh, let's get acquainted before we get down to business. Tell me a little about yourself."

"Not much to tell." I tell him I've lived in Jarrett Creek my whole life, married right out of college, and we came back here to settle down. "Jeanne passed away a few years ago."

"I'm sorry to hear that. You have kids?"

"We weren't fortunate enough to have children." I could tell him that we raised my nephew Tom, but I'd like to shorten the conversation.

"My wife and I have two kids, a boy and a girl. The girl lives in Houston. She's an architect. And my boy is at UT in Austin, studying to be an engineer, like me."

I'm interested in spite of my impatience. "What do you mean, like you? You're a preacher."

"Now I am, but I was an engineer for almost thirty years. Five years ago, I got the call to minister to a church. I went to seminary and here I am." That explains why a man his age has been assigned to such a small church. Usually the men who get assigned to the Jarrett Creek First Baptist Church are either young men just starting out or older men ready to call it quits.

"Well, I welcome you. I hope it's a good place for you."

"I'm sure it will be. I'll let the Lord be the judge of whether I'm good for the place." He chuckles. "Now, on the subject of the rodeo."

The abrupt change of subject startles me. "Yes?"

"I understand your friend Loretta Singletary spoke to you about my concerns."

"Yes, she did."

"She said you weren't enthusiastic about standing with us on the issue. I'm wondering whether I can be of help in urging you to reconsider."

"It's unlikely. As I told Loretta, I figure if the Baptist Church gets to be a co-sponsor, then other churches are going to want in on the action too, which could make a mess. Besides, I'm truly puzzled why you want to get involved in the rodeo anyway. It's not like it's a big religious event."

He lets out that hearty laugh again. "You have me there." He uncrosses his leg and leans forward. "But I disagree that it isn't a religious event. Everything in life has potential for us to bear witness. We don't ever know where the Lord is going to speak to us, and we have to be prepared. I don't want to say anything against Catholics. I'm sure there are good ones. But the Catholic Church grabs people up with their glitter and ceremonies. Those of us in less showy churches have to be on our guard not to let people be sucked in by all that. Do you know what I mean?"

One thing I know is that he loves the sound of his own voice. "Have you seen the Catholic Church here in town?" Glitter is the last thing it brings to mind. It's a tiny little structure with one stained glass window.

"I can't say that I have, but the local church doesn't have to have a grand building to entice people. People get drawn in by big cathedrals like the Catholics have all over. And Catholics have a lot more leeway in their religious life than we do in the Baptist Church. When they sin, all they have to do is tell the priest, and he fixes them right up. Baptists don't have the luxury. We have to go directly to God. All this means is that we have to use every opportunity to make sure we don't lose people to the Catholics way of life. I would not be a proper shepherd of my flock if I didn't pay attention to their needs."

"If you say so. But I find that most of the people in this town are pretty good folks, and I'll let them make their choices."

"Oh, no, no, no." He waves his hand in a munificent gesture. "Don't mistake me. It's not whether you're a good person; it's whether or not you are saved. I hate to put it bluntly, but not everyone who is a good person is going to heaven."

I hadn't heard Maria's car drive up, and I'm surprised and relieved when she steps inside. I get up. "Maria, let me introduce you to the new Baptist preacher, Reverend Becker. Reverend, this is Deputy Trevino."

He rises too and says hello, but he doesn't offer to shake her hand. And I see a curious thing happen. Becker has dropped his jovial manner and is decidedly cool to Maria. I would say it looks suspiciously like he is affronted by having a woman in the room, and a Hispanic woman at that.

It's all I can do not to announce to Maria that Reverend Becker was just telling me that, her being a Catholic, she was unlikely to go to heaven. "The Reverend is here on a mission."

Maria looks puzzled, and Becker looks like he swallowed something unpleasant.

"I was going to run over to the Dairy Queen and get a hamburger," Maria says. "I didn't have time for lunch. You want anything?"

"No, you go ahead. But we have things to discuss when you get back." And I hope she hurries.

"Did you find out something?"

"I did. Don't be gone long."

She cuts her eyes at Becker. "I'll be back in ten minutes," she says.

When she leaves, I say, "Reverend Becker, I apologize, but I need to put this discussion on hold. You may not be aware, but a member of your congregation, Loretta Singletary, is missing."

He nods. "I heard that. She's a busy lady. I imagine she has gone off on a little jaunt and forgot to tell anybody."

So much for the shepherd tending his flock. "I'm afraid it's more serious than that, and right now I need to concentrate on finding her.

We'll have to save this rodeo discussion for another time." I'm still standing to emphasize to him that the meeting is over.

"I think we could . . ."

I interrupt by sticking out my hand. "Thank you for coming by. As soon as Loretta is back home, we'll talk."

He tries for one of those sparkly smiles but falls a little short. "Before I leave, there is one thing I promised my wife I'd ask you."

"What's that?"

"She heard that you have a nice art collection. In Houston, she practically lived at the art museums, and she said she'd give anything to see your art."

My wife Jeanne's mother was a serious collector of contemporary art, and Jeanne got me interested in it. We enjoyed finding new artists, and over the years we put together a nice collection. I'm proud of it, although hardly anyone in a small town appreciates what I've got. It would be nice to show it to an art lover.

"Tell her she can call me anytime. I'd be happy to give her a tour."

CHAPTER 12

While I wait for Maria to get back from the Dairy Queen, I look up names of coffee shops in Bryan. I find one that, as Kathy suggested, sounds "Greek." Mykonos Café is in the heart of the student district near Texas A&M.

I wonder if Wendy knows the café, and that gives me an excuse to call her to see how she's getting on with her daughter. "Wait a second," she says. "Let me . . ."

I hear her footsteps and a sliding door open and close. "Oh, my heavens!" she says. "This girl. She knows every one of my buttons and pushes them pretty much nonstop." Wendy always says that the two of them are too much alike, and that's why they frequently quarrel.

"You could come on home." I try not to sound hopeful.

"Good try!" She giggles. "No, I can't. Even though she and I drive each other crazy, it would hurt her feelings if I left. We'll work it out. Anyway, I'm glad to hear your voice."

"I called for a specific reason. Do you know a coffee shop called Mykonos Café?"

"I know of it, but I've never been there. It's pretty much a student hangout. But I have been to Mykonos. What a beautiful island! We should go sometime. Why are you asking?"

"It's something that came up in an investigation."

"This isn't about Loretta, is it?"

"Yes, it is."

"Oh, dear. I hoped she would be back in her house by now."

"You and me both."

We only have a few more minutes to talk before Maria comes in, and I have to get off the phone.

Maria plops down with her burger and a milkshake. "What did the Baptist preacher want? Was he worried about Loretta?"

"Far from it. He's much more concerned with the goat rodeo."

"You're kidding."

"I wish I were. Seems like the kind of man who's used to getting his way."

"And who's used to only dealing with lily white people, especially men."

"You noticed?"

"How could I miss it? He looked like he wanted to run screaming from the room. I'd like to know what his wife is like." She shudders. "Well, no matter. Did you give in to him?"

"Sent him packing," I say. "I told him I had something more important on my mind—namely, finding Loretta. Now, let's compare notes."

"I didn't find out anything worth sharing."

"Well, I did." I tell her that a woman who Loretta takes painting classes with shared a few things with me. "She told me that Loretta planned to go out with a couple of different men." I tell her there were two coffee shops where the dates were supposed to happen. "She was meeting one man at the one in Bryan-College Station last Sunday and the one in Bobtail on Tuesday. I asked her last Saturday why she was dressed up, and I think she was meeting someone that day too."

"We should go to the one in Bobtail first. We know she survived the ones over the weekend because she changed the calendar on Monday." Maria is ready to jump in the car now and get on over there.

"No, I'm going to Bryan first," I say.

"Why?"

"First of all, we don't know that she didn't meet a guy there and cancel the one in Bobtail. And second, it's Saturday today. Loretta was going to meet the man last Sunday afternoon. It's likely that the same staff will be on duty on weekends and more likely to recognize Loretta's photo. I'm also going to take that photo with me that we found in her desk."

Maria wads up the paper from her hamburger. "Then we better get going."

"Not we. Me."

"What? Why can't I go too?"

"Because we aren't a big enough department to team up. You're not going to miss any action, and you're on duty this afternoon. You need to stick around here. Suppose Loretta shows up?"

She glares at me. "This is not just an excuse to go see Wendy, is it?"

"No, Ms. Busybody, it isn't. Wendy is out of town."

I stand up and Dusty leaps to his feet, ready for action. I look down at him. "I'll tell you what," I say to Maria. "I'll leave Dusty with you."

She loves Dusty, but even that gesture doesn't satisfy her, and by leaving Dusty, I've left two disappointed individuals.

The Mykonos Café is teeming with students, most of whom look to me like they ought to be in junior high school—or what they call middle school these days. The youthful energy in the room is contagious. I suddenly get a flash of nostalgia for the days I was in school at A&M.

I hang back and wait for a lull in the coffee line before I approach the counter and show the staff Loretta's photo that I took off the dating site and the man's photo we found in her desk. Although I don't think Loretta's photo looks like her, Maria said if she fixed herself up to have her picture taken, most likely she fixed herself up to meet a date too.

Both the young women and the young man behind the counter give the photos a fair look, but none of them recognizes Loretta or the man. "We get a whole lot of people through here every day," one of the girls says. She has a sweet face and tattooed arms.

"Not so many old people though," the other girl says, and then blushes as if she's said the wrong thing.

It's possible that Loretta didn't come to the counter at all. Her date might have gotten her a cup of coffee. I survey the room and turn back to the counter staff. "Can you point out anyone who is a regular here? Maybe someone else noticed her."

They pick out a half-dozen people who are here all the time. I visit each of their tables in turn, and on the third one, a woman who looks a little older than the students says she recognizes Loretta's photo.

"I remember seeing her, maybe last weekend?"

"Are you a student?"

She laughs. "No, I'm an assistant professor. I live near here though, which is why I come to this place for coffee. It's so chaotic that every time I come, I tell myself it's the last time; but it's convenient."

"Can you tell me if this woman was with anyone?"

"Why don't you sit down?" she says. I take the seat across from her, and she closes her computer. "What is this about?"

"The woman is missing."

"Ah. Well, I can tell you who she was with. I think that's why I noticed her. She was with Professor Leonard Raymond. His students call him Leo the Lecher. He's always hitting on his female students."

"I thought that was frowned upon."

She shrugs. "It is, but he stops short of harassment. He's just annoying."

"What does he teach?"

"He's in the History Department. He teaches European History, and he actually has a reputation as a pretty good professor, despite his roving hands."

"I suppose I won't be able to find him in his office on a Saturday."

"Probably not, but it's worth a try." She gives me directions to the building where he's likely to have an office. "At least you can find his office hours, and it's possible he has posted a phone number."

"Did you notice anything in particular about the professor and this woman?"

"Honestly, I didn't pay much attention except to think that he usually goes for the hot young things, and she didn't fit that category. Still, they were having what looked to be a lively conversation."

I find Professor Raymond's office easily enough, but as I feared it's closed for the weekend. There's a note on the door that says his office hours are Tuesday and Thursday. But as the woman at the coffee shop suggested, there's also a phone number and email address, "in case you find yourself in desperate need of a history lesson."

It's four o'clock on Saturday afternoon, and I'm not surprised that the professor doesn't answer his phone. Still, I leave a message in case he's out on an errand, and I decide I'll hang around for a while in case he does get back to me. While I wait for him to call, I retreat to a coffee shop I've been to with Wendy, one that's a lot quieter, to have a slice of pie and a cup of coffee. I won't wait forever, but I can put in an hour. I pick up a campus newspaper and am reading it when my phone rings.

"This is Professor Raymond. To whom am I speaking?"

I tell him who I am. "I'd like to ask you a few questions. Are you at home?"

"Questions concerning what?"

"It's a police matter. I can meet you at the downtown Bryan Police Department if you'd prefer. Or we could talk in your office."

There's a long silence. "I prefer my office. It will take me 20 minutes to get there." From the hesitation in his voice, I suspect he's worried that one of his students has complained about his "roving hands."

It's actually thirty minutes before he comes rushing up to unlock his office door. He's around fifty, 5'8" and trim, with a bushy brown and gray mustache and longish hair pulled back in a short ponytail. He's wearing wire-rimmed glasses, jeans and a blue work shirt, and loafers with no socks.

His small office is cramped by bookshelves filled to capacity. A quick glance tells me it's mostly history books with a shelf reserved for classics of Greek literature and poetry. But his desk is relatively clean and littered with oddities—a cowrie shell, a dish of marbles, and a small Japanese statue.

"Sit down, sit down." He eases into the leather and wood desk chair and then points me to a straight-backed side chair that I imagine is for students who come to visit and is designed so they don't overstay. "Now what is this police matter?" He smooths his mustache, a nervous gesture rather than preening. His eyes are watchful.

"Have you ever signed up for an online dating site?"

"I?" He's startled. "No. I wouldn't even think of it."

"Why not?"

"I meet plenty of women. I don't need to fish around on a dating site."

"Married?"

"Divorced. Why?"

I take out the photo of Loretta and see the relief that flits across his face. "Have you seen this woman?"

"I . . ." He blinks. "I may have, but I don't remember where. Who is she?"

"Someone recognized her as a woman you were having a conversation with at Mykonos Café a week ago."

"Right. I remember now. Nice lady." He's relaxed now that he knows I'm not here about something to do with his students.

"Can you tell me how you met her?"

"I didn't exactly meet her, at least not intentionally. She was sitting at a table alone, and there were no empty tables in the café, so I asked if I could join her."

"You didn't arrange to meet her?"

"No, of course not." His lip curls as if he's caught wind of an unpleasant odor. "I'm sorry, you didn't say what this is about."

"Had you ever seen her or spoken to her before you saw her at the coffee shop?"

He studies me. "Did something happen to her?"

"Answer the question, please."

"No, I had never seen her before, nor have I seen her since. Like I said, she was a nice lady, but we had nothing in common, no reason for me to know her. In fact, she was a bit of a chatterbox, and after a while I was sorry that I had sat down with her."

"What did you talk about?"

He leans back and steeples his fingers under his chin. After thinking a minute, he says, "It was not a scintillating conversation. She told me she was meeting someone. She told me she had lived in Jarrett Creek her entire life. She asked me if I was married and had children. I told her I was divorced and had two kids." He throws up his hands. "Nothing more exciting than that."

"Did she say anything specific about who she was meeting?"

He draws a deep breath. "She said she was early and that whoever she was meeting wasn't going to be there for another half hour, and that's why she said it was okay for me to sit with her." He takes a couple of marbles out of the bowl on his desk and starts to roll them in his fingers, absentmindedly.

"While you were there, did the person she was meeting come in?"

"No."

I take out the photograph of the man Loretta had in her desk. "Recognize him?"

He shakes his head. "Something did happen to her, didn't it?"

"She's missing, and I'm trying to find her."

"I'm sorry to hear that. I wish I could be of more help."

"You've at least verified that she was in Bryan a week ago."

I stand up and hand him my card. "If you think of anything else that came up in the conversation with her, please give me a call. No matter how insignificant it seems."

He looks at my card, and I see that he's troubled. I wasn't inclined to care much for him, but the fact that he is willing to give a thought to Loretta is in his favor. He gets to his feet. "I certainly will. What could have happened to her? She was cheerful."

His words give me a pang. I've known Loretta so long, and we're such good friends that I realize I've taken her for granted. Seeing her through this man's eyes has made me aware that I would be devastated if anything happened to her in my jurisdiction.

When I get back to headquarters, Maria has left a message on the front door with her cell number in case anyone needs her. I call to find out what she's up to.

"I'm driving around," she says. "Did you find out anything?"

"A little. Driving around where?"

She sighs. "Looking for Loretta's car."

CHAPTER 13

Twenty minutes later, Maria walks in looking discouraged. Dusty is right behind her, as happy as ever. He rushes over to me and leaps up again and again until I crouch down and ruffle his ears and tussle with him. "Where were you looking for the car?" I ask Maria.

"I was driving around all those little roads that lead off the main road between Bobtail and here. I figured that because no one had found her car and she hadn't bought gas anywhere on her credit card, she must still be around here."

I stand up. "Maria, you know you're not going to find her car by wandering around looking for it."

"I know it, but I couldn't sit around the office doing nothing."

"You do have a case you're working on." I glance pointedly at the stack of files on her desk that she was supposed to take back.

"I know, I know. I'll take them back Monday." She pokes at the stack with a listless gesture.

"Let me tell what happened this afternoon."

She listens intently. "Do you think the professor was telling the truth?"

"I think so. The woman who told me she saw them together at the coffee shop knew him. According to her, he's more interested in girls his students' age. The guy who hits on young girls is not likely to be interested in an older woman."

"I suppose. Too bad that was a dead end. Chief, we can't wait until next week to go to the other coffee shop."

"Remember I told you that Elaine Farquart, the woman missing from Bobtail, was supposed to meet a man in a coffee shop? And that he called to say he had hurt his ankle and asked her to get groceries for him?"

"Yes."

"Suppose he pulled the same thing on Loretta?"

Maria perks up. "That would account for her leaving her house in a hurry."

"But even if she left in a hurry to go help this man, it doesn't explain why she packed a suitcase. I can't see her making a plan to spend the night with someone she has never even met."

She props her chin on her hands, her momentary excitement deflated. "Maybe she thought he'd need care overnight? No." She answers her own question. "She'd get someone else to help, or she'd call you or me."

"You're right," I say.

She shakes her head. "That doesn't work anyway because there were no phone calls to her house the day before she disappeared that matched any of the men."

"Were there any calls that morning at all?"

"Couple of marketing calls, that's all." She sighs. "Meanwhile, she's out there somewhere, and there's nothing we can do."

"I'm still holding out hope that this other woman going missing is just a bizarre coincidence, and that Loretta has gone off on an adventure."

"You're trying to make me feel better, I know."

"Maybe a little bit. But I'm trying to think positive for myself too." I snap my fingers. "Oh. One thing the woman I talked to from her painting class reminded me about. We need to distribute flyers asking if anyone has seen Loretta."

She sits straighter. "I'll make one up."

I tell her it can wait until tomorrow, but she waves me away. "I want to have it ready first thing in the morning to get it copied." She grimaces. "I wonder if there's a copy place open in Bobtail tomorrow."

"I doubt it. We'll have to copy it here." We both look toward the ancient, balky copier.

She groans. "That will take forever. Never mind. I'll get to it right now. I'll do half tonight and half tomorrow morning. And I'm going to put out a notice on Facebook and Twitter."

"You think that will help?"

"Can't hurt."

I offer to stay and help her print the flyers.

"No, take Dusty home and feed him. He's a growing dog."

She's right. When we get home and I set his food out, he eats as if it's the first food he has ever had.

I take a steak out of the refrigerator and put it in a pan to sear. I'm thinking of whether to bake a potato in the microwave or open a can of pinto beans to go with it when my landline phone rings. Most people have taken to using my cell phone, so this time of night it's probably a telemarketer. I almost don't answer, but it could be someone calling about Loretta.

But it's a telemarketer, wanting to let me know the IRS is on my case. I find it more irritating than usual.

I open a can of beans and throw them in a pot, and while I wait for the steak to cook, I begin to pace. Loretta could be anywhere. Even after Elaine Farquart disappeared, in the back of my mind I was betting that Loretta would come back on her own and laugh at how silly we all were to worry about her. My thoughts lead me to darker and darker places, and before I know it, I'm agitated. I get myself a drink of water and try to calm myself down. Then I pour myself a shot of bourbon. It won't do any good for me to let myself thrash around. Focus is what I need.

I turn off the burner under the steak. I'm not hungry, but I force down some of the food. It has no taste.

Dusty is watching me anxiously. He knows something is bothering me. I reach down and pat him and feed him a bit of steak. "You're a good dog." He goes to the door and whines. "All right, we'll go for a walk."

As I walk down the steps, I glance down the street toward Loretta's house, feeling a sense of despair. I stop short. I'm sure I saw a light in the house. It flashed on and bobbed around and then turned off, as if someone is using a flashlight. I watch the house for a minute but don't see a repeat of the light. It could be my imagination. It's not fully dark yet, but that shade of twilight where everything looks spooky. Maybe a car was driving by one street over and its lights momentarily reflected in a window. Or it could be that Scott decided he can't stay away and has come back. However, there are no cars parked in front, where he usually parks. And why would he use a flashlight and not turn on the lights?

"Uh-oh," I say out loud. "Dusty, maybe some kids know Loretta isn't there and have broken in. Let's go see what's up." I pause to consider calling Connor or Maria for backup, but I'm not even sure I saw anything. Still, it will only take a minute for Maria to get over here. It's probably better for me to phone her.

Dusty makes up my mind for me. He has been dancing down the street in front of me, but as we near Loretta's house, he takes off toward it at a dead run.

"Dusty! Here boy! Come back."

I could have saved my breath. Usually he would be stopped by the gate, but it has been left ajar, as has the front door.

He runs straight up the front steps without making a sound. I've noticed that when he is intent on something, he moves without barking. That's the Border Collie in him.

I run into the yard and pull the gate shut behind me. Whoever is in the house could have an innocent excuse for being here. If so, why didn't they turn on a light?

Dusty has disappeared into the house. I take the steps up to the porch two at a time but pause outside the front door. Suppose whoever is in there has a gun? They could shoot my dog—or me.

"Who's in there?" I shout. "Dusty, come!"

From inside, I hear a snarl, a hoarse shout, and then a yelp.

Dusty comes flying out onto the porch, leaping at me with excitement. I hear a drawer slammed shut and another opened and someone scrabbling through papers. Then there's another flash of light.

Grabbing Dusty's collar and pulling him along with me, I creep inside, moving toward the kitchen. It's much darker inside the house than out. I'm trying to remember exactly how the furniture is laid out when I nudge a table. It wasn't much of a nudge, but it's enough for a knick knack to fall over. No way the intruder won't have heard it. I've brought my flashlight, and as I flick it on, he explodes out the kitchen door, running past me, knocking me down. I fall awkwardly, hitting the side of the table I nudged and sending a cascade of knick knacks to the floor.

I'm not hurt, but I'm not as physically quick as I used to be, and by the time I pull myself to my feet, I hear the intruder crash into the gate and Dusty barking hysterically, with a few snarls thrown in for good measure. I run out onto the porch and see the guy sprinting down the street. Whoever he is, he's stocky and doesn't move like a kid. Dusty is hot on his heels. The man kicks backward, and Dusty barely leaps out of his way.

I know there's no way I can catch the runner. If I had my flashlight, I could turn it on and maybe see who it is, but when he knocked me down, I dropped it and didn't stop to pick it up.

The man turns the corner and disappears from sight, Dusty right behind him, still barking. Soon I hear a car start up and roar away from the curb. I tense, hoping Dusty has sense enough to get out of the way.

"Dusty, come!" I yell. It takes a couple of calls before he comes trotting back to the gate, panting. I tell him he's a good boy. I crouch down and feel around for any tender spots, but he seems fine.

When I go back inside, I take him with me. I flip on lights as I go. In the kitchen, one of the desk drawers is open. What could the guy have been looking for in Loretta's desk? Only one thing occurs to me. Suppose this is the man she was meeting, and he was afraid she had kept a photo of him? Or information about him? I don't touch the desk. It will have to be fingerprinted. I'd rather wait until tomorrow to do it in the daylight, but there's no way to guarantee he won't come back in the middle of the night to finish his job, and our little police department doesn't have the manpower to stake out the house overnight.

It's lucky I still have my cell phone with me. I call Maria and tell her what happened. She arrives a half hour later with the forensics kit to take fingerprints.

"I hope we get a useful print," she says, and then gets a puzzled look on her face. "What did you do to your arm?"

I look down and see a gash in my forearm that leaked a fair amount of blood but has since congealed. "I must have scraped it when the guy pushed me down. I'll clean it up when I get home." My back and side are starting to feel sore from the fall.

"What do you suppose the guy was after?" she says. It's not really a question. She's asking the air. "And how can we find out?"

"I don't know, but we're going to do what we always do. We're going to take it step by step."

"I wonder how he got in," Maria says.

"It couldn't have been the outside key. I took it with me last time I was here. I was afraid she might have told other people where it was. I didn't want them to come in and poke around."

We go back to examine the front door. It was ajar, which first alerted me to the break-in. There's no sign of the door being jimmied or otherwise forced. "I suppose there could be a second hidden key that the intruder was aware of," I say. There is one other possibility. I left before Scott did this afternoon. Maybe he forgot to lock one of the doors. He was sweating. Maybe he opened a window and forgot to close it.

We go back to the kitchen, but there's no sign that a break-in occurred there either. We split up and go through the house looking for windows that might have been opened, but when we come back we report that all windows were locked up tight.

"Still," I say, "it's possible that one of them was open and when he climbed in, he locked it after him. That might account for why he opened the front door, to give himself a way out."

"There's one other possibility," Maria says. She looks stricken. "It could be that he got the key from Loretta."

We're silent for a few seconds, contemplating that dreaded possibility.

After that, we set to the business of taking prints, dusting not only the front and back door, but the windowsills as well. If the intruder doesn't have prints on file, then it won't be of any use, but at least it makes us feel useful for now.

"Do you suppose he was here to get that photo we found?" Maria says, as we're packing up.

I nod. "It's possible."

"You said the Farquart woman had shown her neighbor a photo of the man she was supposed to meet, but you didn't find the photo in her house. Maybe he broke in and got it and he was planning to do the same thing here. "

"I'll phone over to the Bobtail Police Department tomorrow to tell them what happened here and get them to take prints in the Farquart woman's house, including the desk."

After Maria leaves, I go through Loretta's desk one more time, taking out the drawers in case something is stuck and looking behind the desk for anything that might have fallen. For once, I'm annoyed that my friend is tidy. "Loretta, where are you?"

I spend a restless evening at home and go to bed early after taking ibuprofen to help with my aches and pains from the assault.

I don't usually dream a lot, and I don't remember my dreams the way some people do, but in the middle of the night, I wake up with a gasp, heart pounding. I sit up and my dream comes back to me full force. In the dream, I answer my phone, and it's Loretta:

"Samuel." She talks in a whisper.

"Who is this?"

"It's me. Loretta." The same whisper.

I strain to be sure it's really her. "Where are you?"

"I don't know. There's nothing around here." She whimpers, "You have to find me. Please!"

"Well, tell me . . ."

"There's another woman here too."

"Elaine? Is that her name?"

"I have to go." Her voice fades.

"Loretta, no, wait!"

The line goes dead.

I frantically dial Star 69 to get the number she called from, but I get a message that says, in a sing song voice, "Sorry, the call return feature cannot be used to return your last incoming call." I dial it again, and this time the phone bursts into flames.

I get out of bed, still not quite believing it didn't happen. I walk into the living room to the front door and peer out. Now I understand the impulse that grabbed Maria this afternoon. I have an urge to run out the door, jump in my car, and start looking for Loretta. I keep remembering her voice from the dream, plaintive and scared. Now I worry that she might really try to call and I won't be here. I picture her listening to the phone ring, willing me to pick up.

CHAPTER 14

I wake up sore from the tumble I took, and I'm achy and grumpy. The dream I had last night has stuck with me, and I have to remind myself it wasn't real. I take more ibuprofen before I leave for headquarters.

Because we're a small police department, there's no one scheduled to work on Sunday, but I don't have the place to myself. Maria is already here when I arrive, churning out flyers. I hope our antique printer can take the strain.

I call Bobtail Police Department and talk to Hogarth. He's frustrated that they haven't found any solid leads to Elaine Farquart's disappearance. "We have got to find them," he says. "I'm already getting calls from panicked women, wondering if they're next."

"You may not like it, then, but my deputy has made up flyers, and some women from Bobtail are going to distribute them."

He sighs. "I may not like it, but that doesn't mean I don't think it's a good idea. We're planning to do the same. I'll just have to deal with any fallout."

"There's been a development on this end. Last night I surprised an intruder in Loretta's house." I tell him that he knocked me down and managed to get away. "He was searching for something when I discovered him. I wondered if he might be worried that Loretta had a printout of his photo that could identify him. Elaine Farquart's neighbor said Elaine showed her a photo of a guy she was going to meet, but we didn't find it in her house. It occurred to me that the same guy may have broken into Elaine's house and stolen it."

"We didn't see any signs that anyone had broken in, but I'll send somebody over to her house right away to check it out. We didn't take fingerprints because it wasn't really a crime scene, but we'll do that now. Do you know how the guy got into Loretta's house?"

"As far as we could tell there were no locks jimmied on the doors or windows. My deputy suggested that if the intruder were the kidnapper, he might have gotten the key from Loretta."

"I don't like the sound of that, but it makes sense, and he may have gotten Elaine Farquart's key as well."

"Tomorrow I'm going to call the FBI and see what legal means they can use to get information from the dating website."

"I hate to tell you," Hogarth says, "but I already did that, and they said we'll have to get a court order, and that's not easy. We don't really have probable cause."

"Maybe we can appeal to the better nature of whoever runs the website."

He snorts. We both know how likely that is.

"By the way, I do have a possible lead. Loretta confided in a woman. She told the woman that she had made appointments with men she met on the dating website." I tell him I went to the coffee shop in Bryan and talked to a potential suspect who turned out not to be suspicious after all.

"That's more than we've managed to uncover."

"This afternoon I'm going to the coffee shop in Bobtail where Loretta was supposed to meet the second date. Can I drop by and get a photo of Elaine Farquart? If they don't recognize one, they might have noticed the other."

"Absolutely, and we can give you a copy of the sketch that came from the description Elaine Farquart's neighbor gave us too."

"Have you located her car?"

"No."

"I was thinking the cars might be in a garage."

Hogarth agrees. He tells me to let him know if there's anything he can help with.

Maria is printing out flyers, and she calls Kathy Weinman to arrange to get them to her. She isn't home, so Maria leaves a message.

"If she's at church, she probably won't be home until after noon," I say. Since Maria isn't technically on duty, I tell her to go home and wait for Kathy's call.

It's not even ten o'clock. I'm not going to the coffee shop in Bobtail until this afternoon, to try to catch the same people on duty, so I've got time on my hands. I brew myself a pot of strong coffee and sit back to think.

Elaine Farquart was abducted from Bobtail, and Loretta was supposed to meet someone at a coffee shop in Bobtail, which means logically we should focus on the Bobtail area to search for Loretta. If we found one of the cars, we might be able to narrow the search, but the fact that neither of them has been found suggests they are tucked away. If both cars are inside, it means the abductor either has a two-car garage, or larger, or maybe has a big place to keep cars, like a warehouse or barn. Barn suggests countryside. There are more than enough big barns and out-buildings around to make finding the cars highly unlikely.

Elaine and Loretta are around the same age, widows who both happened to use the same dating website. Are there other things the two abducted women have in common? Was it possible that they knew each other? The dating site they used wasn't the biggest one, so why did they choose it? I think back to the comment the FBI officer made— that women who go on those sites change their appearance before they dip into online dating. Maybe they bought clothes in the same shop. Loretta loved to shop, and she usually liked to go to the outlet mall down near San Antonio. But I don't even know what shops are in the mall, much less where Loretta might have gone. Maria might have more luck than I would trying to trace something like that.

I'm ready for an interruption, so I'm glad when I see someone drive into the parking lot. But then I see that it's Father Sanchez. He must have come here straight after morning mass. Here we go again.

Dusty is thrilled to have company and leaps around the priest's feet. Sanchez crouches down and makes a fuss over him, which the Baptist preacher didn't do.

"What are you doing here? Don't you have services?"

"We Catholics like to get that over with early. Mass is over by nine. At least in my church."

"Well sit down and have a cup of coffee. I imagine I know why you're here," I say.

"I expect you know at least one of the reasons."

"The rodeo?"

"That's number one."

Sanchez accepts a cup of coffee, and we sit down at my desk. He's mid-forties, wiry with a shock of dark hair. He's wearing jeans and a shirt. His only concession to the priesthood is a collar.

"I'm not sure how to handle this rodeo situation," he says. "I suppose I should give in and let the Baptist preacher have his way."

"As I pointed out to Reverend Becker, it won't stop with the Baptists. If they get their part, then all the other churches will want a hand."

He gives a shout of laughter. "Everybody will want a hand in, and they'll squabble over every job, like it's going to get them into heaven." He waves his arm up in the air like he's at a meeting. "I want the peanut concession. No, I want it. You can have the soft drinks. No . . ." He swats his leg. "I sometimes think I'm not cut out for the priesthood. The idea of all that confusion kind of appeals to me in a perverse way."

"Maybe you're right. But I'll tell you what. I'm going to give you my usual check, and you can organize the rodeo however you want to. I don't want to get involved with church politics."

"Thank you, but it isn't going to solve my problem."

"Maybe you could talk to the Methodist preacher and get him on your side? He seems like an easy going man, and he has been around for a long time. I bet he'd be willing to help you."

He brightens. "Not a bad idea. Although I hate to put him in Becker's sights."

"What do you mean?"

Sanchez looks uncomfortable. He gives a half-shrug. "I don't want to badmouth the man. Something about him bothers me though. I've never met a preacher who's so relentless. Maybe it's because he's ambitious."

"Ambitious? Then being sent to a small town like this will be his worst nightmare. No wonder he's itching for something to keep him occupied."

"Chief Craddock, all of us religious leaders have to go where we're sent, especially in our first few postings. Some of us are luckier than others and end up where we should be. All those years ago when I first came here, I was disappointed, and I hoped I'd be moved before long. But then I got to really know the place, and when they asked me whether I wanted to go elsewhere, I told them I was content."

"I'm glad you stayed."

He nods in acknowledgment of our friendship. "The fact that Reverend Becker is too big for the town may be the reason they chose it for him. To take him down a peg or two. He told me he came to being a preacher only recently and that they put him here in a small congregation to test him."

"He said something similar to me," I say.

He grins. "The citizens of Jarrett Creek better watch their step. I suspect he wants to reel in a few new members so he can make the case that he should be moved to a bigger church, where he can have more of an impact."

"Either way, you're the one who has to make the decision whether to include him in the rodeo." I take out my checkbook and make out my usual donation. "Now you said there were two reasons you came."

"The second one is more in your ballpark, thank goodness. I've got two brothers who are at each other's throats because each of them wants his son to be the flag bearer in the opening ceremonies."

A light dawns. "Two brothers? This wouldn't be T.J. and Robert Caisson, would it?"

"Yes. How did you know?"

"I just know." I wonder if he knows that Robert shot T.J. "Are they Catholic?"

"Oh, no. In fact, I'm not sure they're churchgoers at all. The school decides who gets to be the flag bearer. It has to do with grades and attendance. Both these boys are good students and have good attendance records."

I'm surprised to hear it, but I'm glad. Sanchez tells me that because Robert's son is the older one, he should theoretically be the flag bearer. "But he got held back a grade because he was sick a lot in kindergarten, and now he's a grade behind T.J.'s son. T.J. thinks that because his son is in a higher grade, he ought to be the bearer."

"Have you suggested any solutions to them?"

"I suggested they flip a coin, and I thought they were both going to attack me." He laughs. "I'm afraid they're going to come to blows."

"I'm glad you have a sense of humor about it. You may not feel that way if I tell you that Robert shot T.J. last week."

"Shot him! How did I not hear that news?"

"If they were normal people, I would think it's because they were embarrassed to come to blows over something as silly as that, and they kept it quiet."

He groans. "This puts a different light on it. I have to think of a way to calm the situation."

We sit quietly for a minute, thinking. He's a companionable man, and the silence is easy. Then I have a thought. "Have you ever had a girl as flag bearer?"

Sanchez sits up, a big grin splitting his face. "No, we have not. And it's high time we did!"

"I agree. You think the school will go along with it?"

"I'm pretty sure I can persuade them."

"How are you going to break it to the Caisson brothers?"

"That's easy. I'll tell them a woman's committee came to me and demanded that a girl be allowed to do it. Men like them are cowards. They won't dare go against women."

I wonder whether Robert's wife will take it the same way the men will. We'll see.

After Sanchez leaves, I take care of paperwork that has been piling up. Dusty watches me, and every time I get up to pour another cup of coffee, he races to the door in hopes of an expedition.

By noon it's still too early to go to the coffee shop in Bobtail, but I'm too restless to stay around, and I decide to go back to Loretta's house. Maybe in the daytime I'll pick up something that I didn't notice last night.

First, I stop at the next-door neighbor's place. When I pull up, they're just arriving home from church. Sharon tells me to come inside and asks me to stay for Sunday dinner. "I put on a roast before I left this morning, and it should be ready to eat."

I eye Dusty, deciding if I should let him stay on the porch or leave him in the truck with the windows down.

"You can bring the dog in. We had dogs for years. Our last one, Maxie, died last year, and I miss having a dog."

I take her up on the dinner offer. While we eat, I tell them about last night's break-in and ask whether they saw or heard anything.

"We weren't home. We went over to a friend's house for supper last night and didn't get home until almost ten. Did they take anything?"

"No. I surprised the guy in the act, and although I didn't catch him, he didn't get away with anything." I tell them I'd appreciate it if they keep an eye on the place. "If you see anybody going in there though, don't try to stop them. Just call me."

"I wouldn't try to stop them," Sharon says, "but I can't speak for Ken." She narrows her eyes at him.

"I promise not to be a hero," he says.

When I leave, I walk around the perimeter of Loretta's house, hoping for a clue. Any clue. A footprint. A dropped item, a piece of clothing snagged on a windowsill. But there's nothing. Dusty busies himself with staring up into a tree where a squirrel holds forth with his opinion that a dog shouldn't have appeared in his usually dog-free yard.

Before I leave, I turn the hose on Loretta's garden for twenty minutes, not an activity I usually enjoy, but I'm doing it for Loretta.

I'm climbing into the car when I get call from a number I don't recognize.

"Chief Craddock? This is Marlene Becker." Reverend Becker's wife has a timid voice.

"Your husband said you had an interest in art. Is that what you're calling about?"

"Yes, it is. I don't want to impose, but I'd love to see your collection if you don't mind. At your convenience."

I'm eager to get to Bobtail, and I didn't plan to go until mid-afternoon, so I still have an hour to spare. It occurs to me that if I get in the good graces of Becker's wife, she might persuade him to back off the goat rodeo. I tell her I'm free if she wants to come over now.

"Oh, could I?" She sounds almost desperate.

I tell her I'll be at home.

She's a tiny woman of fifty, wearing her Sunday church clothes, a prim blue suit with a white blouse, and tiny silver earrings. "You sure this is convenient?" she says, standing on the porch, her enormous brown eyes beseeching. "I don't want to put you out."

"No, I rarely meet anybody who has an appreciation for my art. I'm happy to show you around."

It turns out that she does have a fair amount of knowledge of art and is especially taken with the Diebenkorn. "You're right," she says. "It's not one of his finest pieces. But I have to say the worst Diebenkorn is better than the best of most other artists. This one has those beautiful blues and greens." She has relaxed as we look at the art, becoming almost chatty.

We compare notes on the art museums we like best and agree that the one in Houston has improved a lot over the last few years.

"I keep meaning to take a trip to Houston to go to the museum, but there's too much to do here in town, being the preacher's wife." Her anxious expression returns.

"Have you met Ellen Forester? She has the art gallery and workshop downtown?" I hesitate to call it downtown. Our downtown is one block long.

"I heard her mentioned. I haven't had a chance to meet her yet, but I'd like to."

"Maybe the two of you could plan a trip to Houston."

"Oh, well, I don't know. She's . . ." She swallows. "My husband doesn't think it's a good idea for me to spend a lot of time with a woman who, well, who's divorced."

"I see. Well, maybe one of her art students . . ." I feel annoyed. Ellen is a friend, and judging her by her marital status seems foolish. But then I'm not a Baptist.

"I guess I shouldn't let him tell me who I can be friends with." Marlene's face has flushed, and I feel sorry for her.

"I think you'd like Ellen," I say.

Marlene Becker takes her leave quickly after that. I wonder what her husband would have to say if he knew I was having a fling with a woman "out of wedlock."

CHAPTER 15

I've been at the Hot Spot Coffee Shop in Bobtail a few times because it's near the courthouse. Seems like an odd place to meet a person someone plans to kidnap. But I remind myself that the man didn't actually meet Elaine Farquart here. Instead, he lured her to his house. And the same thing could have happened to Loretta. Again, I flash on why she would have taken a suitcase with her. And why she left dishes undone.

I'm disappointed when the two young women working behind the counter say they only work weekends. If Loretta was here on Tuesday, then they wouldn't have seen her. Still, I show them the four photos: Elaine Farquart and Loretta, the composed sketch of the man Elaine's neighbor described, and the photo I found in Loretta's desk. Both of the girls say they've never seen any of them. I leave them with my card and the request to call me if they see the man.

I'm walking out when one of the baristas calls out, "Wait. Come back." I go back to the counter. "She works here on Tuesday." She points to a woman in a corner, huddled over a laptop and a cup of coffee. "I forgot she was here."

This woman is older than the other two, around thirty, with tired eyes. I introduce myself and tell her that I'd like her to look at a few photos to see whether she has seen any of them. Still standing, I lay the pictures out on the table.

"Who are they?"

"These two women had arranged to meet this man." I'm hoping that's enough of an explanation.

She peers closer. "I've seen this woman." She points to Elaine's photo. "But I couldn't tell you where. She live around here?"

"That's right."

"What about this one?" She points to Loretta.

"She lives in Jarrett Creek."

"She doesn't look familiar at all. Why am I looking at these?"

"Both of the women are missing."

"Oh my God. And you think one of these men might have kidnapped them?" Her voice is suddenly loud, and conversation stops around us.

I lean closer. "We really don't know."

"Oh." She sounds disappointed not to be looking at the photo of a kidnapper. She shrugs.

"And the men? Have you ever seen either of them?"

She picks up the composite and shakes her head, then picks up the photograph. "I think I've seen him, but I don't know where." She starts to put it down and then looks again. "Maybe in the newspaper?"

I hand her my card. "If you see any of these people again, I'd appreciate a call."

It occurred to me when I was driving over to Bobtail that the man who hurt his ankle might be legitimate and someone else grabbed Elaine Farquart—someone who had nothing to do with the dating site. And if his ankle was hurt, he might have gone to the emergency room. It's a longshot, but it's important to cover all the bases. My next stop is the hospital in Bobtail.

The waiting room is busy, as it always is, and the frazzled duty nurse tells me it's unlikely that anyone would remember seeing the man. She waves her hand to indicate the waiting room. "It's like this all day every day. Pretty soon, all faces blend together." She sighs. "Let me look at the photo."

I hand her both the composite sketch and the photo. She rears back when she looks at the photo. "Of course I've seen him! I see him all the time. He's on the hospital board."

I have to wait to hear more while the nurse deals with a young guy who has come in bleeding. She hustles him back for emergency help, and by the time she gets back, she has two more people waiting. It seems to me that standing here at her window is a good place to get a hefty dose of germs. People all over the room are hacking and coughing, moaning, and looking stunned.

When the nurse finally has a break, I say, "Can you just tell me his name?"

"He's Douglas Black. Owns several businesses in town. He's a big hospital donor, which is why he's on the board."

She says a skeleton crew works in the administration office even on Sunday. I flee the germ zone and head over there to find out how I can track him down.

In the hospital administration office, I talk to the receptionist, and she says she'll be glad to tell me anything I need to know. "I expect you can find Mr. Black in his office tomorrow morning. He owns three stores and two office buildings downtown." The way she says it, she thinks of him as a titan of business in a thriving metropolis. She writes down the address of the building where his office is located.

"How long has he been on the hospital board?"

"Couple of years. He's such a nice man. A widower, poor thing. We all love him to pieces." She's a middle-aged woman, neatly put together. I notice she is not wearing a wedding ring. I suspect she has designs on Mr. Black.

She also gives me his home address, and I drive out to the house, but there's no one home. I'll go to his office first thing in the morning.

On the way home, I get a call from Maria, who says she heard back from Kathy Weinman. Kathy's out of town today, but they're going to meet tomorrow to distribute the flyers. "I've been taking flyers around town here in Jarrett Creek—the grocery store, places like that."

I doubt that will help because pretty much everyone probably already knows Loretta is missing, but at least it has given Maria something to do.

A RISKY UNDERTAKING FOR LORETTA SINGLETARY

I spend a restless evening at home. The only bright spot is a call from Wendy. She'll be home next week. "You know I love my daughter," she says. "But young people have a different kind of energy. Kind of overwhelming sometimes."

CHAPTER 16

A phone call early in the morning is not a good sign. My cell phone rings while I'm down in the pasture. It's Hogarth. His voice is husky. "Thought you'd want to know. Elaine Farquart's body was found early this morning."

I reach out for a fencepost to steady myself. "Where?"

"She was found on the road between Jarrett Creek and Bryan just before dawn. Somebody ran her down."

"You mean it was a hit and run?"

"No, it was deliberate. It's a strange story. Whoever did it ran over her, then backed up and ran over her again."

What if it had been Loretta? I bow my head. I'm too old for this. "You sure it was her?"

"We ID'd her from her photos, and we found her purse in a ditch. Family will make a positive ID later."

"Her purse intact?"

"Nothing missing. She had money and credit cards. Looks like it wasn't a robbery, unless she had something of value with her that we don't know about that got taken."

"What was she doing out there on the road?"

"Not a clue. We'll know more once the medical examiner has a go at the body."

I shudder, thinking that I'm glad it wasn't Loretta. But then I am ashamed. What kind of thing is that to think? "Who called it in?"

"Truck driver on his way to do a soft drink delivery in Bryan. He called Bryan PD and when they saw she lived in Bobtail, they called us in. The driver was coming from the distribution center out near San Antonio. Shook him up pretty bad. He's not a suspect."

"What's the next step?"

"The woman's daughter and son have been notified. One of 'em out in Lubbock and the other one in Brady. They'll be here later today. I'm hoping they can give us information that might help, but they didn't even have any idea she was on that dating website, much less that she was going out with a man she met through it."

"Have you told her neighbor?"

"I'm going over there now."

When I hang up, I walk back to the house, feeling like I've aged twenty years. All sorts of scenarios are running through my head and none of them good. I dread telling Maria the news, but I don't wait. I call her right away. She sounds groggy.

"I'm sorry if I woke you up, but I needed to tell you something."

"No! Not Loretta."

"Calm down. No, it's not Loretta, but it's bad." I tell her what happened.

"I'm coming in. I'll see you soon."

"No. Wait until your shift this afternoon. We'll know more by then. If you come right now, that will be two of us moping around."

At headquarters I go over and over the sequence of events that got Elaine Farquart killed. If the same person took Loretta, how did he overpower them? Did he drug them? It could be that they walked into the man's house and he had a gun on them, or maybe he sweet-talked them and then tied them up. My imagination can think of too many bad scenarios.

How did the man get Elaine out of the car and onto the road? Was she drugged and then driven out to the highway, told to get out and walk, or maybe she jumped out to try to get away? And then she was run down. It's a sickening scenario.

I consider going to Bobtail to see whether I can get in on the interview with Farquart's neighbor, but Hogarth will fill me in. I have a lead that I need to question right away. I leave a note for anyone who needs me to call my cell.

Douglas Black's office building is substantial, twelve stories of concrete and glass, the bottom floor of which is adorned with local beige and tan stone. Mr. Black's office is on the top floor, floor twelve, a high rise in these parts. I arrive in the elevator and step into a spacious entry that leads to a long counter. Apparently, his office takes up the entire top floor.

I introduce myself to the serious-looking receptionist, one of those willowy young women who look like they don't get enough to eat. "I wonder if I might have a word with Mr. Black."

"Do you have an appointment?" She must know the answer is no since she's the chief of this little domain, but she asked it pleasantly enough.

"No, but I need to see him right away regarding a police matter."

She takes that in stride, as if police officers come in to see him all the time. Maybe they do. "I'll see if he's in." Another thing she probably knows, but she feels the need to go through the motions.

She turns away from me and speaks quietly. When she clicks off the intercom and turns back around, she has the air of a woman who is preparing to tell me I've won the lottery. "He can see you. He doesn't have much time, but he said I should bring you back, he can spare a few minutes."

As I follow her down the interior hallway, I think what it would be like to have a position where I needed someone to run interference for me. I don't think I'm cut out for it. Even when I was in business, I preferred to do my own meeting and greeting.

"Thank you, Liz." Douglas Black is standing behind his desk when she shows me in.

Black is older than he looked in the photo that I found in Loretta's desk. He used an old photo on the dating site. Still, he is a healthy-looking man, with a head of gray hair that's thicker than mine, broad shoulders, and good proportion to his features.

He has the good grace to ask if I could use a cup of coffee, which I accept gladly. Then he takes his seat behind his substantial, but not ostentatious, dark wood desk, and I settle into a comfortable chair across from him.

"It's unusual for me to get a visit from a police chief. What is it I can do for you?" he asks.

"I have a couple of questions for you concerning a case I'm working on."

"Ooh, sounds interesting. Tell me more." He folds his hands on the desk in front of him and raises his eyebrows as if he thinks we're playing a game.

"First of all, let me get a little background. I understand you own a few stores here in Bobtail. What of kind of establishments are they?"

"Well, sir, I don't know how this can help with your investigation, but I have a very nice women's clothing store, a men's western store, and a large discount shoe store."

Women's clothing. "Do you ever work in the stores?"

"Not these days. When I was getting started, I surely did. Worked long hours in all of them. But I'm happy to say that I had good success, and I haven't needed to be on the floor for many years."

"You never meet any customers?"

"I wouldn't say that. I do stop by from time to time to keep my eye on the way the inventory moves. And I have a few old customers who call me to take care of them personally. But the inventory is my bailiwick. You can depend on people to do your buying and selling, but there's nothing like your instinct for the new thing. I've always prided myself on having that instinct."

"What kind of ladies do you cater to?"

"I'd like to say all kinds, but the younger girls . . . well, they like to go to the mall. Either in the outlet mall between here and San Antonio or in one of the big, sprawling complexes in San Antonio."

"It's the middle-aged and older women who frequent your stores?"

"I'd say so. You can't try to please everyone. You have to know your community, and I think that's where I've made my mark." He beams with pleasure. I usually like a man who has pride in his accomplishments, but in his case I hesitate because I'm afraid Mr. Black might not be a man to admire.

"Now, surely you didn't come here to find out how you can start your own clothing store. What's up?"

I pull the sketch from my pocket and unfold it. "Do you recognize this man?"

He takes a pair of glasses out of his pocket and puts them on and peruses the sketch. "No. Never seen him before." He lays it down.

I take his photo out and hand it to him. He gives a huff of laughter. "That's me all right. But it's ten years out of date. Where did it come from?" He lays it on the desk. He looks truly puzzled.

"Mr. Black, are you married?" I know he's a widower, but I like to ask all the pertinent questions.

"Widowed. Five years."

"Seeing anyone?"

He takes his glasses off and frowns. "I need to know what all these questions are in service of."

"I'm getting to it. Have you signed up for a dating website?"

The light dawns, but instead of my question making him nervous, it makes him burst out laughing so hard he has to wipe his eyes.

"Well?"

"Excuse me. In a manner of speaking I have, or rather someone has for me. My daughters ganged up on me and signed me up on a dating site. They think I ought to find a lady friend and settle down."

"And you don't want to?"

"Oh, I want to, but I don't need a dating site to help me with that. To tell you the truth, I rather like playing the field, and I haven't had any trouble finding a date." He actually winks at me, which seems a little extreme.

I indicate his photo. "Is this the photo that's on the site?"

"No. There's isn't one. I told them they could say what they wanted to, but too many people know me and they'd recognize my picture. I didn't want to embarrass myself." He grins, but then his expression suddenly sobers. "Why do you have that photo of me?"

In reply, I bring out the photos of Elaine Farquart and Loretta. "Do you recognize either of these women?"

He glances at them and hands Loretta's back. "Not that one, but this one looks vaguely familiar." He continues to study Elaine's photo, frowning. "Who are they?"

I tell him. "Do you recognize their names?"

"Elaine Farquart. Isn't that the woman who was murdered? I heard it on the news an hour ago."

"Yes, that's her. How about the other one, Loretta Singletary?"

His face gets red. "I know her name too."

"From the dating site?"

"Yes. It's pretty embarrassing. After my girls put my information on the website, several women contacted me to arrange a meeting. I think both of those women were among them."

"And did you contact them?"

"Absolutely not. I told you, the whole thing wasn't my doing." His good humor is gone.

"Then can you explain to me why I found this photograph in the possession of Loretta Singletary?"

"What do you mean, 'in the possession'?" He looks wary. "She's not dead too, is she?"

"Not that I know of. But I need to know how she got your photo."

His eyes dart around the room as if he's trapped, and his breathing is heavy. Finally, he speaks. "I'm going to kill those girls."

"I don't get your meaning."

"I mean," he says, his face growing redder by the second, "most likely my daughters sent the photo as if they were me and probably intended to trick me into going on a date with her."

"If that's the case, what happened?"

"I don't know, but I intend to find out." He reaches for his phone.

"Hold it," I say. "We need to talk to your daughters in person. I need to be there."

Understanding dawns. "You think I'd get them to lie for me? You think I had something to do with that poor woman's death? Think again." He hustles out from behind his desk. "Let's go. We're going to get to the bottom of this."

On the way out, he stops at the receptionist's desk. "Liz, I need you to locate my daughters and tell them both I want them at my house right this minute. No excuses."

"Yes, sir." The look she sends his way tells me she's not used to him speaking roughly to her.

"I'm going to be out for the afternoon."

"You're supposed to see Marybeth O'Toole at four o'clock."

"Reschedule," he snaps.

CHAPTER 17

Black wants me to ride with him, but I tell him I've got my dog in the car and I'll follow him. It's never good to get in the car with a suspect, no matter how unlikely his guilt. And I'm growing less inclined to believe in his guilt by the minute.

As we're walking to our cars, I say, "How can you be sure your receptionist can reach your daughters?"

He seems brought up short by the question. "Dammit, I shouldn't have talked to her that way. She's a gem. I'll have to get her flowers tomorrow." He shakes himself. "In answer to your question, if it's humanly possible to find the girls, she'll do it."

When we reach his house, a one-story ranch house on the south edge of town, two cars are parked in the driveway: a black BMW and a red sport convertible. He strides toward the garage, not waiting for me, but pauses when he reaches it. He turns and calls out, "You can bring the dog in. I have a dog, and we'll put 'em in the back yard."

Dusty and I follow him through the garage and into the kitchen, where we find two leggy young women in their twenties. They look like human racehorses, sleek and muscular. One is wearing black tights and a T-shirt. Her face is pink. She was probably called out of a workout session. The other one is dressed in a skirt and blouse. She looks like the older of the two and more serious. Both girls eye me nervously. The young one has a package of cookies out on the counter and is slitting it open. "Hey, Daddy," she says, running over to kiss his cheek. "What's going on? Liz said you were on the warpath." Her voice has a forced cheerfulness.

"I hope this is important," the other one says, petulantly. "I had to cancel a meeting."

"Let's go in the living room, and I'll tell you what's up. And I warn you, it isn't good. At least not for you two, it's not." At the tone of his voice, the girls exchange swift glances of alarm.

Dusty and Black's golden retriever are frisking around, and when we get into the living room, Black opens the sliding glass door and sends them into the backyard.

Once we're seated, Black introduces us. The older girl is named Caitlin, and the younger is Jessica—Jess, she puts in. "I'm going to turn this over to Chief Craddock to ask you a few questions," Black says.

I normally would prefer to be speaking to each woman individually, but now that I've seen their reaction to his stern demeanor, I'm pretty sure Douglas Black was telling the truth about them being responsible for his involvement in the dating site.

"I'd like one of you to tell me how your daddy got involved in Smalltownpair," I say.

The younger one, Jess, says, "Uh-oh."

"You're damn right, 'Uh-oh,'" her daddy says. "Now answer the question."

Caitlin sighs.

"We thought Daddy ought to widen his circle of lady friends," Jess says. She avoids looking at her father.

"*You* thought," Caitlin says.

"No, not just me. You can't blame it only on me. You're the one who brought up that he should be seeing women more his own age."

"Girls!"

"All right." Jess is turning surly. "We signed him up. He didn't want to, but we thought it might be fun."

"And he got some replies," I say.

"Yes. Really good prospects," Jess says. Her sister rolls her eyes.

"Did you show your daddy the replies?"

"Yes," Caitlin says.

"And?"

The girls exchange glances. "Look, Daddy refused to go out with

125

any of them, so we picked out a few and made dates with them. One of them was . . ." She swallows.

Jess says, "It was that woman, the one who was killed." Her voice is trembling. She looks down at her hands, which are clasped in her lap.

"Oh, my ever loving . . ." Black puts his head in his hands.

"Daddy, we were going to tell you tonight," Jess says. Her lower lip trembles and she scoots closer to her older sister, who puts an arm around her.

"Jessie, we didn't do anything wrong." She looks from her father to me. "The date we had set for her with dad was supposed to be tomorrow. We were going to tell dad and make him go, and then we saw the news this morning."

"We didn't mean to cause a problem," Jess says.

"Look," Douglas Black says, going over to the girls and sitting down next to them. "What happened to this woman isn't your fault, but you can understand how surprised I was when Chief Craddock here came to my office to question me."

I pull out the photo of Loretta. "Did you also reply to this woman?"

The girls look at the photo. "I remember her picture. Yes, we got back to her too," Jess says. "She said she had to think about it."

"You hadn't arranged anything with her?"

Both girls shake their heads.

"Did something happen to her too?" Caitlin asks.

I hesitate to say, but I don't know why it would hurt for her to know. "She's missing."

"Oh, my God." Both girls turn stricken eyes on me.

"I'm sorry we dragged you into this, Daddy," Jess says.

"Is there anything we can do to help?" Black asks.

I tell him that the police are doing everything we can to find Loretta.

He nods. "Girls, I want you to resign me from that dating site, or whatever it is you have to do to get me off of it right now. We've had enough of this nonsense."

Maria is meeting Kathy Weinman at the Hot Spot Coffee Shop at eleven to arrange to distribute the flyers Maria made up over the weekend. I go off to join them and question the weekday baristas.

I'm at the coffee shop early, and I show the regular baristas all the photos, but the only person they recognize is Elaine because her picture has been all over local news this morning. Although Loretta was supposed to meet someone here last Tuesday, apparently she didn't—or at least no one remembers it if she did.

Ever since I had the dream about Loretta calling me on my landline, I've been worrying that if she actually did get the chance to call, I might not be home. While I wait for the women to arrive, I call the phone company and give them my identification number as a police officer. I tell the woman I need my landline to ring through to my cell phone.

"No problem."

It turns out to be a little bit of a problem because I need my account number, and I'm not in the habit of carrying it with me. Why they can't simply get the account number from my phone number escapes me. But eventually the woman gets the number and performs the hocus pocus needed to have the number ring through. I'm ready to hang up when she adds, "It will take a few days for that order to go through."

"No, I need it to take effect immediately."

She digs in her heels, and I ask to speak to her supervisor. That entails a long wait, during which the women, who have brought one man, arrive to get the flyers.

The phone company supervisor doesn't have much more interest in my request than the first one I talk to. It's not the first time I've run into petty phone company bureaucrats determined to wield their bit of power.

"This could mean a matter of a woman's life," I say.

"Yes, sir, I'm sure. We hear that a lot."

"Do you hear it from the chief of police?" I repeat my ID number. "If the missing woman manages to call, and I'm not at home—which I can't be all the time because I am, in fact, the chief of police, the consequences could be fatal. We already have one woman dead. I suspect that the phone company won't be thrilled to get the kind of publicity that would go with causing a woman's death."

"Publicity" seems to be the operative word. By a miracle, the phone company can take care of the matter right now.

"Good for you, boss," Maria says when I click off my phone.

I introduce Maria to Kathy and the gang she has brought with her, all armed with staplers and tape. The flyer looks good, but seeing it makes Loretta's disappearance all too real. I think about people who have lost children and parents and have put up flyers, desperate for their return. I've never seen statistics on how effective they are, but I don't have high hopes.

If it is effective, it may well be due to those who have come to tack up the flyers. They are as well prepared as a small army. They've brought maps that lay out specific parts of town, and they tell me they will enlist others in neighborhoods. They know the parks and grocery stores. They know where people congregate.

"It looks like you've done this before," I say to Kathy.

She shrugs. "Mostly for lost pets. But Alicia's dad had Alzheimer's and he went missing last year for two days." She indicates one of the women. "Thank goodness the weather was mild and somebody found him in a park. They said they had seen a flyer and recognized him. So, we know it can work. Let's just hope somebody has seen Loretta."

CHAPTER 18

When the women leave to distribute the flyers, Maria stays behind so we can discuss our next moves. Before we can get started, my phone rings.

"Chief Craddock? This is Ray Sanchez. We need to have a talk about Robert and T.J. Caisson. They didn't take kindly to the suggestion that a girl lead the opening parade for the Goat Rodeo this year."

"Who did you choose?"

"I don't think who I chose is the problem. The problem is that she's a girl."

"When you say 'didn't take kindly,' what do you mean exactly?"

"T.J. threatened to kill me. Not that I take it seriously," he adds hastily. "But I thought you ought to know."

"I'm going to have to get to the bottom of it," I say. "But don't be alone with either of them."

"I'm not worried about it, but I worry that they will threaten someone at the school."

When I get off the phone, I tell Maria that the Caisson brothers threatened Sanchez. "How can it be so important who leads the parade for the Goat Rodeo?"

"They *threatened* Father Sanchez?" Smoke could be coming out of her ears. She is a good Catholic, attends mass, and adores the priest. "I told you we hadn't heard the end of it with those brothers."

"I've got a good mind to run them in and keep them locked up until the rodeo is over," I say.

"Then you'd have to deal with Darla. I'm not sure that's much better. Let me deal with them," she says grimly.

"No, I'm going over to the garage right now and tell them I'm not going to put up with anymore aggravation over this rodeo."

"What should I do while you're gone? I could help with the flyers."

I tell her I'd like her to go to the big outlet mall an hour away, on the road to San Antonio, and show Loretta's and Elaine Farquart's photos to the clerks in the clothing stores. "We've got to find out if there is another connection between those two women—why they were both chosen."

"I hate that mall," she grumbles.

"Do you have a better idea?"

"No. I'm not saying it's not a good idea. I'm just saying I don't like it."

"Who do you think I should send? Connor?"

She snickers. "I'd like to see his face if you made him go."

The Caisson Brothers' Garage is on the north side of Bobtail. It's a big outfit, the kind you usually associate with car dealerships. According to the sign out front, they are a full-service business—not only repairing engines but doing bodywork and smog certificates as well. There's a big barn-like building with a dozen slots for car repair, all filled and in various stages of work. It's a surprise to me that these two clowns manage a thriving business.

When I drive up in my squad car and park outside the structure, a young man in coveralls comes over, wiping his hands on a rag. "I hope you're not needing a service today," he says. "We're plumb full up."

"No, I'm here to see T.J. or Robert. Either one of them around?"

"In a manner of speaking," he says. His tone is dry, but he seems more amused than mad. "They're around back with a new toy."

As I round the corner to the back of the garage, I hear a buzzing sound. The Caisson brothers are there along with two other men. They're all looking up at the sky. T.J.'s arm is in a sling, and his brother has the controls of some contraption. I look up and at first don't see anything, but I follow their gaze to a small apparatus a couple hundred feet off the ground that looks like a big mosquito.

One of the men says, "You can use that thing to spy on your girlfriend, Robert."

"I don't know," one of the others says. "Look out for Darla. If she catches you, I don't give two cents for your chances of escaping with your life."

Chuckles all around, and then they notice me. "Chief Craddock, what are you up to?" T.J. asks, grinning.

Robert gestures to the sky. "Look what we got. What do you think of that?" Apparently, he doesn't hold a grudge over spending a night in jail.

"Is that a drone?" I ask.

"Sure is. Look at this." Robert fiddles with the control in his hand, and the contraption veers toward us, slows down, and settles on the ground nearby.

"That's quite a toy," I say. "What kind of range does it have?"

"This is a cheap one," Robert says. "It only goes 15 minutes before we have to recharge it. But it can fly a good distance in that time."

"We have to get a camera on it," T.J. says. "That way we can see what it sees."

"Yeah, but that will weigh it down too much," Robert says. "Then it won't go very far."

"Well why do you care if it goes far if it can't let you know what it's looking at?"

I tune out their squabbling because their toy has triggered an idea. We can't cover a lot of territory looking for Loretta's car on the ground, but suppose we had a drone with a camera? I have no idea whether the Department of Public Safety uses drones, but I'll find out.

Robert picks up the drone and brings it close. I've never seen one before, and it looks awfully small to do surveillance. "Are there larger ones?" I ask.

"Oh, yeah," Robert says. "You can get them a lot bigger and more complicated than this one."

"I'll bet the U.S. government has some big ones, and they're using them to spy on us," one of the men says.

The others grunt.

Robert looks at his contraption as if he sees it in a new light. He takes it over near the building where a big charger is set up with a long cord that snakes around from inside the building and plugs it in.

"How long does it take to charge up?" I ask.

"Fifteen, twenty minutes," he says. "As soon as I get good at this one, I'm going to get me a better one."

"Always have to have something better than anybody else has," his brother snipes.

"Listen, before you two get tuned up again, I need to have a word with you. Privately." I give a pointed look to the two men with them.

"Say no more," one of them says.

"What is it?" Robert says when they're gone. "That priest complain to you?"

"What would he complain about?" I ask.

"I don't know, but sometimes people don't care for straight talk."

"Straight talk like threatening him?"

"We didn't threaten him," T.J. says. "We just told him we didn't think it was appropriate for a young lady to lead the goat parade."

"Why not?" I ask.

"It's not right. A boy has always done it."

Robert shoots his brother a warning look. "That's not the point. The point is that Sanchez is trying to figure out a way to keep our boys from doing it."

I look over at the drone. My mind is on that, hatching an idea, and not especially on the silly spat between these brothers. "Makes sense to me," I say. "Since the two of you are making such a big deal out of it, practically ready to kill each other, Sanchez is right to try to find a better solution."

"Well goddammit, that's between us. Why should he horn in?"

"Because he's the one who puts in all the work, and then for his trouble he gets threatened. I'm not sure I care anymore what the two of you do to each other, but threatening to kill the priest is another matter."

"We didn't threaten to kill him," Robert says, but T.J. seems to have found something interesting off in the distance.

"See to it that you don't. In fact, I want you two to stay away from him until after the rodeo. And furthermore, you're going to have to live with the fact that a girl is leading the opening ceremonies, which may not have happened if you had managed to settle your fight without gunplay and threats. Now that the idea has been floated, the ladies will be all for it. You sure you want to tangle with them?"

The brothers look like they could spit fire, and I leave them squabbling about whose fault this was.

CHAPTER 19

Back at headquarters, Connor is holding down the fort and says it has been quiet. "You look like you've got a fire under your tail."

"An idea."

I sit down at my desk and dial Luke Schoppe's number. He's an old friend who has been a Texas Ranger from the time when it used to be a separate organization. Ever since it was put under the umbrella of the Texas Department of Public Safety, he keeps threatening to retire, but he never gets around to it.

He isn't in the Bryan office, but I reach him on his cell phone. "Schoppe, I could use your help."

"Tell me what's up."

I fill him in on Loretta and Elaine Farquart going missing. "Both women were set up to meet men they contacted through a dating website."

At that Schoppe grunts. "That's so risky."

"Risky is right. The Farquart woman was found dead this morning. She was run down by a car."

"I heard that, but I didn't know somebody from your neck of the woods was also missing."

I bristle at the idea that he hasn't heard that Loretta is missing. He works out of Bryan. He should have known. "I don't understand how you can't have heard about it."

"I'm not in the office. I'm up in Austin and have been for the past week. Someone called me with the news about the Farquart woman just before I left to head home. They called because it happened on the highway out from Bryan."

"I don't understand why there hasn't been more action from the Department of Public Safety. They aren't paying enough attention to this!"

"Samuel, that isn't like you. Now you have to calm down. It won't do your friend any good if you have a stroke."

"Listen, Schoppe, you know as well as I do that time is of the essence here." As soon as I say it, I'm stabbed by the memory that at first I didn't take Loretta's disappearance seriously myself.

"Do you know for sure the same person took both women?"

"No, but the MO is the same, and it seems damn likely to be the same person."

"Samuel, I'm telling you, you're too agitated."

"Of course I'm agitated. This woman is a personal friend. I have to find her, and I'm no closer than I was when she went missing."

"You're too close to the victim. You aren't thinking clearly. You caught me driving on my way back to Bryan, but I'm coming to you. Hold tight."

"Wait. I had a specific reason for calling. Does the DPS use drones for surveillance?"

"Drones? Not that I know of. The FBI might. What are you thinking?"

"Nobody has spotted either woman's car. And there hasn't been any activity on their credit cards, so the likelihood is that Loretta is still around here. I'm thinking if her car is out in the open, a drone might be able to spot it. Or maybe a helicopter."

In the background, I hear the hum of his car. "You know they aren't going to send out a helicopter for that, and the drone is an unlikely scenario too. Like I said, I'm coming over there. We'll talk it over when I get there. Should be forty-five minutes."

When I hang up, Connor says, "I thought kidnapping was a federal offense. You'd think the FBI would get involved."

"That's only if a victim is taken across state lines. Or if it's a child. I phoned them as soon as we knew Loretta was missing, but they have to have more evidence that someone was actually kidnapped, and the county sheriff in Bobtail has to ask for help before they'll do anything."

But another thought strikes me. It would be appealing to turn over the search to a big federal organization, but would they have the same urgency that Maria and I do?

When Schoppe arrives, he swoops in like a hero on a white horse, striding in with purpose in his step. He doesn't waste time on small talk.

"Tell me everything you've done to find her."

I take him through it from the beginning, starting from when she didn't show up to meet Ellen last Wednesday, finding dishes left undone in her house, and noting the missing suitcase and toiletries. I tell him that none of her relatives has heard from her, but that was no real surprise. "It took a while before we took it seriously. And that's when we found out she had met a few men through the Internet dating site."

"Okay, you've threaded all the needles so far. No leads at all?"

"A couple that fizzled out." I tell him about the professor and the man whose daughters plugged him into the website.

He laughs, but it's mirthless. "I know it's not funny, but I can imagine how aggravated that poor man must have been. What about another connection between the women? Any chance that Loretta and this Farquart woman knew each other?"

"I'm working with Brent Hogarth in Bobtail. We haven't been able to come up with any real connection between them. And there might not be one," I say. "Hell, for that matter, whoever killed the Farquart woman may not have contacted her through the dating site at all. But we're working on that assumption for now."

"Makes sense."

"At the moment, Maria is off at the outlet mall showing photos of the two women, hoping somebody remembers seeing both of them—seeing them together would be even better. And there's a posse of women putting up flyers in Bobtail asking if anyone has seen her. My deputy and I have been questioning men she had contact with on the website, but nothing has popped out. Beyond that, I don't know what to do. The Department of Public Safety was supposed to be on the lookout for Loretta's car, but I don't know how much manpower they've put into it. I'll be glad for any suggestion you might have."

"And you were hoping that you could send a drone around to go from house to house instead of driving around." Schoppe smiles kindly. "You understand how unlikely it is that her car is out in the open, right?"

"I do. I guess I'm clutching at straws." I haven't felt like a rookie in long time, but I've been acting like one. I'm beginning to realize that in my agitation, I've lost my usual steady way of doing things, and Schoppe is helping me get it back.

"I'll tell you what we ought to do," Schoppe says. "Let's go back through that dating site and zero in on anybody who lives around here."

"The addresses aren't available to users," Connor says. He has been following our conversation eagerly. "People have to volunteer information on where they live, and they don't usually do that until they get a match."

Schoppe's face gets red. I've seen that in him, that he doesn't like it when he gets snagged by a bureaucratic roadblock. "We'll see about that," he says.

He gets on the phone to an office in Austin, but when he gets off the phone, he shakes his head. "It's a privacy issue. I should have known that."

"I wonder where the dating site is headquartered?" I say. "Could we appeal to them to do a civic duty?"

"Ha! Good luck with that," Connor says. "All those people are interested in is money. Civic interest doesn't enter into it."

"Okay," Schoppe says. "If you need to, you can try to get a court order, but for now there's no use getting hung up on something we don't have control over. Let's move on. Have you heard how the Bobtail Police Department's investigation of the Farquart woman's murder is going?"

"Haven't had a chance to talk to them since Hogarth called me this morning. I'll tell you one thing I can do," I say. "I'm going to question some of Elaine Farquart's close friends. Maybe they'll know if she ever met Loretta." I'm sure Hogarth will talk to the friends, but I want to focus on Loretta.

"Look into whether they both went to the same professionals—eye doctors, dentists, podiatrists, that sort of thing."

"Good thought. And I sent Maria to the outlet stores because I know Loretta liked to shop there, but we'll talk to clothing stores in Bobtail too."

"You have to look into women things too. Did Loretta go in for manicures? Maybe they went to the same place. And how about her hairdresser? According to my wife, a woman's hairdresser knows everything there is to know about a client."

"That's an interesting thought." I remember a few months ago, when Loretta started wearing her hair different, she told me she went to Houston to have it done and was going to look around here for a hairdresser who could do it the same way. She said she knew she couldn't find anybody here in Jarrett Creek, but that's the last I heard of it. Maria will know whether she found somebody. If her new hairdresser is in Bobtail, then maybe both she and Elaine went to the same one.

"Even if they didn't go to the same salon, it's possible one of them told her hairdresser something that could be a lead."

"I'll get right on it. I knew talking to you was a good idea." All at once, I realize that Schoppe looks tired. He said he'd been in Austin all week, probably been working hard on another case. "Listen, I've called you away from getting back home. I appreciate your putting in your two cents. It helped me focus."

"I hope it helps." He pulls himself to his feet, and I notice the effort.

"You didn't say what you were up to in Austin."

He settles his hat on his head. "No, I didn't. But I'm tired and ready to get home. Glad I could help, although I'm not sure what good it did. Don't hesitate to call me if you want to discuss it more."

When he walks out the door, I'm left with an uneasy feeling that I missed something. But my problem with Loretta shoves it away.

I call Maria and get her on her cell phone. "Do you know if Loretta ever had manicures or pedicures?"

"She didn't. She said it was a waste to get manicures because she works in the garden every day, and she didn't like people fooling with her feet. Besides, she said nobody ever sees her feet because she doesn't wear sandals. Why do you ask?"

I tell her what Schoppe said. "You know where she gets her hair done?"

"I don't. But I'll bet she has a telephone number in her house."

CHAPTER 20

Pursuing the theory that Loretta and Elaine Farquart must have had some common point of intersection, I phone Elaine Farquart's next-door neighbor, Amy Martin. She's eager to help in any way she can. She knows Elaine's two closest friends and tells me she'll phone them to see when they are available to meet me. Within minutes she gets back to say that they want to talk to me right away. "We all want to find out what happened to Elaine. It's so horrible."

I swing by Loretta's house to look at her calendar and list of phone numbers to see whether there's a name or number for a beauty shop. Two weeks back, there's a Tuesday afternoon appointment for "hair." That's not helpful. The list of phone numbers is by name, almost all first names only. No more helpful than "hair." Turning to her credit bills, I find a payment for "Darlene's Beauty Shop" in Bobtail. She paid $85 to have her hair done. Seems steep to me. Douglas Heckman still gives me a $15 haircut in his barbershop.

I arrive at Amy's just as two of her boys have gotten home from school. The oldest one has stayed for baseball practice. She sends the two upstairs and tells them they are not to disturb us, reinforcing her admonition with an armload of snacks. When the doorbell rings, she whispers, "Carol and Misty are good friends, but you wouldn't know it. Be prepared; they pick at each other constantly."

Carol Johnson and Misty Lovell are in their sixties, Elaine's age. Carol is a big-boned widow with steel gray hair and posture a model would envy. Misty is plump and pink-eyed, reminding me of a nervous rabbit. Neither of them recognizes Loretta's name or her photo. The two of them sit side by side on the sofa.

"Elaine had many interests," Carol says, speaking precisely as one would expect of the English teacher that she was for forty years. "It's quite possible she knew your friend and I wouldn't have met her."

"What was she interested in?"

"She played bridge and was a bird watcher—went down to King's Ranch every year for bird count season."

"I believe she also went to Costa Rica once to look at birds," Misty says, casting a nervous glance at Carol.

"Of course she did," Carol says. "Don't say you believe so when you know perfectly well she did." Her tone is scolding.

Amy widens her eyes in my direction.

Carol says, "She used to volunteer at the animal shelter, but she said seeing all those unwanted pets upset her, and she had to quit." They both eye Dusty, who has sprawled at my feet.

"She loved her cat," Misty says, dabbing at the corner of her eye. "I hope somebody will take care of it. I'm allergic, or I'd take it."

"If her daughter doesn't take the kitty, I will," Amy says.

"Did Elaine have a church affiliation?" I ask. It's possible she met Loretta at a church function.

The two women exchange a glance. "I don't think she went to church," Misty says.

"You know she didn't, Misty." Carol fixes her with a severe look.

"She was a Baptist at one time," Amy says. "But she said the church got too strict for her taste, and she didn't have the heart to look for another church home."

Carol's eyebrows shoot up. "Well, Elaine and I were friends," she says, "but she was a little free-thinking. She might have been better off if she'd met a man through church instead of putting herself out on that website."

Misty blinks her pink eyes furiously. "Carol, that's not fair, and you know it."

Carol sniffs. "I suppose you're right."

"You know I am."

Amy meets my eye, and I can see she's having trouble stifling a laugh.

I should be amused too, but it's hard to find my sense of humor with Loretta missing.

Although the women seem eager to please, they have no answers that I find helpful. I thank the women for their time, but it seems wasted. Loretta didn't play bridge, and as far as I know, she wasn't interested in birds.

When they've gone, Amy's mood plunges along with mine. "I wish I could be of more help."

"Do you know where Elaine had her hair done?"

Amy looks blank. "I know she liked the woman who did it, but I don't know where it was."

"Did she shop at any particular clothing store in town?"

Amy grimaces. "If she mentioned one, I don't remember. There were a lot of years between us, and we didn't dress the same." She blinks. "Wait. I remember a few weeks ago, she came over for coffee and said she had been to a new store in town and she thought I might like it too. Raven Black or Black Raven or something like that. No. It was Blackbird. I thought it was a funny name for a clothing store."

As I'm leaving, I get a call from Maria. She is leaving the outlet mall and says she's discouraged. I tell her to meet me at Blackbird.

"It will take me an hour to get back this late in the afternoon. They might be closed by then."

"You sound out of breath."

"I'm walking to my car."

I tell her I'll go over to Blackbird and make sure they stay open until she gets there. "I think you might have a better handle on what kind of questions to ask at a woman's store than I will."

"Oh, don't be so squeamish just because they sell women's clothes. Act like you'd act if you were questioning a man's clothing store. It's all the same."

In my car, I put in a call to Hogarth and ask him whether they have Elaine Farquart's credit card bills and bank records. "I'm looking for any connection between her and my friend Loretta. It's possible they went to the same beauty shop."

"That's a good thought. Come on by the station. I'm on my way out, but I'll have Marks get you her credit card bills."

It's four-thirty when I get to the Bobtail Police Department. I'm in a hurry. Blackbird closes in an hour. But Hogarth is as good as his word. The duty officer hands me a sheaf of printouts.

I scan them as I'm walking back to my car. "Bingo," I say. Both women went to the same beauty shop.

I key in the name of Darlene's Beauty Shop on my phone and see that it's out on the edge of town. I'm torn whether to go straight there or stop by the Blackbird clothing store. But a call to the beauty shop answers the question. They're closed on Monday.

I don't want to wait until tomorrow to talk to the owner. I want to question her now. Hoping she leaves a home number, I dial the shop's phone, and sure enough the message gives an emergency number.

"Yeah?" A man's voice answers.

"I'm looking for the owner of Darlene's Beauty Shop."

"This is her number, but she's not available at the moment. I can take a message."

"I need to talk to her pretty quickly." I identify myself.

"I don't know what to tell you. I'm her husband. We're in San Antonio. She's in a department store. I bailed out, and I'm waiting for her in a coffee shop."

"How soon will you be back home?"

"We're going to have supper here at the Crab Shack, so I don't imagine we'll be home much before nine depending on traffic."

"Do you know if she'll be in the shop tomorrow?"

"Bright and early."

"Thank you. I'll talk to her then."

"Can I tell her what it's concerning? She'll be curious."

"I have a few questions about one of her clients."

Blackbird is downtown, on a block that has been newly renovated. Everything looks modern, lots of steel and glass and bright colors, like stores you see in Houston or San Antonio. I can already see the effect on neighboring areas. Scaffolding is up on a tired-looking building down the block, and a couple of stores have "Closing Soon for Renovation" signs. Bobtail is coming up in the world—or at least in the county.

One step inside Blackbird, and I know I'm lost. A young woman with a head full of curls, who makes me think of what Wendy must have looked like when she was young, glides over to me. She has kind eyes and an amused smile. "How can I help you?" Her tone implies that she thinks I might be lost.

I pull out the photos of Loretta and Elaine Farquart. "I wonder if you've ever seen either of these women?"

Her smile disappears, replaced with a somber look. "That's Elaine. Yes, we knew her. What a tragedy."

"How about this woman? Her name is Loretta Singletary," I add, thinking that even if the photo doesn't jog her memory, her name might.

She studies the photo. "I don't remember her. That doesn't mean she hasn't been here. We get a lot of people in who browse and don't buy anything. Or she might have been in when I wasn't here." Her gaze lingers on me. "If you're asking about her and Elaine, that's not good, is it?"

"No, it isn't." I muster a smile. "Good deduction on your part. Loretta is missing, and I'm trying to find out if there was any connection between the two women."

"I never saw the two of them together. But again, that doesn't mean they weren't here when I was off."

I find out that there are three other possible clerks: two who work on weekends and another one who works during the week. "And there's the owner, Shelly Wycoff. She's in and out."

I've brought copies of the photos and leave copies with her. "If anyone has seen Loretta, with or without Elaine Farquart, have them give me a call."

I'm standing outside wondering whether I should ask in any other shops when Maria wheels up. She gets out looking grim and frazzled. "That damn road between here and San Antonio gets worse every time I travel it."

I don't like hearing that. Maria is close to her family in San Antonio, and I worry that one day she'll decide the commute is too much for her and she'll transfer to the San Antonio Police Department. "It was rush hour," I offer.

I tell her that the young woman in Blackbird wasn't able to help.

"But there is one thing." When I tell her about the connection with the beauty shop, she's excited.

"Let's go talk to her."

I tell her the owner of the shop is in San Antonio and won't be back until late.

"Let's see if there are any other clothing stores around here that Loretta might have shopped in." She glances at her watch. "We have a few minutes before people will be closing up."

A block away, in a row of older, more traditional-looking stores, we pass a clothing shop that even I can tell sells clothes that probably appeal to an older crowd. We go in and startle a curvaceous woman in her sixties. She's making a last stand against age with bright lipstick and heavy eye makeup.

I introduce the two of us and pull out the photos.

"Why yes, I recognize both of those girls. Loretta has been coming in here for years. Not that she buys that much, but she likes to browse."

"And the other woman?" I ask.

She cocks her head to one side. "Yes, I recognize her. She's the woman who was killed. Her picture was on the news. But I don't think she was ever in here."

"Is it possible that she was here when another employee was working?"

"No, it isn't. I'm the only one who works here. I'm the owner, and I had to let my last employee go last summer." She turns to Maria. "You probably noticed there are fancy new shops going in. I can't keep up. I'm going to have to sell, but I'm putting it off as long as I can."

"It's a nice store," Maria says. "I imagine you have long-time customers who will be sorry to see you close up."

The woman's eyes widen. She nods and purses her lips. I have the feeling that if she spoke, she'd start to cry.

I tell her why we are asking about Loretta. "Oh, my goodness. She's missing?" She glances at Elaine Farquart's photo again, and I see her make the connection that if one was killed, the other might be too.

"Did you ever have any conversations with Loretta?" Maria asks.

"Not really. I knew she was from Jarrett Creek and that she has two sons . . ." Her voice trails away. "Come to think of it, it has been a while since I saw her."

Because Loretta had started wearing more youthful clothing.

Tomorrow will be a week since Loretta disappeared. In the evening when it's time to check on my cows, I realize that I'm too distracted to do a good job. If something was wrong with one of them, I'd hardly notice. I'll call Truly Bennett tomorrow and see whether he's home yet and hire him to do a thorough job of examining them.

On our evening walk, Dusty and I pass by Loretta's house, and I think again about the man I disturbed inside. There was no way to figure out who he was. No fingerprints. I got no visual on him—just that he had some strength and moved faster than I did. It was dark when I encountered him. He had parked a car around the corner, but he zoomed away before I could get there.

I'm staring at the house when the neighbor on the west side comes out on the porch. He waves at me, and I walk over to greet him. He's a lanky widower with barely a wisp of hair on is head. He wears thick glasses, but he still peers at me as if he has trouble seeing. His hearing is almost nonexistent, but if you yell you can get through to him.

"Hey, Irwin," I say.

"No need to yell," he says. "He points to his ear. Got me some hearing aids."

"That's good. How are they working?" I go up on the porch with Dusty.

"Pretty good. I had to get them so I could talk to my grandson on the phone. His mamma told me he was tired of yelling at me. Else I wouldn't have bothered."

"Well, maybe you can help me out. I guess you know Loretta is missing."

"That's why I come out here. I wanted to tell you what I seen." He gestures toward Loretta's house.

My heart quickens. "What's that?"

"Last Tuesday morning, I come outside to turn on the sprinkler, and I seen Loretta back her car out of her garage and drive away like her tail was on fire."

"Which way did she go?"

"Toward town." He nods toward the east, where the highway runs through town.

"But you didn't speak to her."

"No. I probably wouldn't have anyway. She was in a hurry. You know Loretta. Always busy, always running here and there."

"Did she have a suitcase with her?"

"No, sir. That came later."

"What do you mean?"

"Tuesday evening, I put on my sprinkler and got to watching TV and forgot about it. At 11:00 p.m., I remembered, and I came outside to turn it off. Somebody was coming out of Loretta's place in a big hurry, carrying a suitcase."

"A man?"

He scrunches up his eyes and looks over toward Loretta's house. "Dressed like a man, but . . ." He draws a breath, and I wait while he gathers his thoughts. "Something about the way he walked put me in mind of a lady."

"Tell me how he was dressed. Or she."

"Slacks. A shirt, maybe tan or brown. And a baseball hat."

"Could you see if the hat had a logo?"

"It was too dark, and it all happened fast."

"Why didn't you call me to tell me this?"

"I only heard at church this past Sunday that she was missing. I suppose I should have called after that, but . . ." He shrugs. "Figured it was her business if she's gone off with a man."

I think again of the man I caught here. At least I thought it was a man. Irwin doesn't see very well, which could account for his uncertainty. "Have you seen anybody hanging around here in the past few days who you don't recognize?"

"Only her son. He comes outside to smoke. I can understand that. If he smoked inside, Loretta would have his hide."

"Anyone else?"

"You're thinking somebody might break in and steal something with her away?"

"Not sure. If you happen to see anything unusual, though, give me a call."

CHAPTER 21

Tuesday morning Dusty is frisky, and when we go down to check on the cows, he dashes around like a wild dog. He manages to scare up a squirrel and chases off into the woods after it. Between his frantic barks, I hear it in the trees, chittering. He won't come when I call him, and I have to walk back into the woods and haul him back by the collar until we're close enough to the house that he forgets about the squirrel.

I've been thinking I need to put time in training him. He's a smart pup, and Maria keeps scolding me and telling me he'll be unruly if I don't train him now.

Maybe because it has been a week since Loretta disappeared, I feel a particular sense of dread as I walk back toward the house. I think of all the times I've walked back just in time to meet Loretta coming to my front door with baked goods. I always enjoy seeing her familiar face, smelling and sampling the results of her hard work, and sharing a cup of coffee and a bit of morning news with her. It's satisfying above and beyond eating the baked goods. It's about knowing someone for a long time. I have never really considered how early she must get up to do the baking. Does she do some parts of it before she goes to bed? Does she set her alarm and get up in the wee hours and then go back to bed while dough rises?

Another thing I never thought about is that it must be expensive buying all the ingredients. Why does she do it? It has to be a labor of love. And to think that I have never thought to pitch in financially. I take her out to dinner occasionally—at least I used to before I met Wendy, but that hardly makes up for it. I've taken her for granted.

It's only seven-thirty, and Darlene's Beauty Shop opens at ten, so I have time to kill. When Hogarth told me that Elaine Farquart's body was found, he described the location. I want to go out and see the spot for myself. Not that I think I'll find anything that the Bryan and Bobtail officers haven't already gone over, but I want to get a sense of the place.

As usual, Dusty is thrilled to go for a ride. I take my pickup instead of the squad car because it sits up higher and I can see more. It's a beautiful day, and I have the windows down. Dusty sticks his head out the side window and lets the breeze flap his ears back.

Hogarth described a couple of markers, and I slow when I see an abandoned shed on the left-hand side of the road. He said a quarter of a mile beyond that is a culvert, and 200 yards farther is where Elaine's body was found. He said I'd see yellow tape that they put up for the crime scene. Sure enough, there it is, looking jaunty and waving in the breeze. It has been affixed to a couple of pipes stuck in the ground.

Other than the yellow tape, the site is desolate. This is not fertile ground, and the whole area is overrun with knee-high weeds, interspersed with a few hardy wildflowers—long leggy white ones, a few stray bluebonnets, and tiny, pale buttercups. There are no buildings close by. I feel hopeless surveying the landscape. There are miles and miles of this kind of acreage in the county. Loretta could be held anywhere.

I make Dusty stay in the car. There's not a lot of traffic on the road this early, but what traffic there is goes fast. Dusty is still a youngster, and I don't want to worry that he'll wander out onto the road. But he doesn't like being confined and starts barking when I shut the door.

I walk up and down the graveled verge fifty feet in each direction, scanning for anything odd. There's litter along the road—mostly cans and bottles and a couple of yellowed advertisements. And there's a dead possum that has been here long enough that he doesn't stink anymore.

I try to picture what happened to Elaine Farquart. Was she put out of the car and thought she was being let go, and then her kidnapper came back and ran her down? Did she escape and try to run out onto the road, hoping to flag down a driver who would save her? In the weedy, hard-packed ground off the road, I see no tire tracks or drag marks, no stirred-up ground that would indicate she struggled with anyone. Finally, I give up and get back in the pickup, feeling frustrated. Dusty seems to sense my mood. He nuzzles up to me and licks my hand, then lies down in the seat, his eyes trained on me. I drive farther on, seeing a farmhouse here and there and a few small storage sheds. My impulse is to go knock on doors and peer in windows, but Hogarth said they questioned people in the houses closest to where the body was found.

I'm at Darlene's Beauty Shop, on the west side of town, when the doors open. Maria wanted to come with me, but she had a meeting set up this morning with the former employer of the man she suspects of murdering the victim in the cold case.

The shop is in a wood-shingle house painted white with green trim. The yard is surrounded by a picket fence, with a small sign out front that looks hand-painted. As I approach the door, I wonder whether I should have waited until Maria could come with me, but I don't want to waste time.

Dusty usually stays outside with no trouble, but this morning he whips inside the salon the second I open the door, tail wagging and frisking around like he has been here a dozen times. There's no one in the front, so I call out. A woman in her forties wearing a tight dress with a smock over it and block-heeled shoes comes out from the back and immediately zeroes in on Dusty.

"You have to get that dog out of here! I could lose my license!" She starts shooing him away, and I grab for him. Instead of backing up and heading out the door like he usually does, he leaps on her and starts barking with excitement.

"Dusty! Down!" It's the only command I've used consistently, but it makes no difference. He's leaping and bounding, and the woman squeals more in annoyance than fear.

I manage to grab his collar and take him outside. I get a leash from the car and tie him up to the fence in front of the salon.

Back inside, I apologize, but she's not happy. "How could you have let that dog in here?" she says. "You're a lawman, you ought to know better." I'm wearing my uniform shirt this morning, which is how she knows I'm a lawman.

"You're right. He usually behaves better than that, but he's a pup, and today he seems full of energy." I actually don't know anything about beauty salon regulations. I suppose there must be health department standards for beauty salons, but it's a surprise to me that dogs can't come in. I suspect that even if it is true, if one of her best clients came in with a well-behaved poodle, she'd be fine with that.

"You're the chief of police who called yesterday?"

"That's right."

"What can I help you with?" she says, still frowning. She's eyeing my hair as if she's got ideas. If she does her own hair, I'm surprised that women take it as a sign that she's good at what she does. It's flat on the top and frizzy on the sides. I can't imagine anybody who would look good with hair like that.

"I need your help with a police matter," I say.

I'm pulling out the photos to show her when the door opens and a woman walks in. Dusty has set up a racket outside, and the woman says, "What is that dog doing out there?"

"He's mine," I say. "Sorry about the racket."

"Humph. Oh, Darlene, I'm in a hurry this morning. I hope you can get me out of here in an hour." She's at least sixty, but her hair is dyed jet black, and she is wearing a low-cut blouse and skirt that hits above her knobby knees.

"Of course I can, Louise. Sit down in the shampoo chair." Darlene takes a plastic drape out of a cabinet and arranges it around the woman's shoulders, then runs her fingers through her hair looking at the roots. "I guess we can get by without taking care of those roots for another week."

"I hope so. I don't have time to sit while the color sets."

As if she had hoped I would disappear, Darlene turns back to me. "What is it you said you need help with?"

"I'd like you to take a look at these photographs and see if you recognize them."

She makes an impatient sound as she snatches them from my hand. "Oh." She looks up at me. "Yes, I recognize them. They're both clients of mine. You know that one of them was killed?"

"Who's that?" the woman in the chair says. "Is that poor Elaine?" She sits back up and cranes her head to see the photos.

"Yes, it is."

"That was terrible," the woman says, her sharp eyes glittering. She gets out of the chair for a closer look. "Who's the other woman?"

"That's Loretta Singletary," Darlene says. "She hasn't been coming here very long. Only a few months. So I don't know her very well."

"Why do you have her picture?" the client asks me, apparently forgetting that she was in a hurry.

"She's missing, and I'm trying to find out if the two women knew each other. Do you know if they were friends?" I ask Darlene.

She shakes her head. "I don't know. But Loretta wasn't actually my client. She gets her hair done by the other girl, Lucy."

"Is Lucy working today?"

"She usually only comes in on Wednesday, Thursday, and Friday, but she has a couple of clients later today."

I groan inwardly. It has already been too long since Loretta disappeared. I can't afford another day. "I'm going to need a way to get in touch with her," I say.

"I don't like to give out my employees' home information," she says. "You can talk to her this afternoon or tomorrow."

"It's too urgent for me to wait. I need to get her address and phone number from you."

She sighs. "Just a minute." She goes into the back room.

"Missing?" the client says. "You don't think . . ." Her question dies away as she sees the look on my face. "Well, I don't envy her having Lucy do her hair. Between you and me, Lucy's a sourpuss. Always complaining." She says this as Darlene returns.

"Louise, don't say that. You know Lucy has a perfectly good reason for being cranky. She's bitter, and I don't blame her after what that husband of hers did to her."

"I know it, but she shouldn't take it out on everyone else."

"Her clients like her fine," Darlene says. "Now, if I'm going to get you out of here in time, you'd better sit down."

The woman scurries back to the shampoo chair. Darlene hands me a piece of paper. "Here's Lucy's phone number and address. I don't even know if she's home today. She might have gone away for the weekend. I usually try to get out of town on my days off."

Darlene walks over to her client's chair and turns on the water with enough force that I'm surprised the client doesn't protest.

Back outside, I retrieve Dusty and climb into the squad car. I get out my phone to call Lucy, but Dusty lunges for the piece of paper with her information written on it. I have to pry it out of his mouth. "What has gotten into you?" I say. His nose is working overtime. I sniff the paper, but I don't smell anything. Doc England, the vet, told me that dogs have a much greater capacity to smell than people do. Maybe because Loretta has been in the shop, the paper has retained a faint scent from her. Or maybe Dusty is being a teenager.

I decide Dusty did me a favor by grabbing the paper. It's probably better to surprise the woman rather than calling first anyway. Although I know Bobtail pretty well, I don't recognize the street name, so I put the address into my phone's GPS. Even with the directions, it's hard to find. It's a small house that must have been built at least fifty years ago. There are two cars parked in front, both small Toyotas.

There is only one house nearby, right next door, in poor repair, with a sagging porch and a roof that looks like a good wind would blow it off. It looks like nobody lives there. Other than that, the nearest neighbors are a block in every direction. I wonder if they're tearing down these houses for a new subdivision.

The assessment that Lucy Nettleman is a sourpuss was well-founded. She's Darlene's age but with a deep cleft in her forehead between her eyes that tells me she's accustomed to frowning. Besides that, she's all angles, with a sharp pointed chin, and wrists and elbows that seem to poke out of her skin.

"You the lawman Darlene called me about?"

So much for surprise. "Yes, I'd like to ask you some questions about one of your clients."

"I don't know why this couldn't have waited until this afternoon when I'm in the shop, but I guess you'd better come on in." She's dressed in jeans and a loose-fitting shirt, which along with her close-cropped hair and square face gave her a mannish appearance.

Despite her ill-humored manner, her living room is welcoming, with a butter yellow sofa and comfortable easy chairs. Family photos decorate the walls, along with a couple pictures of Bible scenes. I hear kitchen noises from the back of the house. "Someone else here?"

"My daughter. She came over to bake with me. The bread is going to have to be kneaded again soon, so I can't talk long."

The scent in the air reminds me of Loretta's cinnamon rolls, which gives me a pang. "I won't keep you long."

She gestures to one of the easy chairs and sits in the other without offering coffee or water.

"Just to be clear, I'd like you to identify these photos for me."

She recognizes Elaine's photo and confirms that Loretta is her client.

"How long has Loretta been coming to you?"

"Not long. I've only done her hair three or four times. I could look up the exact times if you come to the shop later."

"Why did she choose you?"

Lucy sits back, eyes flashing. "Because I'm pretty much the only stylist around here who trained in a city salon, and I know what I'm doing. I can do modern hairstyles, which not everybody can do."

"How did she find you?"

She looks past me, lips pursed, considering. "I believe it was Sheila Fenton who told her."

"And how do you know Sheila?"

There's a crash from the kitchen. Lucy jumps up and without a word rushes out of the room. I don't hear individual words, but I hear Lucy's tone, fussing at her daughter.

When she returns, Lucy's face is red. She stays standing. "What do you actually need from me?"

"I understand that you don't want to take the time to talk to me, but I'm afraid you're going to have to. We have a woman who was murdered and another woman missing, and I don't want her to be the next victim. The missing woman is your client. I'm sorry if you're inconvenienced."

I don't usually lose my temper, but in this case I can't help it, and it works to my advantage. She creeps back to the chair she vacated and eases into it. "All right, I didn't mean to be short with you. My daughter is all thumbs in the kitchen, and I hate to leave her alone too long. I'll do my best to help you, though, as long as you don't mind if I run off to check on her every now and then."

"It won't take me long. I was asking how you know Sheila, the woman who introduced Loretta to you."

"We're all Baptists. The Jarrett Creek Baptist Church Ladies' Circle was the guest of Bobtail First Baptist—this was in October and Loretta came. She said she had gone over to Houston and gotten a new hairstyle and wanted to know if anybody around here could copy her new style. Sheila has been a customer of mine for a long time. She likes to keep up on the latest styles, so she comes to me. She told Loretta I could do it."

"How long have you worked for Darlene's Beauty Shop?"

The question was innocent enough, but she flushes bright red. "I went to work for Darlene last summer."

"Where were you before that?"

She thrusts her chin out. "Before that I had my own shop. But my husband ran off with my money, and I couldn't make enough money to keep it going. After a while, I had to close up and go to work for Darlene."

That explains Darlene's reference to Lucy's bitterness at her husband. "How is that working out?"

"Darlene's okay. She has a clean shop, which not everybody does. I'd like to be closer into town, but I had to take whatever job I could get in a hurry."

Her daughter starts humming in the kitchen, which makes Lucy give a quick glance in that direction. It's an annoying sound, high and tuneless.

"Can you tell me if Loretta and Elaine Farquart knew each other?"

She shakes her head slowly. "I'm sorry, but I don't have any idea. I don't know either of them personally, so I can't tell you whether they were acquainted."

I remember Amy telling me that Elaine wasn't much of a church-goer. "Did Elaine ever come to any of your Baptist activities?"

"Not that I know of."

"Did Loretta ever mention to you that she had joined a dating website?"

"I believe she did." Her cheeks grow pink, and I wonder whether she's embarrassed at the idea that a woman Loretta's age would look to strangers for a date.

"Do you recall what she said?"

She gives a thin-lipped smile. "If I remembered everything my clients said to me, I wouldn't have room for my own thoughts."

"She never mentioned any men in particular who she planned to go out with?"

"Not that I recall."

Suddenly Lucy's daughter appears at the door to the living room, looking frazzled. Although she looks like Lucy, she's bigger. Her apron and hands are covered with flour, with patches of flour on her face. "Mamma, this dough doesn't look right."

"I'm sure it's fine."

"No, it's not! It's a mess." The girl has her hands on her hips, and she's practically yelling.

Lucy jumps up, glancing at me and then back to her daughter, torn between the two of us. "It's all right. I'm coming right now."

I stand up. "I'll let you get back to your baking. Do you know how I can get in touch with Sheila Fenton?"

Lucy edges in her daughter's direction. "Her information will be at the shop. Darlene keeps all the records."

I thank her and leave my card on an end table. "If you think of anything or hear something that might be of interest, I'd appreciate a call."

"Mamma, I need you now!"

"I can see myself out," I say.

I drive away, thinking that Lucy has her hands full with her demanding daughter. At least I've found a tiny link between Elaine and Loretta, but it's not enough. Maybe I can find out more from Sheila Fenton.

Darlene is cutting someone's hair while another woman sits under the dryer and yet another is sitting in a chair reading a magazine, flicking the pages as if they have offended her. As busy as she is, Darlene is once again impatient at my request for information, this time about Sheila Fenton. She brings a rolodex from the back room and thrusts it at me. "It's in there."

CHAPTER 22

Another dead end. Sheila Fenton is perfectly willing to co-operate, but she doesn't know a thing about Loretta. She says the only time she ever met her was that time when she introduced her to Lucy. She praises Lucy's skills, and she does have a nice-looking head of hair, so I guess she's right that Lucy knows what she's doing. As much as I know about it.

After I talk to Sheila, I swing by the Bobtail Police Department to see whether my friend Wallace is in. He is, and I tell him I'm about at the end of my ideas. "Short of going house to house and knocking on doors, I don't know what else to do."

"I saw the flyers all over town. You haven't gotten anything from that?"

I shake my head. I'm so discouraged I can hardly talk.

"That's what Hogarth says too. They don't have a clue what happened to Mrs. Farquart. Whoever took those women had it all worked out. Look, you know as well as I do that you have to keep poking at things and hope something comes of it."

And hope it isn't too late. I have an awful feeling that if it wasn't Loretta in peril, I'd be freer with my thinking. My anxiety about her has impeded my ability to reason things out.

I head back to Jarrett Creek. It doesn't help when I get a phone call from Maria wanting to know whether I had any luck and then, barely keeping her criticism to herself, insinuating that if she had been there to talk to the two hairdressers, she probably would have gotten more out of them than I did.

"You could be right," I say, probably more sharply than I intended.

I'm hungry, but I don't feel like stopping at Town Café. Instead, I go home to fix a sandwich. It's there that I get the first good news of the day.

"Is this Chief Craddock?" It's a woman's voice that sounds almost familiar, with an exaggerated drawl.

"It is. How can I help you?"

"Are you at home or at work?"

"I'm home."

"You can help me by staying right where you are, so I can come over there and jump your bones."

I burst out laughing. "Are you back?"

"Yes, and it's a good thing you guessed it was me, otherwise I would have thought you were ready to hop in the sack with any woman who called."

"Just get over here," I say.

"I'm calling you from the gas station. I was afraid I'd run out of gas two blocks from your house. I'll be there in five minutes."

If anything can momentarily distract me from my troubles, it's having Wendy come squealing in through my front door and wrapping her arms around my neck as she kisses me like it's the first kiss she has ever had. Then she has to crouch down and pay attention to Dusty, who is delirious with happiness at seeing her.

Only after we've gone through a proper greeting, in the bedroom, does she ask me whether we've found Loretta.

"No word."

"Oh, no." She gets up and starts putting on her clothes. "I feel guilty having fun with you while she's . . ."

I put my hand up to stop her. "Hush. I'm trying to savor this moment. I've been a wreck, and I'm trying not to dwell on what might be happening to her."

She sits down on the side of the bed and runs her hand over my chest. "You're right. It doesn't do any good to let your imagination run wild."

I smile because her curly hair has sprung out of its clip. "Speaking of wild." I reach up and ruffle her hair.

We haven't had lunch. I make ham sandwiches, which we take out on the porch.

"Would it help if you told me the details of what you've done to find Loretta?"

She has put her hair back in a short ponytail, and she looks at me with such earnest concern that I can't help thinking about the women I've talked to this morning who hardly could be bothered. Wendy is a good person.

I tell her everything that has happened, not only with regard to Loretta, but including the Baptist minister's power play with the rodeo and the brothers who have been at each other's throats—except when they were flying their toy drone.

She's quiet. She knows how to listen. "I know it sounds silly," she says when I'm done, "but part of me thinks you might be right—the only way you're going to find Loretta is to knock on doors."

"It doesn't sound silly, but it's impossible. She could be anywhere—Bobtail, Bryan, right here in Jarrett Creek, or anywhere in between." I picture the acres of land, often dotted with lonely farmhouses, or the sprawl of houses that spreads out from the center of Bobtail and Bryan.

She throws her hands up. "We'll get a posse. We'll get hundreds of people to spread out all over."

I can't help chuckling at her enthusiasm.

"People could knock on doors. It wouldn't be hard."

"I like the idea," I say. "The problem is, we can't put people at risk. That's what law officers are paid for. Suppose some well-meaning person knocked on the kidnapper's door and got shot for their trouble?"

A big, heavy sigh. "I suppose you're right."

I pick up our plates and take them into the kitchen. She follows me. "I haven't asked about your trip," I say. "You came home early. How were things with your daughter?"

"Could be worse. I think I have lockjaw from forcing myself to keep my mouth shut and a big smile on my face, but it kept us from having a major battle. I don't mean to imply it was terrible. We had a few laughs. She even teased me when she knew I wanted to spout an opinion and didn't."

"Where is she off to now?"

She frowns. "She was reticent to say exactly where she's going. I don't know why she didn't say. All she said is she's going to the East Coast to visit a friend."

"At least she's in this country."

She shakes her head. "I guess. I wish I could trust her to tell me the truth. She doesn't want me to worry, so she's always vague about her plans. She doesn't realize that being vague worries me more than if I knew specifics." She laughs. "At least I think it does."

"Does she ever talk to her sister?" Her sister lives in Bobtail, is married, and has a sedate life.

"Oil and water. They're cordial, but they don't really have anything in common."

I'm feeling restless to get back to work again, and Wendy senses it. She puts her arms around me and hugs me. "I'm going to go home now. I didn't even unpack. I came straight here as soon as I got home and set my suitcase down."

Dusty and I stand on the porch and watch her go. When she drives away, Dusty looks up at me as if wondering what I did to send her away. "Come on, boy, we've got to get back to work."

Maria is on the phone when I walk into the station, and she waves me over with vigorous hand motions. "Okay, thank you very much. We'll be there to talk to you in twenty minutes."

She sets down the phone. "A man saw the flyer and called us."

"Suspect?"

She stares at the phone as if it might double as a Ouija board. "Probably not, but you never know. Sometimes a guilty person will try to play cat and mouse. He said he went out for coffee with Loretta on Saturday, a few days before she disappeared."

CHAPTER 23

The coffee shop is a Starbucks in one of the shopping centers that has sprung up in the last ten years on the outskirts of Bobtail. The main store in the mall is a big grocer, surrounded by a dry cleaner, a real estate office, a shoe store, and various other small shops. Just the kind of mall I would imagine Loretta might like to poke around in.

Wade Drummons is a man my age, with scrawny arms and legs and a bowling ball middle. What surprises me is that he has a little fluff of mustache. I can't imagine Loretta going for that. She preferred that men be clean-shaven. I wonder whether the photo of him on the website had the mustache.

Maria orders a frothy coffee drink, and Drummons and I get plain cups of coffee. He also buys a brownie. "I love brownies. I order them anytime I can get one."

We're lucky and the place is not crowded, so we get a table.

"What kind of drink did Loretta order?" Maria asks, after we sit down.

He shrugs. "Some kind of frou-frou drink like you've got." He nods toward Maria's mocha.

"Mr. Drummons," I say, "Before you tell us about your encounter with Loretta Singletary, let me get a few preliminary questions out of the way. Did you and Loretta get in contact with each other through the dating website, Smalltownpair?"

"Yes. I saw her photograph and thought she looked nice, so I got in touch with her, and we agreed to have coffee." He pinches off a bite of the brownie and shoves the plate out to the middle. "Help yourself. They're good."

I wave it off, and Maria eyes it but shakes her head.

"When did you meet her?" I ask.

"It was Saturday a week ago. The flyer said she disappeared the next Tuesday. That's right after I saw her."

"Did you arrange to see her any more after Saturday?"

"No, although we left it open that maybe we'd have coffee again sometime."

"How many times have you met women through the website?"

"Hmmm . . ." He looks at the ceiling while he finishes chewing a bite of brownie. "Six times."

"How did the meetings go? Did you ever see somebody more than once?"

"No, I didn't. I'm particular about the kind of woman I want to date, and I haven't found anybody who is a good match yet." He has polished off the brownie and wipes his hands on his napkin.

"Have you been married before?"

"Yes. I was married twice. My first wife ran off with another man after only a year. But my second wife, Alison, lasted thirty-two years. She died a while back. Heart attack—the silent killer they call it, and that was absolutely right. No idea she had a bad heart, and bam! She was gone." He shakes his head. "She's the kind of woman I'm looking for. My family says I'm too picky, but I think if I found one like Alison once, there's another one out there for me."

"How long ago did your wife pass away?"

He sighs. "Eighteen months ago. It's only in the last few months that I decided I ought to try to start dating again. It gets lonely being by myself after I've had a good woman in my life."

I know what he means, although Jeanne has been gone for a while. "Tell me about your meeting with Loretta. What made you decide to contact us?"

"Okay, okay," he says, nodding. "When I first saw the flyer, I wasn't going to bother you, but then I thought, 'You know, she said something that struck me.' I thought maybe it could be of help to you."

"What was that?" Maria says. I can see she's trying not to be too eager, but we both want to pounce on the little hope he holds out.

"I have to give you a little context. We figured out pretty fast that we weren't meant for each other, but we liked each other. Like I said, we even thought we might meet again sometime, just to talk. She had a funny sense of humor, and we were relaxed. We started talking about our pasts and our families. And then we went on to talk about how we decided to go on the dating site, and how we picked the people we wanted to get to know. We both said we didn't want anybody too young, and we didn't want anybody weird. She said she didn't want anybody with a dog, although she could tolerate a cat. That kind of thing." He looks from one to the other of us to make sure we're following.

We nod for him to carry on. He's chatty.

"Then she surprised me. She said that she would like to meet someone quirky. And I asked what she meant. She said somebody who had an interesting past or an interesting occupation. She had talked to one guy online who had been in the circus when he was young, and she thought that might be interesting. She also said she was thinking about going on a date with a man who had a chinchilla farm." He chuckles. "I asked her if she had ever seen a chinchilla up close, and she said no. I told her they'd drive her crazy. They never stop moving." He laughs again. "She said she would mark him off the list." He shifts in his seat. "But the remark I'm referring to is that she said she was going to meet a man who said he was interested in the fact that she liked baking, and that he would like to learn how to bake."

"Learn how to bake?" Maria says.

"He said he was a chef, and he'd never learned to bake."

"A chef. Did she say where he worked?" I ask.

He shakes his head. "We moved on to other subjects." He leans closer. "She was a nice lady. I wasn't attracted to her, you know, in *that* way, but I'd feel bad if something happened to her. I take it she hasn't been found?"

"That's right. And we really appreciate your coming forward with this. Did she say when she was going to meet the man?"

"That's what perked up my interest. She said she was meeting him the next day, Sunday. She said she was meeting him in Bryan, although she didn't know whether she wanted to get involved with a man who lived that far away."

"We appreciate your coming forward," I say. "Gives us something to work with."

Maria says, "What did you do before you retired?"

"Insurance. Drummons and Son Insurance. Went into my daddy's office right out of high school and never considered doing anything else. It was the perfect job for me. Made a good living. Married a good woman, at least the second time." He snickers. "Me and Alison had a couple of kids, and they're both raising their families right here in Bobtail. I'm a lucky man, if you don't count losing my wife."

After he leaves, I think it's a shame that he and Loretta didn't hit it off. He seems like a solid person, and she could have done worse . . . and in fact, probably has done worse.

"I'll check up on his story," Maria says as we're walking out.

She's right. No matter how upright he sounded, you have to verify everything.

When we walk out of the Starbucks, I see that it's almost five o'clock. "There's one thing I'd like to check on if we can get there in time."

I drive to Darlene's Beauty Shop. Darlene said that Lucy normally works Wednesday, Thursday, and Friday, but that she had a few clients this afternoon. I hope she hasn't left for the day.

Maria goes in with me, and I see Lucy behind a woman in the styling chair, using a hair dryer on her. I assume that means she'll be done soon. She's intent on what she's doing, with that same sour expression on her face. She walks around in front of the client and then cocks her head to look at the hairdo critically. When she starts back around, she glances up and sees me. She looks startled. But then she glances over at a woman sitting in the waiting area, and I realize she is probably worried that we'll take up time she needs to get her clients out.

When the woman she was working on gets up and heads for the pay station, which consists of a little desk, Lucy follows her, saying to me, "I'll be with you in a minute." The woman pays, and Lucy comes back, hands on her hips. She glares from me to Maria and back. "I'm really backed up. I don't have time to talk. I need to get out of here at a reasonable hour."

"One question. That's it."

She glances over at Darlene, who is eyeing us. "Okay, what?"

"Did Loretta Singletary ever mention that she was going on a date with a cook or a chef?"

A funny look flits across her face, like she's alarmed, but then she frowns. "No, like I said, she didn't talk about that kind of thing at all."

I don't remember her saying that, but that's all I needed to know.

When we leave, Maria says, "That is one unhappy woman."

I tell her what little I know about the woman's husband leaving her in the lurch financially.

I managed to fend off Scott Singletary over the weekend, but I could tell he was getting more and more agitated. The dam breaks at 6:00, just as I'm leaving for the day. He calls and chews me out, saying he doesn't know what I've been doing, but it obviously isn't enough. He tells me he's coming back tomorrow, and if I don't have a solid lead by then, he is going to see to it that my job isn't safe. I suspect he has been getting grief from his brother, who must feel helpless living so far away.

I don't tell him that he isn't likely to have much sway in town over my job. The fact is, if I can't find Loretta, and if she ends up dead, I don't think I'd have the heart to continue the job anyway.

"Scott, I wish I had good news for you. Believe me, I'm as frustrated as you are."

"I seriously doubt that." I hear his wife murmuring in the background. It sounds like she's trying to calm him down.

"I do have a couple of very slim leads, and I'm following up on them."

"What leads?"

"I can't discuss it with you. But I promise I'm doing everything I can."

I hang up to find Maria looking as mopey as I feel. "What leads?" she says.

"I fudged. Lead, not leads. The chef."

"How are we going to find him?"

We stare at each other, willing a bright idea. "I guess the only way is to talk to every damn cook in the county and ask if he met Loretta."

But we both know that's absurd. For all we know, the man might not have been a chef at all. Or he doesn't live in Bobtail County. Or when asked whether he met Loretta, he could lie. Even if we did question the right person, he might realize we were hot on his trail and decide that Loretta has become a liability. We might be signing her death warrant if we get too close.

"We're getting out of here for tonight," I say. "But both of us need to come in tomorrow morning with a new idea. I don't care if I have to stay up all night to think of one."

As I walk to my car, I'm thinking that the only way we're going to catch the guy we're looking for is through the dating site. I need to start back at the beginning and recheck every single person who Loretta might have contacted. I'm convinced one of the men she was in touch with is a kidnapper. And I need to figure out a way to smoke him out.

After I gobble down a meal, with Dusty hot on my heels, I head for Loretta's place to retrieve the list of men's names that she considered as possible dates. Maria took them back to Loretta's place after she tried calling the men in case we needed to check them on her computer again. It occurs to me that it may be an incomplete list, and I may have to dig deeper.

The first time Maria and I went through the list and the website, we were not taking seriously the idea that Loretta had been abducted. Or at least I wasn't. Maybe we missed something.

I bring the pages back to my place, pour myself two fingers of bourbon, and get to work. The first thing I do is set up a dummy profile on the dating site, as if I'm a woman looking for a man. If the kidnapper took two women, it's likely he won't stop there. I'm hoping that a new profile will get his interest. Working from Loretta's profile, I create a "woman" by the name of Nancy Helms. Like Loretta, she loves to cook, especially baking, she's a widow, owns her own home, likes to go to live country music concerts, and dabbles in art. I decide to take out that last part, not wanting to make it too similar. I ponder whether to say she's a Baptist but finally say "churchgoer."

I don't have a dummy photo to put in, but I've noticed that a few participants in the website say, "Photo on request." I put that in.

I post the profile and start the second part of my mission. When I went through Loretta's list the first time, I was only interested in the ones that she marked as possible. But what if she changed her mind about one? I begin the painstaking process of matching each name with a profile. Luckily for my search, for each man she was interested in, she wrote down the number associated with his profile, so I have a way of finding them.

My plan is to read through each profile to see whether there are any who call themselves chefs. If that doesn't work, then I'll have to think of other criteria. Reading the profiles is hard work because they are like reading a bad book. Only one or two of them seems to have any imagination. One after another, they list their former occupation and what they like to do in retirement—golf, fishing, and hunting are the biggest ones. One says he does charity work, and another likes to do carpentry now that he's retired. On the first two pages, I find two men who say they like to cook, although they don't mention being chefs. I turn to the third page and stop short. There are only three pages. I'm sure there were four when Maria and I first went through them.

I go ahead and read the profiles on the third page, and nothing pops out at me. But now I have to go back and get the fourth page. I must have left it behind.

It's late, way past my bedtime, but I intend to finish this tonight. Dusty is reluctant to leave his comfy bed, but he also doesn't want me to go out without him. We trudge back to Loretta's house. The evening air is nice. It has cooled down. A few porchlights are on, but most are turned off. Everyone has gone to bed. It's peaceful. Or at least it would be if I wasn't on such a hard mission.

The missing sheet isn't in Loretta's desk. I go through all the drawers of the desk and look behind it to make sure it hasn't fallen back there. It isn't on the countertops in the kitchen. Maybe Maria snatched them up too quickly and left one behind at headquarters. I consider going there to look for it, but my eyes are tired and my brain is shutting down. Tomorrow will have to do.

CHAPTER 24

Wednesday morning, I go straight to headquarters, but I don't see the missing sheet. I call Maria at home and ask whether she remembers where it might be. She tells me she didn't take any of them home, so if it's not at Loretta's, it would be at the office.

"I don't suppose you made a copy?"

"Didn't think of it."

"It's missing."

"Where could it be? Do you suppose that's what the man who was in her house was looking for?"

"It's possible. I can't remember if he was there before or after you took the list back to her house."

"I can't remember either," she says.

"We'll figure it out." I tell her I made a fake account on the dating site last night. "Since he lured two women, I'm hoping he'll be looking for more."

"We can always hope," she says. "And by the way, you should call Elaine Farquart's next-door neighbor and ask if she mentioned going out with a chef." Maria tells me she won't be around for a while. She is meeting Jenny Sandstone in the DA's office in Bobtail late this morning to discuss what more she needs for them to pursue a case against the man she suspects of being guilty in the cold case.

When I hang up, I think about the sequence of events immediately before and after surprising the intruder in Loretta's house. I conclude that we found the list before he broke in. That may have been what he was after. If so, how did he know she had it? She must have told him. If that's what he was looking for, then at least we know that there was something on that list that he didn't want us to find.

I turn on my computer to see what kind of fish I might have caught with my dummy profile on the dating website. There are ten new responses. I see right away that most of them are the same men who responded to Loretta's profile. I try to imagine who these men must be. Are they that desperate for a date? Are they lonely? All I know is that one of these men is up to no good, and it's up to me to find him. At first, I think I can eliminate the new ones, but it occurs to me that the killer might be using more than one name. I have to cross-check names and profiles to see whether I get any matches.

I've barely started when I get a call from Brent Hogarth. "I thought you might want to know about the autopsy report on Elaine Farquart. It's interesting."

"Interesting how?"

"Several things. For one thing, she was drugged."

"Did they say what she was drugged with?"

"You ready for the big words? It was a benzodiazepine called flunitrazepam."

Big is right. "What is that exactly?"

"I had to look it up. It's called a 'date rape' drug. But it's also used clinically for anxiety."

"Sounds like our abductor is a nervous sort?"

Hogarth chuckles. "Who knows? Maybe he's a pharmacist, or maybe he stole the drugs. Anyway, she didn't have enough in her system to kill her, just make her disoriented. Which at first I thought would explain why she was in a position to get run over."

"I'm curious. Why did the medical examiner even do toxicology tests?"

"I asked him to. It seemed too unusual for Elaine Farquart to be walking along a road in the middle of the night. Her family and friends said she wasn't much of a drinker, so it made sense that the guy who killed her drugged her to make her compliant. But it turns out I was wrong. That isn't why she was compliant."

"Okay, I'll bite. What was the reason?"

"She was dead when she was run over. And she wasn't murdered."

"You're kidding. What did she die of?"

"Heart attack. Could have been fear that brought it on, but she had a bad heart. We've confirmed it with her doctor."

"You could make a case that the stress from being kidnapped brought on the heart attack."

"We could. There was another odd thing they found in the autopsy though. Or at least I thought it was odd."

"What's that?"

"There was no sign of recent sexual activity."

"That's a surprise." And a comfort. At least she wasn't raped.

I describe yesterday's meeting with the man who said Loretta mentioned she had a date to meet a chef. I ask him to call Amy Martin to find out whether Elaine mentioned anything similar.

Every time I hear anything new about Elaine, I get more disheartened. And more determined.

I turn back to the computer. The answer is somewhere in the group of men who contacted Loretta. It's up to me to find it. Even though I don't have the fourth page of Loretta's notes, I do have the website's record of her replies. After eliminating the ones that were on the three remaining sheets, I'm left with eight names. Three of those have no profile photo, and not all have email addresses.

It occurs to me that I might get information if I Google the names. It turns out to be harder than I thought. Only a couple of the names are distinctive enough that I can tell they are the men on the site. The rest are so general that it's tedious trying to match the photos on the images with the profiles. I narrow it down a bit. Three of them are not very likely to be my targets. One is ninety years old, one is in a wheelchair, and one is in prison.

I then compare the old profiles from Loretta's list with the new ones that I've recently received, and I am rewarded by one match. The two men go by different names, but the details in their profiles are too similar to be a coincidence.

Bob Beckman, who contacted Loretta, describes himself as "a man of experience who enjoys meeting ladies who like to explore life. My goal is intimacy with a woman who knows how to appreciate a man. I'm financially well off, so I'm not interested in a woman's finances. You have no reason to fear me, as I am a religious man who respects women. I love classical music, art, and enjoy going out for a good meal."

Rob Barnes, who contacted my fake profile, says he "has had many life experiences" and "wants to meet a woman who loves life." And, "I hope to find a woman who knows how to appreciate a man's finer qualities. I respect women and am financially stable, so you have no need to worry about your finances." He goes on to say he loves music and good food.

This Mr. Beckman/Barnes is very interesting. The question is, how do I get him to send me a photo of himself?

Connor is on duty this morning and comes in while I'm working. He pours himself a cup of coffee and comes over to my desk. "I heard that the woman missing from Bobtail was killed. No word on Loretta Singletary?"

"No. I'm going through the names of the men who responded to her online."

He picks up the photos I've been showing around and goes through them. He stops at one. "What are you doing with this one?" He's holding out the composite drawing that was made from Amy Martin's description of the man she and Elaine Farquart deemed "too handsome" to be real.

When I tell him where it came from, he says, "This is not a real person."

"What do you mean?"

"I've seen this man's photo on a couple of the bigger dating sites. It's used as an example of a good profile photo."

"Are you sure?"

"Here let me show you." He commandeers my computer, types in a few words, and one of the big dating sites pops up. Then he goes to the "instructions" section. There it is. The photo of "Andrew."

I sit back, stunned.

"Whoever lured the Farquart woman took this photo off the website and used it," he says.

"How does somebody even do that?"

"It's easy." He frowns and looks at me, calculating. "Well, maybe not exactly easy, but it means whoever did it knows how to use the Internet."

I can't take my eyes off the photo on the website. The man is handsome and looks sincere and reliable and not the least bit threatening. No wonder these women were interested in him. But I'm puzzled. He has a glib smile, which I don't think Loretta would take to. She's down to earth. Her husband was a good man, respectable and responsible, but no Cary Grant.

I thank Connor for his help. "I'll have to call Hogarth and tell him we can stop looking for a man who looks like this," I say.

Hogarth is as surprised as I was. "Sometimes I think we're going to have to turn all our investigations over to youngsters," he says. I agree with him, but to me Hogarth is a youngster.

I talk to Connor a little more, and he suggests that I email each of the men who didn't put in a profile photo and tell them I'd like them to email me a photo. "And let me find a photo for you to send them," he says.

He types some more and eventually comes up with a photo of a woman who looks the right age, who, as he says, is attractive enough to be passable, but not gorgeous enough to scare anybody away. And she has an inviting gleam in her eye. Actually, that reminds me of Wendy.

I write emails to each of the men who replied, personalizing the email with bits of information from their profiles. On the fifth one, I come to a problem.

"Connor, this one doesn't have an email address." It's one of the ones without a photo.

He has been eating a kolache from the bakery down the street, and he wipes his hands. He already has a little weight on him, and eating pastries like that isn't going to take care of the stomach bulge that is threatening to bust his shirt buttons.

He looks at the website again. "Hmmm, probably there's a main email where people can go through the website and be anonymous until they want to make a date. It's probably in the instructions." He taps in a few lines. "Here is it." Anonymous. That gives people a chance to make plans without leaving a trace—at least not in public.

I understand that the website needs to maintain people's privacy, but they also have a duty to make sure people are safe. It can't hurt to contact the website and make my case. At the top I see a "Contact" selection, and I hit it.

As I figured, it's complicated. To get in touch with the faceless person on the other end, you have to type in your profile identification, then you're given a list of reasons you might want to get in touch, and finally it asks how you want to be contacted "within 48 hours." I have the ID, and from the list of reasons I hit "Other," and then give my phone number. At last I'm allowed to write 200 characters for "What seems to be the problem?" I decide short is best: "URGENT. Need to report stalker." Then I change the last part to: "Need to report sexual harassment." I figure that is more likely to get their attention.

Meanwhile, I'm not going to sit around and wait for them to contact me. I send a carefully thought-out message to Rob Barnes, who is going through the anonymous email address: "Your email made me very curious. I don't know if I'm ready to explore, but I am ready to hear more. Would luv to see a photo." It embarrasses the devil out of me to write "luv," but something tells me that the kind of woman who would write "luv" is exactly the kind of woman he's looking for.

CHAPTER 25

Chasing our elusive suspect on the Internet has taken more hours than I thought, and it's late afternoon before I know it. While I wait for Maria to get back and for three return messages—one from Hogarth, one from the website, and one from Rob Barnes—I continue to look at the website profiles. I doubt it will be productive, but I have to keep myself busy.

When Father Ray Sanchez walks in, I'm grateful for the break.

"I hope this is a social call," I say.

"I wish. I'm not sure what to do about this, but the Baptist ladies are on the rampage."

"I'm picturing pitchforks. Can you be more specific?"

"Jolene Ramsey and Ida Ruth Dillard came to see me. They said if the Baptist Church isn't made a co-sponsor for the rodeo, then they and all the Baptist families will boycott the rodeo."

"Was Reverend Becker with them?"

"No, but I detect his hand behind it. And I don't like it. If we could sit down and hash it out, it would be one thing. But he's pulling blackmail, and I don't feel like giving in. At the same time, all the kids in those families are going to be really upset if they can't participate."

There's little enough to do in a small town, and the rodeo has become a central event of the year. I can't help thinking that if Loretta were around, she wouldn't have let it get to this point. But what would she have done? Maybe I should ask Ida Ruth what she thinks Loretta would make of this.

"What is it you'd like me to do?" I ask.

"I thought I should pass it by you, because . . ." he looks to the heavens, which if they speak to him, remain silent for me. "I'm not going to give in to this kind of tactic." He searches my face for a response, but I just nod. "The first time Becker talked to me, I suggested maybe they'd want to start out small and take one part of it this year, and then we'd see how that worked out. But he insisted on full participation. I don't like his bullying."

It comes to me that even though Father Sanchez seems unassuming, he has an ego investment in the rodeo. He may tell himself otherwise, but it's true. "I appreciate your warning me in advance," I say. I must admit I'd be glad if this particular preacher had not come to town.

"You know I never cared much for Reverend Duckworth, as bossy as he was, or that poor boy who was here last year that the congregation fired before his boxes were unpacked, but they never tried to commandeer the rodeo."

I have the feeling Sanchez just wants an ear. "I've known Ida Ruth a long time. She's a good person. I'll have a chat with her and see if I can move things in another direction."

He sighs. "That's more than I hoped for. I appreciate it."

After he leaves, I call Hogarth again at the Bobtail Police Department, too impatient to wait to find out if they talked to Elaine Farquart's neighbor about the chef aspect. He tells me he talked to Amy, and she said Elaine did not mention anything like that. I'm brooding over it when Maria flings herself in.

"It's blowing up to rain outside. Did you see that?"

I haven't been paying attention, and sure enough dark clouds have closed in and the wind has picked up. "Did you get anywhere with your cold case?"

She sighs. "Jenny says I'm going to need more evidence. She said just because Doug Lantana's body was found buried on the ranch doesn't mean Howard Mosley killed him. I showed her what we had—that the hired hand and Mosley had had a very public fight a week before, and that I recently found out that Mosley had taken out an insurance policy on Lantana, but she said that's not illegal, and that it isn't direct evidence."

"Do you know if Mosley owned a gun like the one that Lantana was shot with?"

"No, I haven't investigated that. I thought I'd go talk to Mosley's ex-wife. She lives in Burton. And I'm going to talk to the people who had ranches close to him to see if anybody remembers anything at all. They were all questioned at the time, but I got the feeling the officer who did it wasn't particularly thorough."

"That wouldn't be Rodell Simms, would it?"

She looks surprised. "Yes, how did you know?"

"I knew Rodell a long time, and it fits with his way of working that he let things slide. And he'd misfile papers as well. Be sure you check all the files that might be relevant."

"Good to know."

Instead of tackling the files, Maria sits back and frowns. I know she's back to thinking about Loretta. "You know, we've never considered motive. What would cause a guy to want to kidnap a woman he met through the Internet, like Elaine Farquart? And the same for Loretta. What drives somebody to do that?"

I remind her that the FBI told me usually older women are targeted for money scams. But then I tell her about Hogarth's call, saying the autopsy showed that Elaine wasn't murdered.

"That's no comfort," she says. "But if Elaine was kidnapped as part of a scam, maybe she died too fast for him to follow through."

"If it's money he's after, I don't see how Loretta fits. She's comfortable, but that's because she's frugal."

I get up and pour myself a cup of coffee. It's sludge, so I pour it out and make a new pot.

I think out loud while I work. "Elaine Farquart didn't live high, but she had a nice house. I wonder how much money a scammer would be aiming for."

"A woman who owns a house might look appealing to a guy who rents a place and lives on a shoestring." Maria rubs her forehead. "This gives me a headache."

"Go home. I'm going soon myself."

But after she leaves, I know I'm not ready to go yet. Each time I walk out the door, it feels like I'm abandoning Loretta. Realistically, I know I can do as much from home as from work, but it feels more serious here. I want to make a list of everything we've gone through, starting at the beginning. I want to see in black and white whether I've missed anything.

Dusty has pointedly positioned himself by the front door to remind me that home is where his dinner is. "Sorry, boy, you're stuck a little longer." He flops down with a big sigh.

I get out a pad of paper and begin jotting down a timeline of events as they happened:

1. Ellen tells me that Loretta missed an appointment.

No. I need to back up from there.

1. Loretta changed her hair and the way she dressed.
2. She was not bringing baked goods as often.
3. Ellen says Loretta missed an appointment.
4. She's missing and left the house without washing dishes, and she left no one in charge of watering her yard.
5. Her car, a suitcase, and toiletries are missing.
6. We find out she has been meeting men through the website, Smalltownpair.
7. Elaine Farquart kidnapped.
8. Farquart dies, and her body is mutilated by being run over.
9. Point of connection between the two women: they went to the same hairdresser.

I then write down the dead ends:

1. The professor at Texas A&M who seems to have had an

innocent cup of coffee with her at Mykonos. (Maybe not as innocent as he seemed?)

2. The man whose daughters set up an Internet site for him. (Not as embarrassed as he acted? Took advantage of being on the site?)

3. Wade Drummons. (We only have his word for it that he didn't set up another date with her.)

Finally, there is a short list of odd things that can't be explained:

1. The man I surprised at Loretta's house. Maybe he stole one of the four sheets of paper with names of men who had replied to her profile posting. (Where was he from? Where had he parked his car? What was on that sheet of paper that might have incriminated him? Did she tell him she had written something down?)

2. The man (woman?) who Loretta's next-door neighbor saw carrying the suitcase out of her house. Did Loretta send him to pick up items for her? Did Loretta have a secret stash of valuables? Stocks or bonds? Jewelry?

The last items seem ridiculous. I've known Loretta my whole life. Where would she get anything worth stealing that I didn't know anything about? Maybe she's secretly a master thief and has stored up goods and someone found out. Ha!

Another thing that piques my curiosity is the area where Elaine Farquart's body was found. Why there? I wish the Department of Public Safety could stake out that stretch of highway in case the killer brings Loretta there, but that's impossible. It's twenty miles long.

Then there's Elaine Farquart's body. Have the officers working the case thought of whether they can get tire tracks from clothing? Even if they do, unless whoever murdered her has unusual tires, you'd be considering hundreds of vehicles.

I feel like I've missed something. I go back through the list, paying particular attention to the unexplained items, but whatever it is doesn't jump out at me.

I check to see whether I've had a reply from the man with no photograph, but no luck yet. He might not bite at all. It's like fishing for some exotic species.

As I'm leaving, I remember my promise to Sanchez to try to talk sense into Ida Ruth about the rodeo.

I reach her at home, and she reluctantly says I can stop by. "I can't talk long; I'm cooking dinner. I know what you're calling about."

It's not that late, but the clouds have thickened, making it seem later than it is. When I get to Ida Ruth's, I tell Dusty to stay in the pickup. "I won't be long. You'll get your dinner before long."

Ida Ruth takes me into the kitchen and installs me on a stool at the cabinet. Whatever she's cooking smells odd, like it has got vinegar in it, so I don't ask what it is. I don't want to risk her asking me to stay for dinner.

"Ida Ruth, this business with the goat rodeo has gotten out of hand."

She's chopping celery, and she pauses, like she's thinking. "Samuel, I know it has. But I don't know what I can do to fix it."

"You can lay off Father Sanchez, for one thing."

She lays her knife down and folds her arms across her chest. "I don't understand why he has to be so selfish."

"Let me ask you a question. What do you think Loretta would say if she was here? Do you think she'd have tried to intimidate Father Sanchez?"

She narrows her eyes. "What kind of question is that?"

I wait her out.

"I don't know what she'd do. But I don't think it's fair to bring her into it." There's a hitch in her voice, and when she speaks next her voice is small. "Do you think she's still alive?"

"I have to believe it."

"But what about that other lady . . . ?"

I don't know whether Hogarth has made it public yet that Elaine

Farquart died of natural causes, so I can't tell Ida Ruth that. But I don't want to dash her hopes. "We don't even know for sure that the same person who took Mrs. Farquart has Loretta."

"You mean maybe Loretta didn't get kidnapped? Maybe she's just gone off and doesn't even know that everybody is upset?"

I hesitate. I don't want to alarm people. "We're trying to find Loretta."

She picks her knife back up and attacks the celery as if it has offended her. "Why would somebody kidnap those two women anyway? People say they didn't even know each other." Her voice is miserable, and we are both silent with our awful thoughts for several seconds.

"We're looking into it. But I have to say, Ida Ruth, focusing on Loretta doesn't leave me time for this nonsense between Becker and Sanchez. And it's not like you to be petty." I don't know if that's true, but it doesn't hurt to butter her up a little.

"Reverend Becker came to the Ladies' Circle last week, and he . . ." She pauses in her chopping but doesn't look up. "He told us that if we were good Baptists, we ought to be on his side." She shoots me a quick glance and then chops more vigorously. Why do I have the feeling she had started to say one thing and then changed her mind?

"Do you really think that has anything to do with being right with God?"

"I know it doesn't. But we have to make allowances for Reverend Becker. He's new and doesn't know how things work."

"You'd think if he didn't know how things worked he would be a little more careful not to horn in on the way things have been done in the past."

She sighs and scoops up the celery and throws it into the pot. "I'll see if I can get a chance to talk to him. But he's . . . well, he's persuasive."

Again, that odd feeling that she meant something else. Maybe I need to chat with some of the other women to see if others have a different sense of Reverend Becker.

CHAPTER 26

I t's dusk when I get home. The wind is blowing, and I feel the rain in the air. I want to hurry and get my chores done before the rain sets in, so I leave Dusty in the house while I go down to feed the cows.

When I get back, I feel world-weary and sad. There's a message on my home phone, and I grab for it, hoping it's Loretta. But it's a telemarketer, wanting to sell me a new roof. Which isn't a bad idea.

"Woof."

I'm so upset that I've forgotten to feed Dusty. I crouch down and rub his ears. "Sorry about that, boy."

He submits for a few seconds but then pulls back and races into the kitchen. I feed him and throw an enchilada into the microwave.

While I eat, standing at the kitchen counter, I consider whether I should call Wendy, but even the prospect of seeing her doesn't help me climb out of my mood.

Hoping I've gotten a bite on my website profile, I pour myself a beer and sit down at the kitchen table with the computer. To my surprise, I've gotten five new emails from men interested in my dummy site. I feel a certain stupid pride in that. The profile I wrote must have been pretty good. But none of the five is the man I'm looking for. That doesn't mean the kidnapper isn't among them, but a quick perusal of the emails tells me it's not likely. One asks if she's taken Jesus as her savior and invites her to visit his church congregation because, "I wouldn't consider a woman who was not in my church family." Another wants to sell her insurance. Two ask for another bunch of photos "to help me know more about you," and one says he wouldn't go out with her on a bet. That one makes me laugh. Some people are just odd.

I'm ready to shut off the computer when another email comes in. I open it.

"I don't usually send my photo so quickly," Rob Barnes says, "but you were persuasive. If you are interested, we can meet somewhere discreet."

Eagerly I open the attached photo, and for a few seconds I wonder whether I've made a mistake. I recognize the man, and I'm completely stunned. It's a photo of Arlen Becker. The Reverend Arlen Becker. This has got to be a joke. My thoughts veer wildly, trying to imagine who might be playing this kind of trick. A member of his congregation? A Catholic who's angry that Becker is trying to horn in on the goat rodeo?

I force myself to settle down and be rational. What makes me think it's a trick? Just because Becker is a minister doesn't mean he's not capable of playing around. I sit back and take a sip of beer, contemplating what this means. The reason I was interested in the man to begin with was that he used two different names, and I was sure from the profiles that it was the same man. Beckman and Barnes. It makes sense that Becker would vary his name only slightly. No doubt he did it to avoid anyone making the connection with him as the Baptist minister.

But is there more to it than that? Could Becker be the man who lured Elaine Farquart and Loretta? Why would he do it? He certainly would have recognized Loretta's photo. No, it makes no sense for him to have preyed on Loretta. Maybe on Elaine Farquart but not Loretta. She's a member of his congregation. He'd stay far away from her.

Becker said he was an engineer before he became a minister. He said he was "called" to be a minister. Now I'm suspicious. What did this "call" consist of?

I Google his name and "engineer." There he is. He was employed by a Houston firm as a mechanical and structural engineer, working on bridge projects. But then I see that he had another engineering job with another firm. And then another. He bounced from job to job. Why? The engineering jobs stop five years ago.

I enter his name and "minister." The next entry for him is at a church in Waco. A larger church in a big city. What happened that he moved quickly from job to job when he was an engineer and then as a minister got taken from a mid-sized church in Waco to this tiny town? I have a hunch it's a problem that involves women. Harassment?

Becker's wife must have suspicions that something bad happened for her husband to be sent on his way again and again. And I would be surprised if she weren't fully aware of the nature of his transgressions. Why would she be loyal to a man like that?

And of course, the big question is, is Arlen Becker a killer? Is he the man who lured Elaine Farquart to her death? Was he responsible for Loretta's disappearance? At the risk of feeling disloyal, I wonder why those two women? It isn't as if they are glamorous babes. Or wealthy.

Finally, I mull over what I remember of the man I caught in Loretta's house. He was built like Becker. Did Becker break in because he sent his photo to Loretta by mistake? Or is it more sinister? Did he kidnap her and know she had a photo that could lead to him?

My heart is tripping double-time. I can't sit still, so I stand up and begin pacing. This is a long way from what I thought I would be dealing with. I remind myself not to jump to conclusions, although it's hard for me to come up with an innocent explanation for why Becker is attempting to meet online with the woman he thinks my profile represents.

The question is how to approach this. Let's say the worst scenario is that he has kidnapped Loretta and is holding her for whatever reason. If he finds out I'm onto him, would that lead him to get rid of her? I have to proceed very carefully to investigate him.

First, I want to find out why he left one company after another when he was an engineer. That's a safer start. If I start snooping into why he left Waco, he's likely to find that out. I'm not even sure why I think that's the case. I just suspect that the Baptist ministry is a close-knit group, and even if one of their preachers is troublesome, it's possible they stick together if threatened from the outside. They wouldn't be the first religion to circle the wagons when one of their members is accused of wrongdoing.

I can think of one "innocent" reason that Becker might be conversing with these women. Maybe in his zeal to save people from sin, he thinks women are "loose" if they go on dates with men they don't know. But even as the thought runs through my head, I reject it. There are other ways to preach to people without being nefarious.

I hesitate to bring Maria in on this until I have a clear plan. It could be that Becker is guilty of nothing more than being a sleazy man. I sit back down at the computer and read carefully the snippets of information covering Becker's stints at various companies. He seems to have been able to get one job after another, which means two things are probably true. He was good at his job, and whatever got him fired was covered up. Tomorrow, I'll call human resources in each of the companies to see whether I can get a handle on what he did. I hope I don't have to go to Houston and confront his ex-bosses in person. That would take time I don't want to waste. I'm painfully aware that each passing minute puts Loretta more at risk.

I suddenly notice that Dusty is pacing with me. When I stop, he sits down with a sigh. I crouch down, and he flops over to show me his belly. I scratch it. "You don't have to worry with me," I say. He turns his head to look at me, and I swear he's thinking that I'm wrong. It's his job.

It's ten o'clock, so I tell him it's time for bed. The phone rings and I grab for it, hoping it's Loretta to say she's back home.

"Hey, are you mad at me?" Wendy's voice is half-joking.

I groan. "No, I haven't called because I'm not fit company. But that's no excuse for not calling you. It's this case that has me off-kilter."

"I didn't mean to bother you. I just wanted to hear your voice."

For a wild moment, I entertain the thought of jumping into my truck and high-tailing it over to see her. "You're not bothering me a bit. Hearing your voice is the best thing that's happened to me today."

I tell her I don't want to go into the details of what's going on, but that I need to put my personal life on hold until I find Loretta.

"I understand. But listen, even if you don't have time to come over, call me anytime."

We make small talk for a while. She's going to meet an old friend for lunch tomorrow, and the next day she's going over to her daughter's house for dinner. "She sounded excited, like something's up," she says, "but I don't want to jump to conclusions." Wendy has told me she'd love to be a grandmother, but that her daughter who lives in Bobtail hasn't shown any interest in having children. I know she's hoping the "something's up" is a grandchild.

"Don't get your hopes up. She might have invited you over to introduce you to a new puppy."

She laughs. She has such an easy laugh. It eases my mind. I thought I wouldn't be able to sleep for worry about Loretta, but morning comes before I know it.

CHAPTER 27

Carrie Olivier, the woman I finally get to talk to in the human resources department at Holcomb Construction, tells me that there's nothing untoward in Arlen Becker's file. "It says he parted with the company by mutual agreement," she says.

"What does that mean, 'mutual agreement'?"

She clears her throat. "I can't say exactly. I wasn't here back then, so I don't have any special knowledge of it."

I ask the name of Becker's immediate boss, and she gives it to me, but she says he has retired and she has no contact information for him.

The next company has gone out of business. They say the third time is the charm, and although it's not exactly a charm, it's a step forward. This time the human resources person is a man, Stanley Cash. "Look, I can't be specific, but since you're in law enforcement, I feel like I ought to cooperate. I can only say that Mr. Becker was terminated without notice."

"That sounds serious."

"Mmm. Yes, problems. I'm afraid if you want to find out more than that, you'll have to get a court order for the records."

I have a feeling that if I ask the right question, he might be inclined to say yes or no. "Problems with female staff?"

He hesitates. "I didn't say that."

"The kind of thing that gets companies in trouble with lawsuits these days?"

This time the wait is longer, but finally he says quietly, "Let's just say that no company wants that kind of trouble. Are we clear?"

I'm making these calls at home, and I'm not surprised when I get a call from Maria at 10:30. "Boss, where are you?" She's annoyed.

"I've been making some calls. Hang on and I'll be in. Anything I should know at your end?"

"Only that Loretta is still missing. Nothing important." She couldn't be any more sarcastic.

"I'll fill you in when I get there." I hang up before she can demand to know what I'm doing.

Normally, if I had to tackle the powers-that-be in the Baptist Church, I'd ask for Loretta's advice. Because I can't do that, the next best person to ask is Ida Ruth. She didn't come clean with me last night about Becker, and she owes me.

I call and tell her I'm coming over. "I need help."

"Samuel, I'm . . ."

I hang up before she can protest. She won't leave, knowing I'm on my way.

She opens the door and marches into her kitchen without a word. I follow her. I've left Dusty at home, much to his dismay. I left him howling, so my mood is worse than it might have been.

"I'll get you a cup of coffee." She pours a cup for both of us, and I have a feeling we're squaring off as friendly adversaries. She doesn't offer to take me into the living room, and I'm fine standing in her kitchen.

"I need to talk to you in the strictest confidence," I say.

She nods. She knows that I have complete assurance that she will keep quiet. I've known her to keep a secret for forty years.

"I need to know how the Baptist Church hierarchy works. Like who decides that a particular minister will go to a certain church."

She straightens and blinks. I figure this is the last thing she expected of me. "Well, there's an oversight committee that places ministers. When a minister retires or a church congregation isn't satisfied with their pastor and decides they want a new one, the church applies to the committee, who makes the decision."

"Suppose the minister has had problems at another church? Will they tell the new church that?"

"Let's go in the living room and sit down."

We sit in the same chairs we sat in last time I was here, but it feels more formal. She looks tense. I remind her of my question.

"It depends. When a church wants to make a change, most of the time it's because the preacher didn't get along with somebody in the congregation—like the Ladies' Circle, or a deacon who's too big for his britches. Congregations are different. Some like a strict preacher, others like one who is a little more lenient."

"Suppose the problem is more serious?"

She strokes her throat, as if she were wearing a necklace. "You mean like he's embezzling, or . . ."

"Or the preacher is having an affair with a member of the congregation."

"Samuel!"

"Come on, Ida Ruth, don't tell me it doesn't happen."

"Well, people are human. It's not like the Catholic Church, where those poor priests can't take a wife." She sniffs.

"Suppose a preacher pursued a woman in the congregation against her wishes. Would the committee send him to another congregation without telling them?"

I have to wait for my answer while she sips her coffee. "I don't know exactly what they would do. I'd like to think they would dismiss the man from the ministry, but they may think he deserves another chance. After all, I know you've heard the old saying, 'Church is a workplace for sinners, not a museum for saints.'"

"Would they tell anyone in the new church that he had had problems?"

"Samuel, I don't know."

"If they did, who would it be?"

Her face is crimson, bringing out the puckering in the burned side. "The search committee would know. Or maybe just the head of the committee."

"Who would that be at your church?"

She makes a distressed sound, and her look is pleading. "That would be my husband."

"Would he share the facts with you?"

She shakes her head. "Whatever is told to them is in strict confidence, and I would never ask him to break his word."

"Then I'll have to talk to him."

"That would really put him on the spot."

"I can't help it. I need to know. It's . . ."

She holds her hand up to stop my next word. "I can tell you that he was unhappy when Reverend Becker was sent here. He didn't say why. But he told me the only reason he goes to church these days is that he thinks it would upset me if he didn't."

"Ida Ruth, I appreciate your telling me all this."

"I haven't really told you anything."

"It's what I needed to know."

I know she's relieved when I leave. I may have to approach her husband eventually, but first I'm going to tackle the committee that assigned Becker here.

I go back and pick up Dusty, who greets me as if he's pretty sure I had run out on him for good.

I've been trying to think whether there's any way to get Maria involved in investigating Becker, and I've come up short. I'd like to get her to approach Becker's wife, but with what? Maybe when I lay out to her what I found out last night, she'll have a bright idea.

One thing I haven't done is check to see if Becker has a criminal record or a lawsuit has been brought against him. I drive to headquarters, aware that if I'm away much longer, Maria will be hunting me down.

She's fuming when I walk in, but as soon as I tell her that Becker responded to my false profile, she forgets her grievances.

"Do you think he has Loretta?"

"It would make sense, but I can't figure out why he would kidnap her."

She nods, her heavy brows knitted together so hard they practically meet in the middle of her forehead. "Motive. That's what we've been missing all along." She scoots her chair closer to my desk.

"That's the problem," I say. "I can understand if he's looking for someone to fool around with. I don't mean I condone it, but I'm not naïve. But I can't understand why he would land on Loretta. And if he kidnapped Elaine Farquart, that makes it even worse. Even if she died unexpectedly, why run over her body that way?"

"Maybe he really hates women."

"Maybe." I tell her that I looked up his employment history. "That's what I was up to this morning. Calling the companies to try to find out why he hopped from job to job."

"You think he was accused of harassing women?"

"I couldn't get a clear answer from any of the companies, but one of the people I talked to hinted that I was in the ballpark."

"Must have been pretty strong harassment. Most of those things get swept under the rug, and the woman is fired for claiming it."

I nod, thinking how strong a woman has to be to report such a thing, knowing she might not be believed or, worse, might be fired without even a fair hearing. "But in this case, he was let go."

"That may be, but apparently he was given a good recommendation time and again, and he got hired elsewhere." She has that scowl. "Not only that, but the Baptist higher-ups saw fit to pass him on to Jarrett Creek."

"I wonder how many times they'll do that before they've had enough."

She shakes herself as if to slough off all the bad thoughts. "Whatever."

"The question is, how do we investigate whether he has got Loretta without alerting him? I don't want to give him any reason to think getting rid of her is a good solution to his problems."

Maria is chewing her bottom lip. "Maybe if I went and talked to his wife?"

"On what pretext?"

She stares at me, but she isn't seeing me. Her mind is working. "I know. What if I tell her I'm there to brainstorm for a solution to the problem with the goat rodeo?"

I nod. It's a good line. "How would you approach it?"

"I'll tell her I'm a good Catholic, and I want to find out if she has any ideas. I'll bring up that I heard Becker was an engineer, and I'll ask why he decided to become a minister." She shrugs. "After that I'll have to play it by ear." She's on a roll now, and I trust that she'll make it work.

I've often thought that if persistence is the key to success, there's no way Maria can fail. She's like a bulldog. When she has a goal in mind, she's relentless.

"I want to be sure her husband isn't there, though," Maria says.

"Leave that to me."

I call Ida Ruth and tell her I need to make sure that Becker isn't home for a while.

"This is on the subject of what we discussed earlier?"

"Yes. Do you have an excuse to get him down to the church?"

"Don't you worry, I'll think of something. I'll let you know when he's on his way." Her voice is grim. This isn't just about Loretta anymore. It concerns her beloved church as well.

While we wait, I start searching to find out whether there have ever been charges brought against Becker.

My search yields nothing. That doesn't mean Becker was never accused of assault or harassment. Sex crime records are notoriously spotty, sometimes because the cops involved don't take it seriously, other times because nothing came of the charges. It could be that companies paid off disgruntled women to keep them quiet.

It occurs to me that I could call Luke Schoppe and have him root around in the Texas Ranger databases, which are more thorough than Department of Public Safety files, but I'll wait until I've talked to the Baptist Church selection committee.

I understand why a company would want to keep harassment or assault charges quiet. But I don't get why the church would ignore such charges. If Loretta were around, I'm sure she'd have a thought on the subject, but she isn't.

CHAPTER 28

Ida Ruth is as good as her word. She gets back to me within twenty minutes and says Becker has been called in to solve a tough problem involving a member of his congregation. I'd love to know what excuse Ida Ruth came up with, but it hardly matters as long as she got it done.

Maria reaches Marlene Becker at home. She says she'll be glad for Maria to drop by.

I'm fired up now to talk to the Baptists in charge of placing ministers, so as soon as Maria is out the door, I call them. It's a big bureaucracy, though; big enough to rival any state government agency, and it takes being passed from one secretary to another before I reach the proper office.

"I'm afraid Mr. Todd isn't able to take your call right now." What a surprise.

"When would he be available? It's important."

"Let me see. I think I can schedule a phone appointment with him next week, maybe Tuesday?"

"It has to be today. I'm investigating a serious crime, and I need to talk to him right away."

"I do understand. But you know this is a church organization, and we're protected by state laws against being forced to answer to law enforcement."

"Are you saying the Baptist Church would take the side of a criminal?"

"We don't know that the person you're calling about is actually guilty of anything."

I've run into pretty good stonewalling in my time, but this woman is a master at it.

"This involves the minister of a church here in my jurisdiction, and if it turns out he has murdered someone and that your boss refused to help me, the newspapers are going to have a field day."

"Is this a threat?"

"It's a fact." I've never had blood pressure problems, but I could be driven to high blood pressure by this woman.

"All right, let me convey your concerns to Mr. Todd, and I'll get back to you. May I have your phone number?"

I give it to her. "I'll expect a call back within fifteen minutes." I ring off before she can give me a smart answer. I'm too mad to let it rest. I hate to call on Ida Ruth's husband to step outside his confidentiality agreement, but it may be necessary. I'll wait the fifteen minutes to get a call back from Todd but not a minute longer.

Five minutes later, without the least trace of capitulation in her tone, Mr. Todd's secretary calls back to say that Mr. Todd has a few moments to speak with me.

"Chief Craddock, I'm sorry I was otherwise engaged when you telephoned before. What can I do for you?" A kindly, soothing tone, which I imagine goes down well when he's sending a preacher to a place he doesn't want to go or placing one in a church that has expressed doubts about him.

I'm prepared to challenge him, but for now I match his cordial tone. "Mr. Todd, I'm Chief of Police of Jarrett Creek. You may not know of it. We're a small town in the center of the state. I have a concern regarding the minister of the Baptist Church here in town."

"Oh? That's the First Baptist Church?"

I refrain from snapping that it's the first and only. "That's right."

"Let me see. That would be . . ."

"Arlen Becker."

"Reverend Becker. Oh, yes. A fine man. What are your concerns?"

Sometimes a blunt question takes people by surprise. "I want to know if he has ever been accused of sexual assault or sexual harassment."

"Well, now." He clears his throat. "That's quite an accusation."

"I didn't say I was accusing him. I said I want to know if anyone has accused him."

"I see. Well, I'm afraid that's a confidential matter."

"Are you saying you refuse to cooperate? Do you prefer that I get a search warrant for your files?"

"I don't believe that will be necessary, but I do need a little time to look into it. You understand that I don't have this information off the top of my head."

"You're telling me this happens often enough that you can't keep it straight?"

"I don't think there's any need for you to be insulting."

"Just asking. It seems to me that if it's a rare matter, you'd remember it."

He sighs. "Chief Craddock, you'd be surprised how many little oddities happen in the daily life of a minister. At times when ministers are trying to comfort or counsel a woman, she gets the wrong idea and thinks that his gestures of comfort are meant as sexual invitation. More than one good minister has been shocked to find out that a woman took his kindness for interest."

"Is that what happened in Becker's case?"

"I'm not commenting directly on Reverend Becker. As I said, I'll have to investigate his records before I can tell you anything specific. But be assured that I'll get back to you as soon as I can with the information."

"How soon is that?"

"I have a very busy schedule this week. I hope to be able to get back to you by early next week."

"That's not good enough."

"Investigating these matters isn't solely in my hands. I have to consult with other members of the committee."

"Mr. Todd, if I'm not mistaken, this is stonewalling, pure and simple. And I won't put up with it."

"All I can tell you is that I'll do my best."

When I hang up, I'm shaking. The man's voice never once wavered from its kindly tone, and yet I felt the full impact of his intention to conceal Becker's past misconduct. I'm nearly at the point where I'm going to call Becker in and get to the bottom of it now.

But before I can make a move, the phone rings.

"Chief Craddock? Brent Hogarth."

"I hope you've got good news."

"The opposite. We've got another missing woman."

"Same scenario?"

"Not exactly. The woman is younger than the other ones."

"When did she go missing?"

"This morning. We got the call a few minutes ago. I'm going out there now to talk to the woman who called it in. I wanted to give you a heads up so you could field questions from anybody who might get wind of it. I didn't want you to get caught not knowing about it."

"I appreciate that. Let me know the details when you get a chance."

"I'll get back to you."

I quickly phone Maria. She's talking to Marlene Becker. I tell her about Hogarth's call. "I don't know how you're going to do it, but try to get an idea of Becker's whereabouts the last couple of days."

"Will do." She's in the room with Marlene and can't say much.

"Don't push it too hard. We don't want any suspicions raised."

Maria gets back twenty minutes later. She looks troubled, and she plops down into her chair as if she's world-weary. "Dusty, come on over here. I could use a friendly face."

"Sounds like it didn't go well. Tell me."

"It was okay. Just hard slogging."

"What did you find out?"

"For one thing, she doesn't like Mexicans any more than her husband does. She was polite, but kind of like she was afraid she'd catch brown skin from me."

"I'm sorry."

"Let's you know who people are. Anyway, once she understood that I was there on a professional basis, and not to apply for a job as a field hand, we got along better."

I grin. I can imagine how Maria let her know in no uncertain terms that she was the law, and she expected cooperation, even on the subject of the goat rodeo.

"I started out by asking how she liked Jarrett Creek. She said she liked it fine, but I'm pretty sure she was clenching her teeth when she said it. I told her we were a nice town and that we liked tradition. She caught on fast—she's no dummy. She knew the rodeo was the real subject. I told her maybe it would be better if people got to know her husband a little better before he started pushing for changes, especially in the way the rodeo has always been done."

"How did she take that?"

"It was interesting. She said she didn't have any say over what her husband did in his ministry. But when I told her that we all know that women are the power behind the throne, she relaxed a little bit. She said she would do what she could to get him to back off."

"And the rest of it?"

She sighs. "I asked her what kind of activities she did, and she said she liked to visit the sick and was planning Easter decorations for the church." She shoots me a meaningful look.

"She said that?" Loretta has been in charge of Easter and Christmas decorations as long as I've known her. It's a point of pride with her. Probably not a good enough reason to kidnap Loretta, but the way things are going, not much would surprise me about Reverend Becker.

"I asked if she had been working with Loretta—you know, thinking I'd introduce her into the conversation—and she said, oh yes, they had discussed it. But she didn't say a word about Loretta being missing. I thought that was strange. Anyway, I brought it up and told her we were worried and looking hard for Loretta. She said she was sure we'd find her. Very breezy."

"That's all she said?"

"That was it. I wouldn't exactly call her a cold fish, but she certainly didn't seem to have much interest in a member of the congregation being missing."

"Did you notice any place where they could be hiding someone? Maybe a shed or a garage?"

"You'll like this. I told her I loved the house and asked her to show me around. She wasn't happy about it, but she couldn't very well turn me down. As far as I can tell, it's just a regular house. It isn't very big, three bedrooms and two bathrooms. It's the house the church provides for them, and it isn't grand, although she had nice furnishings. She even showed me the garage. There were no other buildings on the property. If Becker has Loretta, then he's keeping her somewhere else."

"Did you get around to the subject of her husband's previous job as an engineer?"

"More of that same kind of bland reply. She said he got tired of being in the corporate world and felt he had been called to be a minister. I asked her if it was a big change for her, and she said she had always been involved in church business, so it wasn't much of a change. Then I asked what it was like going from a big church like the one in Waco to the small one here in Jarrett Creek. She said she knew they wouldn't be here that long, that preachers get moved around a lot until they settle into a congregation. I tried to pin her down about the difference in Waco and here, and she said she liked both. Like I said, it was hard slogging. Kind of like she had it all memorized."

"You asked all the right questions. What was your impression? Did you get the feeling she was trying to evade the questions, or was she just not particularly chatty?"

She ruffles Dusty's ears absentmindedly and thinks for a minute. "I wouldn't say she acted suspicious in any way. If I had to make a guess, I'd say she isn't very happy. But whether that's because of her relationship with her husband or she doesn't like being in a small town, I don't know."

I agree with her. When Marlene Becker came to my house to look at my art collection, she was hard to read. But that doesn't mean she is up to anything suspicious—or that she thinks her husband might be. It might mean she has deliberately turned a blind eye to Becker's extramarital activities. "It's hard to believe he could be bounced from job to job and she wouldn't be suspicious that something was wrong," I say.

"Still," Maria says, "some women don't want to know. My Uncle Tito kept a mistress right nearby in San Antonio, and everyone knew it, but my aunt never let on that she had the slightest idea. She was crazy about Tito. But this is different. I didn't get the feeling Marlene Becker is crazy about her husband. More like she doesn't have the energy to make a fuss."

"And his whereabouts the last couple of days?"

"I asked her what his schedule was usually like, and I got the same vague answer I got for everything else. He's out working hard, doing things for his congregation."

"I'm curious how preachers get paid. Surely the church here in Jarrett Creek can't pay him enough to get by on."

"I don't know. I know in the Catholic Church, they can get a hardship stipend, but they're expected to live within their means."

"He might be strapped for cash."

"I wonder if it's worth following him."

"You know we don't have the manpower to do that," I say.

"Yes, but . . ."

"But what?"

"Suppose we got Ida Ruth and a few other people to keep an eye on him?" Seeing the look on my face, she throws up her hands. "I know, I know. It's a terrible idea. I'm frustrated, that's all."

"Look, chances are he's just a cad who sneaks around on his wife."

"And thinks he's God's gift to women."

I agree, although I'm still troubled by my suspicion that he was the man I caught in Loretta's house right after she disappeared. Breaking into someone's home is not the action of a man who is innocent. And the question remains, how did he get in without a key?

"Dammit."

Maria is startled. "What?"

"Something I forgot to do. I keep making stupid mistakes because I'm rattled. Don't look at me like that. Has nothing to do with age."

"I didn't say a word. What did you forget?"

"Hold on. You'll find out."

I dial Scott Singletary's cell number.

"Tell me something good," he says.

"Question. When you stayed at your mom's house, did you open a window?"

"Are you kidding? That's why you're calling?"

"Do you remember?"

Silence. I wait. "Yes, I did. It was stuffy and I was hot. I didn't want to turn the air conditioning on because it was nice outside."

"Did you lock it back up?"

"You're asking because of the man who broke in."

"Yes."

He heaves a heavy sigh. "Chief Craddock, it's likely I didn't close the window. I was upset that . . ."

"I understand. But it does answer a question."

"I apologize for the way I talked to you yesterday. Marcie says I was rude and I ought to be ashamed of myself."

"We're all on edge. I'm sorry as hell we haven't gotten any further in the case. But we will."

I get off the phone, and Maria nods. "One small question answered. That could be how the intruder got in." Unless he got a key from Loretta.

CHAPTER 29

It's late afternoon. Maria has gone home, and Dusty is starting to get antsy when Hogarth calls to fill me in on the woman who went missing. "Not much to tell. This morning the woman she works for called the department to say she hadn't come into work. She said with what happened to Elaine Farquart, she was nervous because her employee was usually very reliable."

"What did you find out?"

"She seems to have disappeared, like your lady in Jarrett Creek. I sent an officer over to her house, in case she was sick or had taken a fall and couldn't get to the phone, but she wasn't there. Everything looked fine, but her car was missing. We reached her daughter on her cell phone. She works over in Bryan at a pizza place. I went over there to question her, but she said she didn't have any idea where her mother was."

"Internet dating?"

"I asked if her mother was involved in any Internet dating sites. She said that was the last thing her mother would do, that she was very opposed to it." He chuckles. "This is funny. She said her mother thinks women who do that are floozies."

I laugh, thinking of Loretta as a floozy. "Husband?"

"She's divorced, and her ex-husband lives in Beaumont. He's remarried. We called him, and he said he hadn't seen her in at least a year and hadn't heard from her. He said they didn't have much in the way of communication. I got the impression it was an unfriendly split."

"So she disappeared like Elaine Farquart and Loretta Singletary but didn't do any Internet dating."

"Right. Like I said, the daughter didn't seem particularly worried.

I asked if her mother was inclined to go off and not call into work, and she said no, but her mother could be impulsive sometimes."

"What's your plan?"

"We'll wait to see if she comes back on her own. I don't like to do that, but with no indication of foul play, we don't have any alternatives."

"Did you happen to find out if the woman is a churchgoer?"

"It didn't come up. Why?"

"I've got a situation here that might be related. I don't want to jump the gun, so I won't go into details. I'll let you know if there's more to tell."

When I hang up, I have a mind to call Mr. Todd back to nudge him again, but I may get more cooperation if I give him more time. Suddenly I realize that I'm never going to hear back from the Baptist Church. They will stonewall. They will give me excuses. They will defend their minister as zealously as the Catholic Church defended its pedophile priests a while back.

There's only one way I'm going to find out the truth about Becker's actions, and that's to confront him with what I know. Hanging back because I'm afraid it might have repercussions for Loretta's safety is a coward's stance. Becker has to explain himself, and I'm the one who has to force it. The question is where to have a meeting with him. I remember the way he strode into this office as if he owned the place. He'll be the same at home—or maybe worse. Same with the church.

It has to be here. I'll at least have the advantage of calling him in to talk rather than him choosing his time and place.

The other consideration is whether to do it now or wait until the morning. I've had a hard day, and I'm flagging. Tomorrow I'll be fresher—but Becker will be too. I at least have the advantage of my anger at the church's obfuscation.

I call his home, and Marlene answers.

"It was nice meeting you the other day," I say. Not many people have an appreciation for my art collection."

"It's wonderful," she says, with a warmth I wasn't expecting. "I met your ... colleague today. We had a nice chat. Although I must say I was curious why she came here. I had the feeling there was more to it than she let on."

"Mrs. Becker, is your husband home?"

"Not at the moment. Can I have him call you?"

"Do you know where I might locate him?"

The silence stretches out. "Actually, I'm not sure where he is. He was going over to Bobtail to meet with the Baptist minister there, but that was around 2:30. He should be home soon."

"Please ask him to give me a call right away."

"Is everything all right?"

A strange question. "I need to ask him a few questions."

"Listen, if ... never mind."

"I'll expect to hear from him."

That little moment at the end tells me all I need to know. Marlene Becker knows what her husband has done in the past. She wanted to make a preemptive excuse and couldn't figure out how to do it. The poor woman.

I look online for the First Baptist Church in Bobtail. There's no answer at the church number, but there's a number for the minister, who is the person I want to talk to anyway.

"This is Reverend Wiley. How can I help?" He has a rough-shod voice, more like a country farmer than a preacher.

I ask him my question. He's flustered, but the end result is that, no, he had no meeting with Arlen Becker today. "I've only met the man once at a regional meeting. I was surprised when he didn't call on me when he moved here. That's protocol. Oh, well, I don't know why I'm telling you that. I'm gossiping, and that's unseemly."

I thank him for his time and hang up. He seems like a man I would like, forthright and self-aware without being self-deprecating.

"Dusty, looks like you and I have to go stake out Reverend Becker's house."

His only answer is to start leaping with excitement when I head for the door. He's not going to like this as much as he thinks he will.

When I drive up to Becker's house, I can see he hasn't arrived home because the garage door is open, and the only car inside is the one Marlene Becker drives. I position my truck down the block and settle in with Dusty's head on my lap. I turn the radio on low to a country and western station for company.

My phone rings a couple of times, but one is a telemarketing call and the other is a wrong number.

At nine o'clock, it occurs to me that maybe I'm wrong and the Beckers only have one car, and he has been home all along. I call Marlene Becker. "I haven't heard from your husband. Is he there?"

"I'm sorry. He's been delayed. I told him you called, and he said he'd have to talk to you tomorrow."

I decide to wait a little longer, curious to know whether he plans to come home at all.

At ten o'clock, Becker still isn't home, and Dusty is yipping at me that he has had enough of this nonsense.

Back home, I feed Dusty first and top off Zelda's cat food. I've taken to feeding her on top of a chest near my kitchen table; otherwise, Dusty would gobble up her food. She takes it as a sign of superiority and gazes at Dusty with disdain while she nibbles.

I poke around in the refrigerator and heat up leftover enchiladas that look like they're still okay. I hardly pay attention to what I'm eating, and as soon as I finish, I head back to Becker's place.

This time I decide to walk. It's only a few blocks away, and it's nice to stretch my legs in the cool night air. Dusty frisks alongside me. I'm glad I have a dog now.

The garage door is closed, and there is one lone light on upstairs. That doesn't mean Becker has made it home. The garage door has panels of glass high up, but I'm tall enough to peer in. I tell Dusty to stay on the sidewalk, but he moves right with me as I walk up the driveway. I peer inside, and sure enough, there's only one car. It looks like Marlene Becker has given up on her husband coming home tonight. I doubt it's the first time her husband has done this.

Where is he? If he's holding Loretta somewhere—and maybe the other woman who has newly disappeared—where is that? Has he rented a place? I'm tempted to rouse Marlene Becker and ask, but by now I'm pretty sure that she has made it her business to know as little as possible about his activities.

CHAPTER 30

Even when I get to bed late, I'm never one to lie around in the morning. As soon as I open my eyes, I'm itching to find out whether Becker got home last night. Shortly after seven o'clock, Dusty and I head back to Becker's house on foot.

The garage door is still closed. It's too early to knock on the door. I'm headed toward the driveway to take another look inside the garage when the door opens and Marlene Becker comes out fully dressed.

"Morning!" I call out.

She jumps like I've taken a shot at her.

"Sorry, I didn't mean to scare you. Just out walking my dog."

She stands frozen, so I say, "You're out early. Big day?"

That moves her. She walks down the steps toward me with a peculiar look on her face. Instead of doing his usual excited dance to greet someone, Dusty sits down next to me, leaning on my leg.

When Marlene Becker is directly in front of me she says, "Don't be coy with me. It doesn't suit you."

"You're right. Where's your husband?"

"I'm assuming he's off doing what he has done for the entire twenty-eight years we've been married—off catting around with another woman." Her gaze doesn't falter.

I'm embarrassed on her behalf. "I'm sorry to hear that."

"You knew. That's why you sent that officer over here yesterday. You wanted her to nose around." Her voice would freeze antifreeze.

"Why would I do that?"

"Maybe you want something to hold over him so he'll stop pushing to be part of that stupid goat rodeo."

"This has nothing to do with the goat rodeo. Where were you going just now? You have somewhere to be?"

"I was going for a drive if you must know. I thought I'd head for San Antonio and maybe do a little shopping. That's what I usually do when Arlen has found himself a new woman to spend time with."

"You mind if we go inside and talk for a few minutes?"

"Very few. I don't want to be here when Arlen comes home."

"Then you can come to my house or down to headquarters."

"I'll come to your house. That way if he passes the police station on his way home, he won't see my car there."

At my house, I sit her down in the kitchen and whip up scrambled eggs and toast. She watches me as if I'm an alien creature. My guess is her husband has never turned a hand in the kitchen.

"Why do you stay with him?" I ask when we're seated.

"My marriage vows were for better or worse. I'm a Christian, and I don't believe in divorce."

"You don't have to divorce him to leave him."

She picks at the eggs. "Yes, I suppose that's true. But every time he strays, he swears it's the last time." She gives a bitter laugh. "I used to think when he got older he'd lose his interest in playing around. No such luck."

"Has your husband ever hurt you physically?"

"No. That's not him. He just likes . . . variety."

"Has any woman ever accused him of hurting her?"

She lays her fork down and folds her hands in her lap. She looks puzzled. "Not that I know of, but I try not to know too much. These are strange questions."

"I know they are. But I have specific reasons for asking them, and I'd rather ask him directly. I'd like to get his cell number from you, and then you're free to go."

She writes down the number and then calls Dusty to her side. She leans down to ruffle his ears. It's the first time she seems to have noticed that he is in the room. "Arlen doesn't like dogs. Maybe I'll get one." She gets up and says, "I suppose I'll see you around."

After she leaves, I'm on automatic, washing up the dishes and getting ready to confront Arlen Becker.

My phone rings, and I see that it's Maria. I don't answer it, but it reminds me that I didn't call Wendy last night. Being a lawman can be all-consuming. My wife Jeanne used to get annoyed when my whole attention was focused on a case. It was one reason that I quit the law and went into the oil business with her brother. Turned out that being a land man for an oil company was consuming in a different way. I traveled more than I wanted to, but it was part of the job. One thing Jeanne knew she never had to worry about, though, was me straying with another woman.

When Becker answers his phone, "This is Reverend Becker," his tone is so oily that if he were standing in front of me, I might be tempted to hit him.

"This is Chief Craddock. I'd like to meet with you down at the station."

"I'm not sure that's necessary. I've been rethinking my position on the rodeo. It was suggested to me that perhaps I've been too hasty. Maybe next year will be a better time for me to sit down with Sanchez." It isn't lost on me that he calls Father Sanchez by his last name without the religious title.

"This concerns another matter."

"Oh, and what would that be?"

"It's best if you come in and we'll talk. Say an hour?"

He doesn't reply right away, and I can picture him frowning, outraged that he doesn't have the upper hand. "Uh, I'm busy this morning. How about two o'clock."

"I'll expect you at ten."

"Well, I'll do my best."

"See that you do."

I get into headquarters and find both Maria and Connor there. They're squabbling as usual, this time with opposite opinions of a movie I never heard of, and I'm not in the mood.

"Look, you two need to get straight with each other. Go have a margarita together one night after work."

They look at me as if I've suggested they run off to a motel together. Naturally, it's Maria who speaks up. "What are you so grumpy about?" Connor would never get up the nerve to ask the question that way.

"Where do you stand on the Mosley case? Did you take the files back to the courthouse? Have you given up on it?"

"I've decided to write it up and turn it over to the Department of Public Safety. They have to decide whether to go after Mosley. He lives out in Amarillo now, and he's out of our jurisdiction."

"And the files?"

She looks murderous. "I have to take them back."

"This morning would be good. I need the room at ten o'clock."

"For what?" She isn't being sulky; she's alert.

"Arlen Becker is coming in."

Her eyes get wide. I know she'd like to sit in, but she knows it's best if I talk to him alone.

"Coming in for what?" Connor says. "He's the Baptist preacher, isn't he?"

"Does Connor get to stay while you talk to him?" Maria asks.

"Connor, what have you got that can take you out of the office?"

"A call came in this morning from Pansy Wilkins. She said there was another wild party next door last night. I'll go over and talk to those boys."

We all know that to Pansy, a wild party means somebody was sitting out on his porch drinking a beer and talking on his cell phone. But having Connor follow up will keep him out of the office.

"How long do we have to be gone?" Maria says.

"I'd say it's safe to come back at 11:00. But if you drive up and see a strange car outside, keep on going."

I must have come across pretty stern because both of them scramble out pronto. They've barely left when I get a call from Hogarth in Bobtail.

"That woman still hasn't shown up," he says.

"What's your plan?"

"Plan? Ha! The usual. Fingerprints, looking through her computer, etc. Daughter gave us permission, but she still doesn't seem all that concerned."

"Did you talk to the woman's coworkers?"

"There's just the two of them, the boss and the missing woman."

"What kind of business?"

"It's a hair salon."

I freeze. It can't be the same shop. I can't believe I didn't ask yesterday what kind of work the woman did. "What hair salon?"

"It's called Darlene's Beauty Shop. Not exactly a snappy name."

"Hogarth, I have to talk to you." Outside, Becker's big Chrysler pulls into the lot. "That beauty shop is the same one that Elaine Farquart and Loretta Singletary went to."

"I'll be damned. How long have you known this?"

"It was in the credit card information I got from you. I didn't follow up because, although they went to the same shop, they saw different hairdressers. I talked to both hairdressers, but I didn't find out anything that looked like it ought to be pursued. So that I make no more assumptions, it's Lucy Nettleman who's missing?"

"That's the one. How soon can you get up here?"

"It'll be an hour. I have a person of interest coming in for an informal interview."

"Who is it?"

Becker is just outside the door. "I'll have to fill you in later. He's walking in the door now"

"You're holding out on me."

"Not intentionally. I'll get back to you."

It's a blustery day, wind kicking up and occasional swishes of rain showers. Reverend Arlen Becker walks in stamping his feet and brushing rain from his zip-up jacket.

"Can I get you something to drink?" I ask. "A glass of water?"

"You can tell me what the heck this is all about," he says, bluster matching the weather.

"Have a seat." I gesture to the chair next to my desk. He eyes it as if he's going to refuse, but then he pulls it away from the desk and eases into it slowly as if to prove that he's planning to resist every way he can.

"Where were you last night?" I decide that the shock treatment would work best.

"I don't know that that's any of your business."

"It is if you've been up to no good."

His lip curls. "I'm not sure I catch your drift."

I printed off a copy of the photo he sent me along with the phony profile I made up. I take them out of the desk drawer and shove them over to him. He takes a long time to look at them, no doubt trying to figure out how to approach his protest.

"That's my photo. How did you get a hold of it?"

"You see the profile of the woman there?"

"Yes, what does that have to do with me?"

"You replied to the profile on a dating website."

"What if I did? There's no law against that."

"Normally, I'd say yes, that's between you and your wife, and you and your church. But this is different."

He has tried to stay cocky, but his bluster is deflating. "Different how?"

"I wrote that profile to smoke out men who might have replied to Loretta Singletary's profile."

He lets loose a nasty snicker. "Why would I be interested in an old biddy like that?"

"I can't answer that. No more than I can answer why a man with a good wife like yours would be prowling around on the Internet looking for action. And why you would describe a loyal member of your congregation in such a mean way." Before he can make something of that, I continue, "I have no idea where your taste in women lies. But that's not important. What's important is that one woman on that website is dead, and two more are missing—one of them from right here in town. And I want to know if you were involved with any of them."

"I don't know where you got the idea that I met any of those women. I never meet any of the women I contact on dating websites in person. I like to talk to them, that's all. It's no crime for me to want to have conversations with women."

I don't believe him, but there's no way to prove otherwise at the moment. "What do you think would happen if your congregation found out you chatted up these women?"

"Is this a threat to get me to lay off Sanchez?"

"That's the furthest thing from my mind. I just wonder what lengths you would go to make sure no one found out." I'm trying to figure out whether he's the man who broke into Loretta's house.

"I certainly wouldn't hurt anyone."

"Would you sneak into somebody's house and steal information about your activities?"

"If I knew they had information like that, I guess I might think of it, but I haven't done that."

"How did you hear that Loretta Singletary was missing?"

He clears his throat. He's starting to get the hunted look that people get when they're backed into a corner. "One of the church ladies must have told me."

"And did she tell you that Loretta had been on a dating website— the same one you had been nosing around on? Wait." I hold up my hand. "Before you answer, consider that I can find this information out other ways, and if you're lying it won't look good."

"She may have mentioned it."

"So, you knew there was a possibility that Loretta had seen your information on the website and recognized you."

"How would she do that?"

"How do I know she didn't ask for your photo and you sent it to her?"

"I told you I have no interest in somebody like her."

"I only have your word for it. And last week I surprised somebody about your size who was rummaging around in her house. For all I know, you have her stashed somewhere and broke into her house to retrieve your photo."

"Absolutely not!" He's practically screaming. "You're talking to the wrong man. I may chat up people online, but I don't break into houses, and I certainly don't kidnap people."

"As I understand it, in the past, your relations with women in the workplace have consisted of a lot more than conversation. You've been fired from one job after another for harassing women. The fact is, I'm not sure what that consisted of—was it simply a matter of chasing women around the break room, or was it more serious? Was it assault? You tell me."

"I don't have to tell you a thing. Those files are confidential, and I'll have the hide of anybody who leaked them to you."

I slam my hand down on the desk. "What I'm telling you is that the little I do know gets me mighty interested in the coincidence of you being on the same small-town website as the women who have gone missing. And if you don't think I'm going to pursue this, you're mistaken."

"You don't have any proof of this. You're trying to pin something on me to get the glory."

"No sir, you're the one who's worried about glory. I don't want to pin anything on anybody. I want to find my friend Loretta, and I'm going to turn your life upside down until I make sure you aren't the person I'm looking for. If you don't want to cooperate, that's your business. But one way or another, I'm going to find out. The first thing I'm going to do is talk to the FBI and tell them everything I know about you and let them take it from there. Glory? Forget it."

His eyes are bugging out of his head, and I can't tell whether his red face is due to fear or fury. It doesn't much matter to me. He's my only lead.

"You can't get away with this," he says. "You're messing with my privacy. I have a right to privacy under the law."

"I don't think you understand. Your privacy doesn't mean a thing if I suspect you of kidnapping these women. Another one has disappeared, and you were gone overnight. Why shouldn't I think you're the one who has abducted them?"

He's breathing hard, and his eyes are cold. "I was with a friend last night. She'll vouch for me."

I pull out a pen and pad and point to it. "Name and phone number. And the hours you were with her."

His eyes narrow. "Who are you answerable to? Who do I report you to for overstepping?"

"You can talk to the sheriff in Bobtail, but I guarantee he's as interested in finding out what happened to those women as I am. You realize that even if you did spend last night with a woman, you are still not off the hook. The minute I saw the photograph you sent me, I knew you were up to no good. And everything points in that direction. You think the sheriff is going to hold your hand and tell you that because you're a Baptist minister you've got special privileges?"

His eyes dart from me to the wall behind me and back. He's trapped, but so am I. I keep flashing back to the news Hogarth told me—that the missing woman is from Darlene's Beauty Shop. It doesn't make sense. Three women all connected through a hair salon. Why would that have anything to do with this minister? Just because he's a snake, guilty of running around on his wife, doesn't mean he's a kidnapper or a killer.

"Look, call the woman I was with. All right? But don't tell my wife. She doesn't deserve what I've done."

"I don't have to tell your wife. She already knows. What do you think she thought when you didn't come home last night? That you were out visiting the sick? She knows you better than that. You've humiliated her every chance you've gotten, and you're right, she doesn't deserve that."

He's rocking back and forth, looking ashamed. But he has been here before. Whatever demon drives him to make a fool of himself and humiliate his wife by pursuing women, this episode is not likely to change things. His shame only lasts a few seconds. "That's between my wife and me," he says, jaw jutting out.

"I'm still not convinced you don't have those women, and I'm going to keep a good eye on you."

"What is it you want? You want me to lay off Sanchez? Is he your good pal and you're going to blackmail me to keep him happy?"

"I want to see the last of you regardless of whether you're guilty. What you do about Father Sanchez and the goat rodeo is of no interest to me." I get up. "You're free to go, but like I said, I'll have an eye on your every move."

He springs to his feet. "How do you think you're going to do that? Small-town cop like you with your little half-time force, that little Mexican girl and the chubby half-wit as backup?"

I think of petty things I could say to him—that Maria is worth ten of him and that Connor is every bit as smart as he is—but he's right, I can't really keep an eye on him. Except. Except, like Maria suggested earlier today, if the Baptist ladies happened to know that I needed a few eyes on him, I wouldn't have to tell them why; they'd be intrigued enough to get right on it.

"Why are you smiling?" He's suspicious.

"You don't have any idea what a small town is like, do you?"

"What do you mean?"

What I mean is that he thinks he can get away with the same kind of nonsense in a small town that he did in a city without people finding out. He's sadly mistaken. "Never mind. Just watch your step, that's all."

CHAPTER 31

"I think I might be losing my mind," I say to Hogarth. "I can't get over that I didn't ask you relevant questions about the new missing woman. It could have saved us time."

"I take it your man didn't pan out?"

"He's a creep, but probably not our creep."

"Who is he?"

"If I tell you, you won't believe it. It's the Baptist preacher."

"Whoa!" His eyebrows shoot up. "How did you figure that?"

I tell him how I laid a trap on the dating website and Becker stumbled into it.

"He's not the first preacher who hid behind his religion. And he's not the first to turn out to be an adulterer. But murder? That's a stretch."

"You're right. I didn't get how he fit in with women connected through the beauty salon, but at the time, it was my best shot at a suspect."

"We may not be any better off with this new disappearance. It's hard to put together what connects her with the other two missing women because she didn't do online dating, and only Loretta was her client. You ready to go ask a few questions at the salon?"

Maria had come back from Bobtail when I was ready to leave, and I had left Dusty with her, so we go in Hogarth's squad car. I appreciate that he's willing to count me in on the questioning. When I thank him, he says, "Tell you the truth, I'm glad for the help. We've lost two officers in the last couple of months. One retired and one took a job in Austin. We're short-handed."

We get to the salon and find a dozen women standing in the front yard in small groups, many of them holding cups of coffee. They grow silent when they see Hogarth and me walk in through the gate. One of them, who seems to have been appointed leader, marches over to us. "What are the police going to do about this? We are all scared to death. First poor Elaine Farquart, and now Lucy has gone missing." She takes in my uniform. "And I understand a woman disappeared from Jarrett Creek too. This is a disgrace."

Hogarth takes off his hat. He looks older without it. "Ma'am, we're not even sure Lucy Nettleman is officially missing. She may have had to take a quick trip, or she may have had an accident. We're looking into it."

"A quick trip? That's ridiculous." The woman is around Loretta's age, sharp-featured with ice blue eyes and a pointed chin. She's wearing a lot of makeup and jewelry. "Lucy needs this job. She wouldn't go off without telling Darlene."

"Ma'am, believe me, we're doing everything we can to find her." He glances at me uneasily and then raises his voice and speaks to address them. "I want all of you to think of any information you have that might be pertinent with regard to Lucy Nettleman. Anything that you think might have a bearing on where she might be, even if it seems insignificant, please tell me now or call me at police headquarters. You can talk to anyone there, and they'll get the information to me."

In the salon, it's business as usual. Darlene is shampooing a woman and says she'll be with us right away. As soon as she rinses her client's hair, she says to her, "Patti, you're going to have to wait a couple of minutes while I talk to these officers about Lucy."

Patti waves her away. "You take all the time you need."

Darlene takes us back to a room that she uses as an office and tells us to take a seat on the folding chairs next to the desk. "I'm going out of my mind with worry. It's not like Lucy to disappear like this. I've had to cancel all her appointments. She wouldn't just not show up unless something happened to her. I'm scared that the same person who took Elaine and Loretta has taken her."

"Let's don't jump to conclusions," Hogarth says. He asks her when she last saw Lucy.

"She left work late Wednesday. She doesn't usually work past five-thirty, but she had a couple of ladies who begged her to take care of them. Then yesterday she'd didn't show up. Didn't call . . ."

"How did she seem Wednesday? Was there anything unusual going on? Her mood the same as usual?"

Darlene covers her mouth with her hand, blinking hard while she thinks. "I swear I don't remember a thing that was different. We're busy. We don't have a lot of time to make small talk. But we do talk to our ladies, so maybe one of her clients could tell you more."

"We need to get a list of the clients who had appointments with her that day."

"And if she's particularly friendly with any of her clients, even if they weren't with her that day, it might be good for us to talk to them," I say.

"Okay, that's a good thought," she says. She draws a breath as if she's going to say something and then thinks better of it. Hogarth catches it.

"What is it you're thinking?"

"Well, I don't know that she has a lot of friends. I'll tell you, she was like a whipped dog when she first came to work here, humiliated by her husband like she was. She didn't want to chat much with anybody. People came to her anyway because she's a really good stylist. They were willing to overlook her not being friendly. But gradually she warmed up. I don't know that she made really good friends with anyone though. That's all I'm saying."

"So, the last time you talked to her was Wednesday?"

"That's right. Now let me get you that list. Do you want all the clients she has seen recently or just her regulars?"

"Let's start with the regulars."

She consults her calendar and jots down names and phone numbers. I'm glad she's organized.

"Did you ever hear that Ms. Nettleman was dating anyone?"

"Heavens, no. I think she's pretty much off men. She's bitter."

"Have you talked to her daughter?"

Darlene frowns. "I haven't."

"When we talked to her, she didn't seem all that worried about her mamma."

"I've only met her a few times. She's an odd girl. She's as mad at her daddy as her mother is. If you ask me, they'd be better off putting their bitterness in the past and moving on. They'd be happier." She gives a cluck of laughter. "Well, they didn't ask me, so I mind my own business."

She hands over the list of Lucy's clients, and we get up to leave.

"Now let me ask you a question," Darlene says. "Did the police go out to Lucy's house to check on her? I worried that maybe she had fallen or was sick."

"Yes, ma'am, we went out there," Hogarth says. "We did that first thing. When we were in the house, we checked in case she had left some clue as to where she had gone, but there was nothing. We left a note telling her we were concerned and to contact us if she returned."

Hogarth and I stop at a sandwich shop in a strip mall nearby and eat a quick lunch. Back at Bobtail Police Department, he turns over half the list of Lucy's forty regular customers to one of his junior officers.

I call Maria to tell her where I am and what I've been doing. "I have a list of Lucy's clients I'd like you to call and find out if they can tell you anything about her. Like if they know whether she dated or was happy working there. Anything that could give us a lead one way or the other. I'll fax the list over to you, and you can call me if you get any interesting responses."

"And what are you going to be doing?" she asks.

"Hogarth and I are going to check out her house and talk to her daughter again. Now that she has been missing for twenty-four hours, it's more serious."

The cop I met at Elaine Farquart's place, David Marks, is already at Lucy Nettleman's. He fills us in, saying they haven't found anything that might help.

"Does she keep a computer?" Hogarth asks.

"It's back here." Marks leads us through the house. I only saw the front room when I was here before. It's a plain vanilla two-bedroom, one-bath place. I note that the short hallway walls are bare of art or family photos, as if Lucy just moved in or didn't have the heart to decorate much.

Lucy's computer is an old one, perched on a scarred wooden desk in her bedroom. She apparently only uses it for email and Pinterest, which she is obsessed with. Her history is full of one Pinterest search after another: hair styles, clothing, fluffy white dog breeds, and recipes for Italian food, salads, vegetable dishes, and soups. She also follows a few romance authors and, surprisingly, violent thrillers.

"There were no phone messages on the message machine," Marks says. "We haven't found any email messages out of the ordinary. No travel plans or emails about secret meetings. No threats, no suspicious exchanges."

I look over Hogarth's shoulder as he scrolls through her recent emails. If she gets advertising or political emails, she discards them. The emails are mostly announcements for church meetings, chatty exchanges with a sister who lives in Virginia, and terse exchanges with her daughter about when and where they might meet or whether the daughter enjoyed a movie she saw. Everything is paralyzingly normal.

Hogarth clicks on the history, scrolling through all the Pinterest files. He stops at one. "This is different." He points to the screen where there's a clump of websites for new kitchen appliances. "Marks, did you find anything indicating that she bought a new appliance?"

"I might have. Hold on." He picks up a file from the desk and leafs through the receipts in it. "Here you go." He sets down a receipt for a new stove.

Hogarth whistles. "Expensive."

I walk into the kitchen and find an old GE range. Returning to the bedroom, I say, "When was the new one bought?"

"Couple of months ago."

"It wasn't delivered. She has an old one."

"Oh. Here you go. It was delivered to an address in Bryan. That's where her daughter lives. She must have bought it for her."

"Has anybody questioned the daughter in person?"

"Not yet. I talked to her by phone yesterday."

"I assume Lucy's car is gone," I say.

"Yep."

Hogarth takes his hat off and scratches his head. "This makes absolutely no sense. How are these women disappearing without us having any clue where they are?"

"Well at least so far there's only been one dead, and she died of a heart attack," Marks says.

That's small comfort. "Any suitcases missing? Loretta packed a suitcase."

"I didn't look," Marks says.

I go into the small hall bathroom. It has pink and green tile, the kind of tile they used back in the 1950s. Her toothbrush and toothpaste are out on the counter, robe on the peg behind the door, and makeup and hair products neatly arranged on the countertop.

When I get back, Marks is peering into the closet. Clothes are crammed in tight, and I see no suitcases.

"How long has she had this place?"

After scrabbling through a couple of drawers, Marks comes up with a file folder marked, "House." "Oh," he says. "She bought it nine months ago."

"I figured she hadn't been here long and that she had downsized."

"She got a divorce several months ago. My guess is they sold the house and she had to buy what she could from the proceeds."

Hogarth shakes his head. "Well, I don't see anything more we can do here. Marks, find her phone bill, get a list of recent calls, and see if anything pops out. Meanwhile, Craddock and I are going over to Bryan to talk to the daughter."

CHAPTER 32

Holly Nettleman works as a cashier at a pizza parlor. She gets permission from her boss to take off fifteen minutes to talk to us. "The lunch crowd is over," he says. "But don't take too long. I've got to get over across town by two o'clock."

There are plenty of empty tables, and we sit down with Holly at one where no one is nearby.

"You haven't heard from your mother?" Hogarth asks.

She shakes her head and starts to chew on her thumb. From the looks of it, she chews on it a lot.

"We want to get an idea of your mother's habits," Hogarth says, in a tentative way. Holly is solidly built, but her expression is so fragile, scared even, that I understand his reluctance to spook her. "Maybe it can help us figure out where she has gone."

"I don't know what you mean," she says.

"Well, she's missing, and unless you know where she is, I think we need to look for her. Do you know where she is?"

She shakes her head. I'm glad we're here talking to her in person because, seeing the confused expression on her face, I'm curious. Hogarth had said she didn't seem particularly upset that her mother was missing, and now I wonder if the girl is suffering from developmental problems. She looks to be in her late twenties, but her job is not demanding. Maybe she hasn't quite processed the seriousness of the situation.

"Well, then," Hogarth says in the same gentle manner, "if we know her habits, maybe we can find her. You know she might have had an accident and be in need of rescue."

"Oh, yeah I guess that's true." She looks over at her boss, who is watching us.

"Can you think of why she would fail to show up at work?"

"Hmmm." She tucks her hands under her thighs and shrugs her shoulders. "Maybe she had to go somewhere."

Hogarth glances at me. I suspect he's thinking, as I am, that this girl is not all that bright.

"Is it possible she went shopping, like in Houston or San Antonio, and didn't make it back in time for work?" I ask.

"I don't think so."

"How often do you see your mamma?"

"I don't know. Two or three times a week."

"You were at her house last week when I dropped by. You were baking."

"I remember that. She didn't like that you didn't call first."

"Exactly. Can you tell me when you last saw her?"

"Umm, last weekend."

"What was the occasion?" I can tell Hogarth is getting impatient.

"Church," she says, her tone implying that anyone should know that.

"And afterward?" he asks.

"We went to her house for Sunday dinner. She makes roast chicken and dumplings every Sunday."

"Did anyone join you?" I ask. It's an idle question, but her response is interesting.

Her eyes widen and she sits up. "What do you mean did someone join us?"

"I mean, did anyone else eat dinner with you?"

"No," she slumps back and studies her fingers.

"Did you expect someone?" Hogarth asks, tuning in to her reaction.

"No."

"Is your mamma dating anyone?"

"Mamma? No. She never would! After what daddy did, she hates men."

"Are you dating anyone?"

Her blush comes on faster than I've ever seen a blush. "No, Mamma would have a fit."

"She doesn't want you to date?"

"Not after what daddy did."

I feel like we're getting nowhere with this young woman, and I can't decide whether she's being deliberately obtuse or she really is confused. "You're sure you don't have any idea where your mamma might have gone?" he asks.

"No way. But she'll be fine." She looks at her watch again. "I have to go now. My break is up."

Hogarth tells her to call if she hears from Lucy, but his words are desultory. We're in the squad car, back on the road, when he says what I'm thinking: "She knows more than she's saying."

"It seems that way. But what? Why would she keep it from us?"

"She does seem a little shy of a deck of cards. Maybe talking to police makes her nervous."

My phone had been off while we were talking to Holly, and when I turn it back on, I see that I have a voice message from Maria. "Call when you can."

I call her right away. She tells me that one of the women on the list of Lucy's clients said she has become good friends with Lucy. "Well, what she said was, she's as good a friend as anybody is with Lucy. She said Lucy is standoffish. But they've gotten together a few times. I guess they're both divorced and have that in common."

She gives me the name and number of the woman, and I tell Hogarth.

He says he needs to get back to the station. "We had a traffic fatality yesterday, and it turned out to be a mess. If it's all right with you, I'll let you take the lead on talking to this woman."

Her name is Mary Robinson and, thank goodness, after our ordeal with Lucy's reticent daughter, Mary is chatty. She's a bustling kind of woman, sitting me down on a bright yellow chair in her surprisingly modern living room. She brings me coffee and cookies without asking, setting the tray down on the glass coffee table between us. She perches on her cream-colored sofa and says, "Now, the woman I talked to on the phone told me Lucy is missing. I have to tell you that is not one bit like her. She is absolutely reliable. When we go out, she is right where she says she'll be at the appointed time."

"That's what her employer, Darlene, said too."

"Oh, Darlene. She's always in everybody's business. If Lucy was one minute late, she'd want to know chapter and verse where she was and what kept her. Lucy knows if she missed a day of work, she'd never hear the end of it. There must be something going on for her not to show up."

"You don't care for Darlene?"

She has taken a bite out of a cookie and waves for me to wait until she has swallowed. "I like her fine. But I prefer Lucy. She's friendly but not too friendly, and not snoopy." She takes another cookie and pushes the plate in my direction. "Have one. I'm proud of my cookies. A lot of people would give anything for this recipe."

They're lemon cookies, and they look good. "Don't mind if I do." I put one on my plate. "When was the last time you saw Lucy?"

"After I talked to your officer, I looked it up. It was two weeks ago. We went to a movie. I called her again last week and asked if she wanted to go to the movies, but she said she didn't have time. I don't know what she was up to, but she . . ." She stops abruptly. "Come to think of it, I remember thinking she was downright curt with me. Like she was busy and didn't want to take the time to talk to me."

"Do you have any idea where she might be?"

She shakes her head. "Not the slightest. I mean we're friends, but not the kind of friends where you share every little thing."

"Do you know if she ever considered joining an online dating service?"

She laughs. "Oh, honey, if you knew her, you wouldn't even ask. After what happened to her, she's off men permanently. And even if she wasn't, the last thing she'd do is look for a man on one of those dating services."

"What does she have against them?"

Her eyes glitter with gossip. "That's how her ex-husband met his new wife."

"A trophy wife?"

"Goodness no. You'd think so, wouldn't you? But that's what drove Lucy crazy. He married a woman older than she is."

For a few seconds, I hardly know what to make of that, so I take a sip of her very good, strong coffee and eat my cookie. She's right, the cookies are good. "Do you know her daughter?"

"I've met her. Strange little thing. I think she's a little shy on the uptake, if you know what I mean."

"She and her mamma get along?"

"Like any mother and daughter, they have their spats." I remember Lucy's combination of annoyance and protectiveness with her daughter when I was at her house. And her daughter's nervous manner with us. Did they have an argument? Maybe they did, and Holly doesn't want to admit that Lucy may have gone off because she's angry. Or is it possible that Holly hurt her mamma?

"Anything in particular that they fight about? Anything recent?"

"Well, one thing, but it's silly . . ."

"Tell me."

"The daughter is in food service, but she doesn't know how to cook. She really wants to be a baker, and she was trying to get Lucy to teach her how to cook. Lucy said she didn't want to teach her."

"Why not?"

She sighs. "That would be the blind leading the blind! Lucy is a terrible cook. She makes a pretty good egg salad for the church lunches, but that's about it. I told her I would teach the girl." She indicates the cookies. "I'm a pretty good baker. But Lucy didn't take me up on it. She said her daughter doesn't want to look stupid in front of a stranger."

I get to my feet and thank her for the cookies. "Now if you think of anything you forgot to tell me, or hear from her, I'd appreciate a call. Or you can call Detective Hogarth at the Bobtail Police Department."

"Detective Hogarth? Every woman I know has a crush on him. He's the cutest thing!" I hadn't noticed, but I'll take her word for it.

Based on Mary Robinson's report that Darlene is a snoop, I decide to go back and see Darlene again, and this time I will insist that she sit down and really talk with me. It's possible she knows more than she's letting on. Or maybe she knows something she isn't aware is important. But before I have a chance to get over there, Maria calls.

"You better get on back here. There's trouble."

"What kind of trouble?

"Just . . . trouble. At the Catholic Church." There's an odd tilt to her voice, almost as if she's suppressing a laugh.

It takes me only fifteen minutes to get to the outskirts of town, where I am stopped cold. As far as I recall, the only time there has ever been a traffic jam in Jarrett Creek was when there was a four-car pileup on the north end of town that took a couple of hours to clear away. But here I am in a traffic jam two blocks from the Catholic Church. I rarely put on my flashers, but this seems like the right time.

The vehicle in front of me, a pickup, takes its time easing aside, and there are ten more cars I have to flash and honk at to get them to move. It's like trying to move a herd of ornery cows. But eventually I round the corner, and the sight that greets my eyes dumbfounds me. There are about twenty women and five men marching with signs in front of the Catholic Church. For a minute I think I see Loretta, but of course it isn't her.

The signs read everything from, "Free the Goat Rodeo" to "Catholic Church Unfair" to "Rodeo Belongs to All." Seeing that all the marchers are Baptists, I'm not surprised that there are no curse words or expressions of hatred. Most of the marchers look serious, but a few are looking at the ground, as if they aren't sure they want to be seen; one man, Gary Coates, is downright laughing. His companion pokes him, and he tries to get serious.

Onlookers far outnumber the marchers, and there's a cheerful air about the whole thing. Behind the marchers going back and forth in front of the church, I see Father Sanchez standing on the steps with Maria. Dusty is at her side. When I park the squad car, Dusty makes a break for it, barking and leaping his way over to me, as if to say, "Isn't this fun?"

We make our way back to the steps. Sanchez barely glances at me, but he sighs.

"How long has this been going on?" I ask.

Sanchez sighs again. "Thirty minutes. I called over to headquarters as soon as I heard what was happening, and Maria got right over here."

"Have you talked to them?"

"Not much to say," Sanchez says. "Their aims are pretty clear."

"What do you think we should do?" Maria asks. "We could ask them if they have a permit to march."

I'd laugh if I weren't worried that it would be taken as a reason for the marchers to get really riled up. "Here's what I think," I say, putting on a serious face and inclining my head toward Maria. "I think we let them keep going, and eventually they'll get tired and go home."

"Not bad, not bad."

"Who's the leader?"

"Who do you think? Jolene Ramsey. She gave a little speech just before you got here. You sure we shouldn't call a meeting with them?"

"No, they've got bigger problems than they know. It won't be long before their interest will be elsewhere."

She shoots me a questioning glance.

"I'll tell you when we get back to the station."

Jolene Ramsey strides up to me. Her elfin face is suffused with the glow of righteousness. "We had to do this, you know."

"Hello, Ms. Ramsey," I say. "You have a good day for it anyway, although it looks like it might rain in a bit."

She gathers herself taller. "The law wouldn't intervene, so we had to take matters into our own hands."

"I can see that. I just hope you aren't planning any kind of violence."

I hear Maria cough beside me, and I don't dare look at her for fear we'll start laughing.

"Of course not. This is a church matter."

"In that case, I'll leave you to it. We've had a few developments in the search for Loretta Singletary, and I'd best keep my mind on that."

"You have? What? Where is she?" The outrage is replaced by hope and fear.

"It's a police matter right now, so I can't discuss it."

"But she's alive?"

"Jolene, I wish I knew, but I don't." I'm sorry now that I bluffed her. And I hope I haven't given a false sense of possibility to her and to Maria. "Get on back to your march. I'll let you know as soon as I know something."

I turn back to Maria. "They'll be out of here in twenty minutes. You want to wait or come with me?"

She turns to Sanchez. "You okay?"

He raises his eyebrows. "I'm not worried about these marchers, if that's what you mean."

"Sanchez," I say, "I think you can relax about this whole matter. It will be over before you know it."

Back at headquarters, Maria confronts me the minute we're in the door. "What happened with the Baptist preacher? Is that why you think the ladies are going to have other things to deal with?"

I tell her everything that went on with Arlen Becker. "I won't be surprised if he skips town over the weekend."

"And you're really sure he isn't responsible for kidnapping those women?"

"The worst he has done is cheat on his wife. No, that's not true. Apparently, he has harassed some women in the workplace. And got his hands slapped."

"The Baptist preacher." Her voice is full of disgust.

"The important thing now is that we still have to find Loretta."

"You told Jolene you had a lead."

"Not exactly a lead. More a piece of the puzzle that doesn't quite fit. I'm going back over to Bobtail to see if I can make it work."

"You're not going without me."

"I don't . . ."

"No. I'm tired of this. You always want to be the hero. Always going off and coming back smug as you please with everything all wrapped up. Suppose this time you don't figure it out? Suppose you could have used me and you didn't, and Loretta gets killed? I would never forgive you for that." She isn't angry. She's frustrated.

"All right. Let's go. I'll tell you what we're up to on the way."

She gets Dusty on the leash, and we head out. As we walk to the car, I examine what she said. Am I smug? Do I have to be the hero? Have I pushed her aside for my own ego?

CHAPTER 33

It's five o'clock when we roll up to Darlene's Beauty Shop. A woman newly coiffed and pink-cheeked is walking down the sidewalk to the gate.

When we get inside, Darlene is sweeping up the floor around the client's chair. She looks up, startled. "I didn't know you were coming back."

"It's an informal talk. This is my colleague, Maria Trevino. We want to ask you a few more questions."

She dumps the hair she swept up into the trash can and bangs the dust pan on the side, making more noise than seems necessary. "I don't know any more than I've already told you."

"Why don't we sit down for a minute. Officer Trevino hasn't been in on our conversations. I want her to go back over a few things with you, maybe get a fresh perspective."

She gives a humph of annoyance but escorts us back in to her little domain. We sit down, and she folds her hands on the desk in front of her. "Okay, now what do you want to know? Keep in mind that I have a husband to get home to and make dinner for."

"We'll be brief."

On the way over, I told Maria I'd like her to take the lead, and she hops right in. "Take us back to when Lucy Nettleman came to work for you. What was her state of mind then?"

"Terrible. She had lost everything. She had her business and a big house, and she was the kind of person everybody pointed to as a real success. When her husband left, he cheated her out of all that."

"I don't understand. Texas is a community property state. Didn't she get half the property?"

"She should have, but he finagled it so he got almost everything. Something about putting property in his name or owning things before they married. I don't know the details. He did buy her that little place she lives in. It was the least he could do. She was desperate. When she applied to work here, I didn't take to her, and I worried that it wasn't a good idea to have such an unhappy stylist work in the shop. But I felt sorry for her. Besides, she had a good reputation and brought clients with her. I figured she'd settle down sooner or later."

"And did she?"

She draws a breath and hesitates. "Mostly. I like a friendly atmosphere, and she wasn't always cheerful, but she really is a good hairdresser, and her clients are loyal."

"Did she ever disappear like this before?"

"Goodness, no. I wouldn't put up with that. She's always on time and does her part to clean up and what not."

"Did you ever go out with her socially?"

"No, that wasn't in the cards, ever. I'm a happily married woman and . . ." She raises her eyebrows. "I don't mean I have anything against a divorced woman. It's not like it was her fault. But if you play cards or have dinner, it's a stray person."

"No girls' night out or birthday lunch, nothing like that?"

"Well, let me see. I think one of her ladies took her out for lunch on her birthday back near Christmas, but that's all. And as for ladies' night out, I don't think my husband would care much for that. He likes me to be at home." She gives a satisfied toss of her head.

"Did she ever talk about her divorce?"

Darlene goes still and then says, "Talk about it! I'll say she did." A little pink appears in her cheeks. "I'm afraid she overshared. I had to have a heart to heart with her after she had worked here a month or so. I had to tell her that people did not want to hear her complain nonstop about her ex-husband. I mean, I didn't say it that way, blunt. I tried to be tactful, you know. But I had to put a stop to it."

"And did she stop?"

"Toned it down. I didn't want to put a gag on her, just wanted her to ..." she waves her hand, as if shooing away the unpleasantness.

"Did her daughter ever come in the shop?" Maria says.

Darlene gives a sharp bark of laughter. "You're getting right down to it, aren't you?"

"What do you mean?"

"That was the other problem. I had to tell her that her daughter could not be hanging around all the time. The two of them were like droopy dogs. I don't think it's good for a shop to have gloom and doom. Besides, I thought the daughter ought to have her own life. What was she doing always hanging around here? I don't mind telling you, I put my foot down on that one. I told her I didn't want her daughter coming here. She only works here three or four days a week, which I thought left her plenty of time off to spend with her daughter."

"It's hard to make ends meet working just a few days a week. Do you know if she works anywhere else?"

"I have my suspicions that she does a few clients at her house, but as long as she has a full schedule here, I don't feel like making anything of it."

Another clue to follow up on.

"I understand her daughter doesn't live with her?" Maria says.

"No, that was funny. I thought that because they were joined at the hip, they must live together, but she said her daughter owns a place outside Bryan. You know that's where the daughter works part time at a pizza parlor."

I'm wondering how Holly Nettleman manages to live on the salary of a pizza place cashier, but before I can ask, Maria says, "What pizza parlor?" She has that look she gets when she's onto something.

"Umm, let me see. I know Lucy mentioned it. Pizza My Heart. Cute name."

"Yes it is," Maria says. "Easy to remember."

I ask, "How can she afford to pay rent when she works in a pizza parlor?"

"That's one of the problems between Lucy and her daughter. Apparently when Lucy's in-laws died, they left their farmhouse to Lucy's daughter. That's how she got a house."

"That's kind of unusual." Maria is good at this. She has discovered that gossip is in Darlene's blood.

"It is. And Lucy told me her husband was furious. He blamed Lucy. He accused her of going behind his back to make sure their daughter got the old home place instead of him. She said he practically had apoplexy over it."

"You'd think he'd be glad to have his daughter inherit the place."

"Lucy thinks he already had divorce in mind, and he wanted every penny he could get his hands on."

"Was he already seeing the other woman?"

"Yes. A woman he met on one of those dating sites. Oh, you should have heard the things Lucy had to say about those women who go on those websites."

"Like what?"

"Oh, that they're looking for a man and don't care one bit if they steal somebody's husband. That they are desperate and will do anything to get a man and his money. We all tried to tell her that it was men who usually were after the women—and their money—but she wasn't having any of it."

Maria glances at me with raised eyebrows.

I take the cue. "Did she ever make any threats with regard to these women?"

She gets right away what I'm driving at. She puts her hand to her neck. "Well no. She's not that vindictive. I mean, she said she'd like to strangle the woman who her husband ran off with, but we all said it's him she ought to be mad at."

Maria stands up. "I think that's all for now. Thank you for your help."

"Wait one second," I say. "You don't happen to have Holly Nettleman's address, do you?"

"No. I might have her phone number as her mamma's next of kin, but I don't know the address."

"That's all right." I remember that Hogarth and I saw the address on the receipt for the stove that Lucy bought. I get up to go because Maria is already halfway out the door, moving so fast that I have to hustle to keep up with her. "Thank you for your time," I say on my way out. "We'll be in touch."

"Well . . ." Her tone of indignation is clear, but I don't have time to soothe her feathers.

As soon as we're in the car, Maria says, "Why didn't you tell me the missing woman's daughter worked at a pizza parlor?"

"Why would I tell you that? I just found out yesterday. What difference does it make?"

"Remember I told you that the morning she disappeared, Loretta got a couple of marketing calls?"

"Vaguely."

"One of them was from Bryan, and when I called to find out why they had phoned Loretta's number, the girl I talked to said they had been having a promotion and were calling a lot of people. The name of the business was Pizza My Heart."

I shake my head. Of all the crazy possibilities. "No way we could have made that connection. But . . ."

"Are you thinking what I'm thinking?" Maria says.

I stare out the front window as I gather my reasoning. "All along we've been picturing a man kidnapping those women; talking about a man, searching for a man. But it could as easily have been a woman."

Maria is nodding as I talk.

"In fact," I continue, "it would have been easier for a woman to lure other women in than it would be for a man." I recall Loretta's next-door neighbor saying that the person he saw carrying Loretta's suitcase was dressed like a man, but moved like a woman.

"But if Lucy Nettleman and her daughter kidnapped those women," Maria says, "what did they plan to do with them? We know one of them died, but what about Loretta?"

"I don't know the answer to that," I say. I don't like where my thought are headed. "But it troubles me that Lucy is missing."

"What do you mean?"

"The women were kidnapped a week ago. Why did Lucy suddenly disappear?"

Maria's eyes go wide. "If Lucy decided to get rid of Loretta, she may have killed her and skipped out. Is that what you're thinking?"

My mind is working furiously. I was thinking that, but another possibility occurs to me. "Hold on. Suppose we have it wrong? It was Holly who made the phone call to Loretta. Suppose she kidnapped the women?"

"Was she capable of that?"

"Maybe. I'm sorry you didn't get a chance to meet the daughter. My take on her was that she was a little off. Suppose she kidnapped them, and her mamma just found about it and threatened to turn her in."

"Oh, my goodness." Maria closes her eyes and shakes her head. "And now her mamma is missing. You think it's possible Holly did away with her?"

"We have to consider it." I start the car. "Let's go out to Holly Nettleman's farmhouse and pay her a visit," I say. "Hogarth has the address."

We stop by Bobtail Police Department, but Hogarth is gone. I call his cell phone, and he directs Marks to give me the information I need from the file on Lucy Nettleman. "You going out to talk to the daughter again?" Marks asks. I tell him I am.

"Can't hurt," he says. "You never know."

When I get back to the car, Maria says, "You don't think we ought to tell them what we're up to?"

"Suppose we're wrong? No need to get them all excited for nothing."

Maybe Maria is right. Maybe my ego is involved. But the truth is, if I told Hogarth what we had in mind, it's likely that he'd want to make a detailed plan that would involve other officers. It would take time that we don't have. I feel like every minute we spend is a minute that might be taken off Loretta's life.

After a brief argument over whether to take Dusty with us, Maria persuades me not to swing by my place and leave him at home. "He has to learn how to behave in all circumstances," she says. Besides, it's evening, so if we have to leave him in the car, it will be fine. We also argue over whether to take my truck or the squad car.

"Both," Maria says. "Suppose they do have Loretta? Not only do we have to bring her home, but we also have to arrest them." Her eyes are shining. She has managed to convince herself that we'll find Loretta alive and well at Holly Nettleman's place.

I'm glad for the opportunity to drive to Holly Nettleman's farmhouse by myself. It gives me a chance to consider what we might find. It's possible that Holly Nettleman and her mother have murdered Loretta, and we can find no evidence of it and never will. That's the worst scenario I can imagine, although close behind is that they killed Loretta, and we do find evidence. Either way, Loretta would be gone.

It's also possible that, as Maria has convinced herself, we'll find her there with them, alive. I try not to dwell on mental images of her bedraggled and thin, frightened out of her wits.

The other possibility I don't want to consider is that they kidnapped her and have her hidden where we can't find her. How would we even prove it? And what would be their motive?

We drive past the site where Elaine Farquart's body was found. The turnoff is only a few miles beyond it, lending even more weight to the possibility that Holly and Lucy are responsible for all this.

These thoughts are banished as I slow to turn off the main highway. We are three miles outside of Bryan, with scattered houses getting more infrequent. It's dusk, and although I've slowed down considerably, I almost miss the sign to Shaker Road. It's paved but not well maintained, and the houses grow sparser as I drive slowly, trying to see the numbers on the mailboxes. The road snakes back to the west, paralleling the main highway and then, at a grove of trees, swings back south. In the trees, it's even darker.

My cell phone rings. It's Maria. "The mailboxes have names, but no numbers. How are we going to figure out where it is?"

"There's bound to be a number on some of them, but if not, we'll stop at one of the houses and ask."

Dusty seems to sense that something is going on. He is sitting at alert with his nose testing the air. I've got the windows rolled up too far for him to stick his head out because I don't want him barking.

A quarter mile farther, we see the number 15562. The farmhouse lies at the end of a long gravel driveway. Lights are on, and a car and pickup are in the driveway. I call Maria back. "Did you see that? We're in the area anyway." We're looking for 17992. A little farther, and there's 17778. Maria flashes her lights to show me that she has seen it, too. Dusty gets up and turns around restlessly, giving a little whimper.

"Easy does it," I say. "We don't have too far to go now." As if he could understand.

Maria and I talk again on the phone and agree that when we find the place, we'll drive past it for a quarter mile and rendezvous. I go even slower, my pulse quickening. We pass a little clump of houses close to the road, all lit up in the darkening light.

There it is. A black mailbox with Nettleman painted on it in white. We drive on, and around a curve up the road there's a wide spot where we can stop. Dusty leaps up. "Quiet," I tell him. I leave him in the pickup, go back to the squad car, and slip in beside Maria.

"What's the plan, boss?" she asks.

"There are two ways we could proceed: sneak up and case the place or knock on the door and confront them."

"If we try to sneak up, suppose they have a dog?"

"We have to risk it. If they do have Loretta, then it's not likely that she'll be where we can see her if they open the door. And if they don't allow us in, we have no right to demand it because we don't have anything concrete to go on."

She nods. She's chewing on her knuckle, which I've never seen her do.

"If we sneak up and a dog starts barking, then we'll go knock on the door." I hope that doesn't happen. I prefer to get a good look around before we have to act.

"I saw a building like a barn when we drove by. It was big enough for a couple of cars. I'd like to get a look at that too," Maria says.

I take my holster out of the glovebox and strap it on, something I've only done a few times the whole time I've been chief of police.

Dusty doesn't like being left, but I speak sternly to him, and he lies down, looking at me with reproachful eyes. I don't look back as we walk away.

CHAPTER 34

There are no cars in sight, but the driveway continues alongside the house and on around back. The front and upstairs of the house are dark, but through the front windows, I see there's a light on in the back. The driveway is paved with shell, so we walk alongside it in the dirt so our footsteps won't make any noise. I keep my eye on the windows of the house in case anybody looks out. When we reach the porch, I nod to Maria to take the north side of the house, and I'll go around the south.

It's full-on dark now, and if there's going to be a moon, it isn't up yet. The area around the house is not kept up well, and the footing is treacherous, clods of dirt and rocks to be navigated. I almost run into a bale of wire that's practically invisible in the dark. Off to my right is the structure that looks like a barn that Maria mentioned. It's big enough to keep more than one car in. The big double doors are closed, though, and there are no windows on the side facing me. The two cars that were parked in front of Lucy Nettleman's house the first time I talked to her are parked nearby. Lucy is no longer missing, I think.

As I near the back, I start to make out voices, at least two. The nearest trees are way at the back of the house, but the tree frogs are making such a racket that it's hard to make out any words.

I step around to the back door and crouch down up against the house to avoid being seen from the windows. Maria is peering around the other side. Light from the windows in the back throws pale rectangles of light onto the bare, grassless yard. There's a chicken coop several yards back toward the trees, but I don't hear any sounds that would indicate the coop is in use.

I take a deep breath to steady myself and then hold up my hand to indicate to Maria that I want to listen to whatever's going on inside. I'm suddenly aware that there are good aromas coming from the house. It smells like stew and maybe bread. It would be quite a comedown if we're wrong and all that's going on here is two women making a meal for themselves.

And then we both hear it, clear as day: Loretta's voice. "I don't know if this is going to be fit to eat, since you forgot to get the carrots." She's alive.

Maria heard it too. Our eyes meet, and she nods vigorously, pumping her fists in exultation.

Loretta's voice sounds normal. I'd be tempted to think she was here of her own volition. A swarm of thoughts races through my head. Will they have a gun on her? Will they shoot her if I surprise them? Are both Lucy and her daughter in on this?

Very slowly, I ease myself up, staying to the side of the window, out of the line of sight. It's possible that one of the women could look out at the wrong time and see me, but as long as I move slowly, I hope I won't draw attention. The strain is almost too much. I'm tempted to just stand up and look inside.

When I get a clear visual, I can hardly believe my eyes. Loretta is standing at the stove with Holly Nettleman next to her. Lucy is sitting at a big, wooden table in the middle of the kitchen. She's watching the two women. I can only see her from the side, but her mouth is turned down. Her arms are crossed tight across her chest.

I risk a few more inches so I can take in more of the women. Holly is intent on whatever Loretta is doing. No one appears to be holding a weapon of any kind, although there is a knife and cutting board on the counter out of reach. It looks as if Loretta is moving freely, so why didn't she just leave? And then I see the iron cuff around Loretta's ankle and the long chain attached to it. It's not a heavy chain, but it doesn't need to be. Loretta is not a big or strong woman.

"Come on," I whisper loud enough for Maria to hear me, gesturing with my arm. "We're going in."

I walk up the back steps and bang on the door. Through the glass pane in the door, I see the three women freeze. I bang again, open the screen door, and try the handle of the back door. It opens and I walk in.

Lucy jumps up, and her daughter squeals and takes off for the front of the house. Maria streaks past me. I'm focused on Loretta. When she turns, I see the toll her ordeal has taken on her. Her face is haggard, her hair bedraggled. "Oh, Samuel," she says, her voice breaking.

I hear shouting in the front room, and only then does it occur to me that Lucy might have been running to fetch a weapon. I charge into the front room and find Maria standing in front of a closed closet door.

"Come out of there!" Maria hollers.

I hear an ominous "click," and I grab Maria and pull her aside at the same time a rifle shot rings out, and a bullet slams through the closet door.

We stumble back toward the kitchen doorway. "Get back there and call Bryan PD," I say. I pull my Colt.

"What are you going to do?"

"Never mind. Just get on back there and call. And try to find a key to get that leg cuff off Loretta."

When she walks away, I realize my hand is shaking. That was a close one. If I hadn't come in when I did, Holly might have shot Maria. "Holly," I say loudly, "I want you to put the gun down and walk out of there."

Another click and another shot. This one is at an angle as if she's trying to reach me.

Footsteps run toward me from the kitchen. I jerk my head to see Lucy barreling toward me. I grab her as she hurtles past, almost yanking her off her feet. She tries to pull free, but I hold her back and force her into the next room.

"Did you shoot her?" she says, wild-eyed.

"I haven't fired my gun. That's your daughter shooting. She's in the hall closet."

Lucy clamps her hands over her mouth, and her face crumples. Her voice rises in a wail. "I didn't even know it was loaded. That was her daddy's rifle."

"Take it easy; nobody's hurt. You know what kind of rifle it is?"

"A regular rifle."

"I mean, how many rounds of ammunition does it hold?"

She looks at me as if I've asked her how many miles it is to Rome. "I don't have any idea."

More than one anyway, but it's probably a basic rifle like most people keep for killing snakes. Which means it likely hasn't got more than a few rounds in it. But I can't take that chance. "Holly, your mamma is here. She's worried about you."

Silence.

I whisper to Lucy. "Say something soothing to her."

She wrestles with her thoughts and finally says, "Holly, you need to come out now. I'm afraid you'll get hurt."

"Stay away from me," Holly snarls. "This is all your fault."

Lucy lowers her head into her hands and whimpers. I wonder how this situation came to be, but now is not the time to ask.

I motion for Lucy to follow me a few steps inside the kitchen. I look back and see Maria hovering over Loretta, who is sitting in a chair at the table, watching us. "Do you have the key to Loretta's leg cuff?"

She nods.

"Then get in there and unlock it."

She shoots me a furious look. "What are you going to do?"

"I'm going to see to it that neither one of you does any more damage."

"You won't hurt her?"

"Seems like she's doing a fine job of that all by herself."

Off in the distance, I hear sirens. I hope they're headed in this direction. I keep an eye on the closet door, with an occasional glance to make sure Lucy is following my order for her to get Loretta free.

As soon as the cuff is off, Loretta stands up and looks toward me.

Her haggard expression pierces me. I'd love to comfort her, but I put up my hand to stop her from coming toward me. She nods, and I see her visibly take charge of herself, straightening her shoulders and putting a hand to her hair to smooth it out.

Maria sits Lucy down and handcuffs her to the frame of the chair. Then she turns off the stove burners, where whatever was cooking now smells like it's scorched. Bizarrely, I notice that it's the new stove that we found the receipt for.

Maria takes a glass out of the cabinet, fills it with water, hands it to Loretta, and says something to her I don't hear. Loretta nods.

The sirens get closer, and I walk back near the closet and say, "Holly, the police are on their way. Things will go a lot easier if you come out of there without the rifle."

"They'll lock me up." Her voice is trembling.

"I'm not going to lie. You will have to pay for what you've done. But trust me, if you surrender willingly, it will make a difference."

"If Mamma had just gone on to work like she was supposed to yesterday, nobody would have known." Which leads me to suspect that Lucy must have been trying to persuade her daughter not to keep Loretta any longer, but I can't know that for sure.

"We can sort all that out later." Cars are squealing to a stop outside, doors slamming. "Listen, if they come in here and you're holed up with a gun, it will be very bad. Now throw the rifle out and then come out of the closet." I try to sound firm and trustworthy, even though I'd like to beg. I don't know many people from the Bryan Police Department, and I don't know whether I'll be dealing with an officer who's a trigger-happy rookie or one who's nervous or cowardly.

I hear voices outside. They're no doubt figuring out how to proceed.

"Now's the time. You don't have any more time to stall."

The closet door snicks open. I move off to the side while I still keep an eye on the door, in case she has a wild idea of coming out shooting.

"That's right. Lay the gun on the floor."

And she does.

"Push it away with your foot."

She does. There's an odd screech outside and then the squawk of a bullhorn.

I still can't risk that she doesn't have another weapon. "Now come out with your hands out in front of you so I can see them."

Gradually, I see the hands, and then she appears, her face a mask of terror.

"Hands up high."

She hesitates.

"Now!"

She complies.

"Now I want you to get down on the floor, face down."

"No!"

"If the police officers outside feel like they have to shoot, you'll be in the line of fire." She glances back toward the closet, and I have to act. I pounce on her and force her down to the floor. "Now, stay there."

"You outside," I holler. "This is Samuel Craddock from Jarrett Creek Police Department. Everything is under control. No need to use your weapons."

"Craddock?" The voice comes over the bullhorn.

"That's right. Who am I speaking to?"

"This is Chief Bob Laguna from Bryan. We've met."

"Good. Let's take this slow. The suspect is unarmed."

"Understood."

From the kitchen, I hear Lucy sobbing. Maria comes up behind me. "You want me to go out with you?"

"That will be good, but be cautious. Open the door a little."

"My deputy is opening the door," I call out. "Her name is Maria Trevino."

She eases the door open, keeping to one side in case somebody gets nervous and pulls off a shot, and then she kicks it wider.

"All right, come on out," Laguna says.

"Get up," I say to Holly. "No fast moves. One step at a time." I pull her to her feet. She's shaking so hard she can hardly stand.

From the kitchen, Lucy shouts, "Please don't hurt her."

"Craddock, what's happening?" Laguna yells.

"My deputy and I are going to bring the suspect out now," I holler back. I motion for Maria to help. "Let's go on each side of her." I take one of Holly's arms, and she takes the other. Holly tries to wrench away, but it's a half-hearted effort. Then she goes limp. We hold on and half-drag her out. Within seconds, we are swarmed by half a dozen officers. They cuff Holly, who starts howling.

From the kitchen, Lucy is screaming not to hurt her daughter. I hear Loretta say, "Oh, shut up." It does my heart good.

Chief Laguna directs a couple of officers to get Holly into a squad car and sends men back inside with Maria to arrest Lucy as well. "What the hell has been going on here?" he asks.

I give him the short version and suggest that the two women be transported separately so they don't have a chance to talk to each other. We have to move away from the squad cars because we can't hear each other over Lucy and her daughter hollering. I also ask him to contact Bobtail Police Department. "Talk to Brent Hogarth. He's in charge of the Farquart investigation. He'll probably want to come over here."

"Take these two women to headquarters," Laguna says to his officers. "I'll be along directly. And don't let them consult with each other."

When they leave, he says, "We're going to have to get the Feds involved, so they may have a wait."

"Why is that? Kidnapping is a state crime as long as they didn't cross state lines, which they didn't."

"That may be, but using the Internet to trap somebody makes it different. The state passed a new law last fall, and I don't know exactly what it means. But I'd rather be safe than sorry."

"You're right. They're lucky it isn't murder too," I say. "I'm going to leave you to it. I'm going to take the victim back home now."

"I don't know whether I can let you do that. We need to get a statement."

"Tell you what. Loretta is pretty shook up. She has been through a lot. I can have Deputy Trevino stay with her overnight, and we'll bring her in tomorrow." I try to act casual and not push him, but I suspect he hears the determination in my voice. Loretta has been through enough. I'm taking her home right now.

"We can work with that," he says. "It will take that long for the Feds to get back to me anyway. For now, I'm going to get a forensic team together to start gathering evidence. You want to be involved?"

"Not necessary. I'm sure you've got it under control."

Maria and I sit in the kitchen with Loretta, Maria holding her hand, until she feels settled down enough to get in the car. We don't ask her any questions, and all she volunteers is, "I was scared to death I'd be stuck here forever." I don't know whether she was afraid of being killed or not, and I don't ask.

I tell them to wait while I go get my pickup. Maria argues that she ought to be able to drive Loretta back because she has the more comfortable car, but I counter with the fact that I've known Loretta a lot longer. Loretta pats Maria's hand and says the pickup will be fine.

Maria plays her trump card. "Dusty is in the pickup."

"Well, that silly dog will just have to move over and make room," Loretta says.

There are still a couple of squad cars outside, and Laguna says the forensics van is on its way. I tell him I want to know if Loretta's and Elaine Farquart's cars are in the barn-like building, and he sends one of his men to open the doors. When I get back with my pickup, the doors are standing open. I walk over to the building, and there is Loretta's car, next to a red one that I expect is Elaine's.

Loretta and I wait inside the house while Maria fetches the squad car. We want to drive back in tandem. It seems important to make a procession of it.

Loretta and I don't say much while we wait. She tells me she needs to be quiet for a while, that she still can't believe her ordeal is over. I'm glad when Maria honks her horn, signaling that she's back.

"There's a cat around here," Loretta says, when we're walking out the door. "Don't leave it without any food and water."

"One of us will come back to check on the cat," I say.

When we get out to my truck, before we climb in, Hogarth comes wheeling up. He and Marks leap out of the car and come over to us. He grabs Loretta's hand, and for a minute he's too overcome with emotion to say anything. Then he clears his throat and says, "I'm Brent Hogarth, Bobtail Police Department. I'm awfully glad to see you made it out of this ordeal."

Loretta looks him in the eye. "You and me both."

He meets my eyes, and we chuckle. "You told me if anybody could survive this, she could."

You would think that Loretta is Dusty's favorite person. When I open the door to the pickup, he jumps out and leaps around joyfully. I'm reminded of when we were in Darlene's beauty shop, and I wonder whether he did that because his nose told him that Loretta had been there.

When I order him into the truck, he leaps onto the seat and lies down, quiet, as if sensing that Loretta can't handle much in the way of excitement. When she gets in, she pets him. "You're a good dog," she says.

We're halfway home before I hand her my cell phone. "You better call your son, Scott. Your boys are half out of their minds with worry."

CHAPTER 35

I know things have gotten back to normal when I get back to the house from feeding my cows and see Loretta walking up the front steps, holding a plate. From the smell, I know she has brought cinnamon rolls for the first time since she got back home a week ago.

"I thought it was time I got back to my routine," she says. On this fine spring day, we sit out on the porch and drink coffee while I savor a roll. She won't have one, as usual.

We talk about nothing in particular. I tell her that Connor and Maria are still squabbling. And I tell her that a representative of the dating website Smalltownpair called to tell me that "management" had decided that if I wanted information on any of their clients, then I'd have to get a court order. We both laugh, but it's an uneasy laughter.

She told me that for now she's too embarrassed to discuss with me what led her to decide to go on the dating website, and she's still upset about what happened to Elaine Farquart. At one point, she said, "If both of us hadn't been foolish and signed up for blind dates, she'd still be alive, and I wouldn't have been scared half out of my wits. It probably took five years off my life." In time I will tell her how much everyone admires how she held up under the pressure of being kidnapped and being held by a young woman who was clearly unhinged.

I still can't quite wrap my mind around what those two women did. I was allowed to sit in on the interrogations. It came out that Lucy was so bitter that her husband had found a new woman on an Internet dating site that she fantasized aloud about how to get revenge. She told her daughter several times that she was going to sign up on a dating site in a man's name and lure women, like the one who stole her husband, to meet her and she'd kill them.

During the questioning, she swore that she never meant it, but in Holly's session, she said she kidnapped the women because she thought it would please her mother. When her mother told her the salon had two clients, Elaine Farquart and Loretta Singletary, who had signed up to meet men on a dating website, Holly took it from there, thinking they were the perfect victims for revenge.

"I didn't know what Holly had done until she called me out to the farm to surprise me," Lucy said under questioning. "And there they were."

"She had already kidnapped both women?"

"That's right." She hangs her head. "It was horrible when poor Elaine had a heart attack and died. But that wasn't my daughter's fault."

"Why did your daughter run over the body?" I asked.

"She wanted to make it look like a hit and run. We thought that would be the end of it."

One of the questions I wanted answered was how they had lured Elaine and Loretta in.

It was pretty much what we had speculated, except instead of a man luring them, it was Holly. She called Loretta, claiming to be the sister of the "man" she was supposed to meet. She said he had had a fall and needed to go to the emergency room, and that she was in San Antonio and couldn't get there right away. She asked if Loretta would go over and take him to the hospital, and she'd get there as soon as she could. Loretta, being a Good Samaritan, said of course she would, but when Loretta got out to the farmhouse, it was Holly who met her, not the man she expected. Holly might not be the brightest person in the world, but she had a certain animal cunning, and she knew enough to make the call from the pizza place and then make up some marketing promotion as cover.

"And she came back to your place to pack your suitcase?" I asked Loretta.

"She was crazy, but she wasn't mean. I told her I had to have my medicine and some clothes, and she went to my house, packed a suitcase, and brought them to me."

"Let me ask you this. I caught an intruder in your house. Could it have been Holly?"

"It most certainly was. I convinced her that I had made notes that might lead you to her, so she went to my house to look for them."

"Why did you tell her that?"

"Samuel, I was desperate to think of something. I thought maybe she'd make a mistake, maybe leave fingerprints so you could identify her. Or maybe somebody would catch her in the act."

"I almost did." I tell her that Holly knocked me down when she ran out when I caught her in Loretta's house.

"See? It almost worked!"

"I wish it had. You must have been scared the whole time. Why do you suppose they spared you?"

"Lucy saved my life. Her daughter had it in mind to kill me."

"She told you that?"

"No, but I know she did. The first couple of days were terrible. She kept whispering to her mamma, and Lucy would say, "No, you can't do that.""

"If she wanted to save your life, then why didn't she just let you go?"

"I don't know why. Maybe she didn't want to upset her daughter. You know, that girl has problems. What Lucy did was set me up to teach Holly to cook. I'm pretty sure she was stalling to buy time to figure out how to get me out of there."

I remembered Lucy's friend saying that she had offered to teach Holly to cook because Lucy wasn't very good at it. "And Holly was all right with that cooking scheme?"

"At first she was, but I didn't know how long her interest would last. She was a terrible student. Had no sense of timing or taste."

During the debriefing at headquarters in Bryan, Laguna had asked whether Holly ever hit her.

Loretta got a haunted look. "She slapped me once when I got impatient with her." She shook herself. "But really, she was just an unhappy girl. I guess she was her daddy's pet, and when he left she went to pieces."

Laguna wasn't having any of it. "You're awful generous, Ms. Singletary, but the fact is that she kidnapped you and put your life in danger. She's going to prison for a good long while."

"Oh, my goodness. I wish she hadn't done that. I have to blame her parents. Her daddy for leaving and her mamma for putting ideas in her head."

Now, sitting on the porch, I say, "I'm glad we got you back."

"Oh, you just like my cinnamon rolls."

"That too. But there was that business with the preacher and all the ladies marching in front of the Catholic Church. We needed you then. If you'd been around, you would have talked some sense into them."

She takes a sip of coffee. "I don't know what got into them. They let that silly Jolene Ramsey talk them into it. I think she was a little bit smitten with Reverend Becker." She chuckles. "Speaking of which, there's a little more to say on that subject."

"What's that?"

"We're going to be looking for a new preacher."

"Well, that's good. I didn't care for him all that much." I've kept Becker's story to myself, figuring I'd give him time to get out of town gracefully.

"He told us his wife couldn't put up with small-town life, and he wanted to move on."

"Move on where?" I ask cautiously.

"He has been hired at a new church out in west Texas. Amarillo."

"What?"

The vehemence of my question startles her. "What's wrong with Amarillo?"

I don't know what to say to her. "Amarillo isn't the problem; it's that the Baptist Church decided to foist him off on yet another congregation. I'm just surprised, that's all."

"What aren't you telling me? What do you mean foist him off?"

So, I tell her. About my venture into the world of Internet dating to try to find her and about tricking the good reverend into sending me a photo. And I mention tracking down his old workplaces and finding out that he had left under a cloud.

"Why did you go to all that trouble?"

"Loretta, I thought maybe Becker had kidnapped you. You don't have any idea how worried we all were."

"I do understand that, but why would you think the handsome and distinguished Baptist preacher would be interested in an old turkey like me?"

I could say it's because I was out of my mind with worry and not thinking straight, or I could tell her that I thought he was after money, not companionship. But Wendy's face comes to mind, and I think I know what she would like to hear if she were in that situation. "Because you look good all fixed up, that's why."

She plumps herself up a little. "Well, I'd better be getting along. We're having a meeting about putting out the call for a new preacher."

"Let me ask you something," I say. "Don't you think it's hypocritical for the church directors to keep sending Becker out to new places, knowing what they do about his fooling around?"

"You know, Samuel, Reverend Becker won't be middle-aged and handsome forever, and one of these days he'll get his comeuppance. That's not for me to decide."

ACKNOWLEDGMENTS

My editor, Dan Mayer, and the team at Seventh Street Books that works hard to put out lovely books deserve the highest praise. I also appreciate my fellow Seventh Street Books authors, even those who have wandered away. You are always there with words of wisdom, encouragement, and humor. You are awesome.

Many writing instructors and authors have helped me become a better writer over the years. There are too many to name, but many of you pop up in my writing life weekly. When I face the blank page, you are right there with me, helping me make the leap.

Acknowledgments would not be complete without a tip of the hat to my agent, Janet Reid. Having a good agent is like standing on bedrock. In a hurricane. Or an earthquake. Feeling that solid ground means that I'll survive.

And always, to David.

Note to Readers: If you enjoyed this book, please consider writing a review on Goodreads or Amazon. Thank you, and happy reading!

ABOUT THE AUTHOR

Terry Shames is the author of *A Killing at Cotton Hill*, *The Last Death of Jack Harbin*, *Dead Broke in Jarrett Creek*, *A Deadly Affair at Bobtail Ridge*, *The Necessary Murder of Nonie Blake*, *An Unsettling Crime for Samuel Craddock*, and *A Reckoning in the Back Country*, the first seven Samuel Craddock mysteries. She is the coeditor of *Fire in the Hills*, a book of stories, poems, and photographs about the 1991 Oakland Hills Fire. She grew up in Texas and is fascinated by the convoluted loyalties and betrayals of small-town residents. Terry is a member of the Mystery Writers of America and Sisters in Crime.